It was just a couple of months ago, mid-December, and Gracie said to me, ''Why don't we give Rodney time off for the holiday season? Why shouldn't he celebrate Christmas, too?''

I remember I had my optics unfocused at the time . . . but I focused them quickly to see if Gracie were smiling or had a twinkle in her eye . . .

She wasn't smiling. No twinkle. I said, ''Why on Earth should we give him time off?''

''Why not?''

''Do you want to give the freezer a vacation, the sterilizer, the holoviewer? Shall we turn off the power supply?''

''Come, Howard,'' she said. ''Rodney isn't a freezer or a sterilizer. He's a *person*.''

''He's not a person. He's a robot. He wouldn't want a vacation.''

''How do you know? And he's a *person*. He deserves a chance to rest and just revel in the holiday atmosphere.''

—from Isaac Asimov's
''Christmas without Rodney''

Books in This Series from Ace

ISAAC ASIMOV'S
CHRISTMAS

EDITED BY
GARDNER DOZOIS
AND
SHEILA WILLIAMS

ACE BOOKS, NEW YORK

This book is an Ace original edition
and has never been previously published.

ISAAC ASIMOV'S CHRISTMAS

An Ace Book / published by arrangement with
Dell Magazines

PRINTING HISTORY
Ace edition / December 1997

The Putnam Berkley World Wide Web site address is
http://www.berkley.com

Make sure to check out *PB Plug*,
the science fiction/fantasy newsletter, at
http://www.pbplug.com

ISBN: 0-441-00491-1

ACE®
Ace Books are published by The Berkley Publishing Group,
a member of Penguin Putnam Inc.,
200 Madison Avenue, New York, NY 10016.
ACE and the ''A'' design are trademarks
belonging to Charter Communications, Inc.
PRINTED IN THE UNITED STATES OF AMERICA

10 9 8 7 6 5 4 3 2 1

We are grateful to the following for permission to reprint their copyrighted material:

"Promises to Keep" by Jack McDevitt, copyright © 1984 by Davis Publications, Inc., reprinted by permission of the author.

"Grandfather Christmas" by Robert Frazier and James Patrick Kelly, copyright © 1994 by Bantam Doubleday Dell Magazines, reprinted by permission of the authors.

"Inn" by Connie Willis, copyright © 1993 by Bantam Doubleday Dell Magazines, reprinted by permission of the author.

"A Midwinter's Tale" by Michael Swanwick, copyright © 1988 by Davis Publications, Inc., reprinted by permission of the author.

"Second Cousin Twice Removed" by Cynthia Felice, copyright © 1991 by Davis Publications, Inc., reprinted by permission of the author.

"The Last Castle of Christmas" by Alexander Jablokov, copyright © 1993 by Bantam Doubleday Dell Magazines, reprinted by permission of the author.

"Christmas Without Rodney" by Isaac Asimov, copyright © 1988 by Davis Publications, Inc., reprinted by permission of Ralph M. Vincinanza, Ltd.

"Space Aliens Saved My Marriage" by Sharon N. Farber, copyright © 1990 by Davis Publications, Inc., reprinted by permission of the author.

"How to Feed Your Inner Troll" by Leslie What, copyright © 1995 by Leslie What, reprinted by permission of the author.

"The Nutcracker Coup" by Janet Kagan, copyright © 1992 by Janet Kagan, reprinted by permission of the author.

All stories previously appeared in *Asimov's Science Fiction Magazine*, a division of Crosstown Publications.

CONTENTS

PROMISES TO KEEP

Jack McDevitt

*"Promises To Keep" was purchased by Shawna Mc-
Carthy, and appeared in the December 1984 issue of
Asimov's; with a cover illustration by Robert Walters
and an interior illustration by Val Lakey Lindahn. Jack
McDevitt would continue to contribute a long string of
important stories to Asimov's over the next twelve
years, as well as making sales to The Magazine of Fantasy & Science Fiction, Full Spectrum, and elsewhere.
His well-received first novel, The Hercules Text, published as an Ace Special, was followed in 1989 by the
critically acclaimed novel A Talent for War. His latest
books are the novels The Engines of God and Ancient
Shores. An ex-naval officer, ex-English teacher, and for-
mer customs inspector, he now lives with his family in
Brunswick, Georgia.*

*Here, in one of the earliest and still one of the most
distinctive of the Asimov's Christmas stories, he takes
us across the solar system to the moons of Jupiter, to
the desolate frozen snowscapes of Callisto, for a very
human drama played out against the cold inhuman im-
mensity of space.*

I received a Christmas card last week from Ed Iseminger. The
illustration was a rendering of the celebrated Christmas Eve telecast from Callisto: a lander stands serenely on a rubble-strewn
plain, spilling warm yellow light through its windows. Needle-

point peaks rise behind it, and the rim of a crater curves across the foreground. An enormous belted crescent dominates the sky.

In one window, someone has hung a wreath.

It is a moment preserved, a tableau literally created by Cathie Perth, extracted from her prop bag. Somewhere here, locked away among insurance papers and the deed to the house, is the tape of the original telecast, but I've never played it. In fact, I've seen it only once, on the night of the transmission. But I know the words, Cathie's words, read by Victor Landolfi in his rich baritone, blending the timeless values of the season with the spectral snows of another world. They appear in schoolbooks now, and on marble.

Inside the card, in large, block, defiant letters, Iseminger had printed "SEPTEMBER!" It is a word with which he hopes to conquer a world. Sometimes, at night, when the snow sparkles under the hard cold stars (the way it did on Callisto), I think about him, and his quest. And I am very afraid.

I can almost see Cathie's footprints on the frozen surface. It was a good time, and I wish there were a way to step into the picture, to toast the holidays once more with Victor Landolfi, to hold onto Cathie Perth (and not let go!), and somehow to save us all. It was the end of innocence, a final meeting place for old friends.

We made the Christmas tape over a period of about five days. Cathie took literally hours of visuals, but Callisto is a place of rock and ice and deadening sameness: there is little to soften the effect of cosmic indifference. Which is why all those shots of towering peaks and tumbled boulders were taken at long range, and in half-light. Things not quite seen, she said, are always charming.

Her biggest problem had been persuading Landolfi to do the voice-over. Victor was tall, lean, ascetic. He was equipped with laser eyes and a huge black mustache. His world was built solely of subatomic particles, and driven by electromagnetics. Those who did not share his passions excited his contempt; which meant that he understood the utility of Cathie's public relations function at the same time that he deplored its necessity. To participate was to compromise one's integrity. His sense of delicacy, however, prevented his expressing that view to Cathie: he begged off rather on the press of time, winked apologetically, and straightened his mustache. "Sawyer will read it for you," he said, waving me impatiently into the conversation.

Cathie sneered, and stared irritably out a window (it was the one with the wreath) at Jupiter, heavy in the fragile sky. We knew, by then, that it had a definable surface, that the big planet was a world sea of liquid hydrogen, wrapped around a rocky core. "It must be frustrating," she said, "to know you'll never see it." Her tone was casual, almost frivolous, but Landolfi was not easily baited.

"Do you really think," he asked, with the patience of the superior being (Landolfi had no illusions about his capabilities), "that these little pieces of theater will make any difference? Yes, Catherine, of course it's frustrating. Especially when one realizes that we have the technology to put vehicles down there. . . ."

"And scoop out some hydrogen," Cathie added.

He shrugged. "It may happen someday."

"Victor, it never will if we don't sell the Program. This is the last shot. These ships are old, and nobody's going to build any new ones. Unless things change radically at home."

Landolfi closed his eyes. I knew what he was thinking: Cathie Perth was an outsider, an ex-television journalist who had probably slept her way on board. She played bridge, knew the film library by heart, read John Donne (for style, she said), and showed no interest whatever in the scientific accomplishments of the mission. We'd made far-reaching discoveries in the fields of plate tectonics, planetary climatology, and a dozen other disciplines. We'd narrowed the creation date down inside a range of a few million years. And we finally understood how it had happened! But Cathie's televised reports had de-emphasized the implications, and virtually ignored the mechanics of such things. Instead, while a global audience watched, Marjorie Aubuchon peered inspirationally out of a cargo lock at Ganymede (much in the fashion that Cortez must have looked at the Pacific on that first bright morning), her shoulder flag patch resplendent in the sunlight. And while the camera moved in for a close-up (her features were illuminated by a lamp Cathie had placed for the occasion in her helmet), Herman Selma solemnly intoned Cathie's comments on breaking the umbilical.

That was her style: brooding alien vistas reduced to human terms. In one of her best-known sequences, there had been no narration whatever: two spacesuited figures, obviously male and female, stood together in the shadow of the monumental Cadmus Ice Fracture on Europa, beneath three moons.

"Cathie," Landolfi said, with his eyes still shut, "I don't wish to be offensive: but do you really care? For the Program, that is? When we get home, you will write a book, you will be famous, you will be at the top of your profession. Are you really concerned with where the Program will be in twenty years?"

It was a fair question: Cathie'd made no secret of her hopes for a Pulitzer. And she stood to get it, no matter what happened after this mission. Moreover, although she'd tried to conceal her opinions, we'd been together a long time by then, almost three years, and we could hardly misunderstand the dark view she took of people who voluntarily imprisoned themselves for substantial portions of their lives to go 'rock-collecting.'

"No," she said. "I'm not, because there won't be a Program in twenty years." She looked around at each of us, weighing the effect of her words. Iseminger, a blond giant with a reddish beard, allowed a smile of lazy tolerance to soften his granite features. "We're in the same class as the pyramids," she continued, in a tone that was unemotional and irritatingly condescending. "We're a hell of an expensive operation, and for what? Do you think the taxpayers give a good goddam about the weather on Jupiter? There's nothing out here but gas and boulders. Playthings for eggheads!"

I sat and thought about it while she smiled sweetly, and Victor smoldered. I had not heard the solar system ever before described in quite those terms; I'd heard people call it *vast, awesome, magnificent, serene,* stuff like that. But never *boring.*

In the end, Landolfi read his lines. He did it, he said, to end the distraction.

Cathie was clearly pleased with the result. She spent three days editing the tapes, commenting frequently (and with good-natured malice) on the *resonance* and *tonal qualities* of the voice-over. She finished on the morning of the 24th (ship time, of course), and transmitted the report to *Greenswallow* for relay to Houston.

"It'll make the evening newscasts," she said with satisfaction.

It was our third Christmas out. Except for a couple of experiments-in-progress, we were finished on Callisto and, in fact, in the Jovian system. Everybody was feeling good about that, and we passed an uneventful afternoon, playing bridge and talking about what we'd do when we got back. (Cathie had described a deserted beach near Tillamook, Oregon, where she'd grown up. "It would be nice to walk on it again, under a *blue* sky," she said. Landolfi had startled everyone at that point: he looked up from the computer console at which he'd been working, and his eyes grew very distant. "I think," he said, "when the time comes, I would like very much to walk with you. . . .")

For the most part, Victor kept busy that afternoon with his hobby: he was designing a fusion engine that would be capable, he thought, of carrying ships to Jupiter within a few weeks, and, possibly, would eventually open the stars to direct exploration. But I watched him: he turned away periodically from the display screen, to glance at Cathie. Yes (I thought), she would indeed be lovely against the rocks and the spume, her black hair free in the wind.

Just before dinner, we watched the transmission of Cathie's tape. It was very strong, and when it was finished we sat silently looking at one another. By then, Herman Selma and Esther Crowley had joined us. (Although two landers were down, Cathie had been careful to give the impression in her report that there had only been one. When I asked why, she said, "In a place like this, one lander is the Spirit of Man. Two landers is just two landers.") We toasted Victor, and we toasted Cathie. Almost everyone, it turned out, had brought down a bottle for the occasion. We sang and laughed, and somebody turned up the music. We'd long since discovered the effect of low-gravity dancing in cramped quarters, and I guess we made the most of it.

Marj Aubuchon, overhead in the linkup, called to wish us season's greetings, and called again later to tell us that the telecast, according to Houston, had been "well-received." That was government talk, of course, and it meant only that no one in authority could find anything to object to. Actually, somebody high up had considerable confidence in her: in order to promote the illusion of spontaneity, the tapes were being broadcast directly to the commercial networks.

Cathie, who by then had had a little too much to drink, gloated openly. "It's the best we've done," she said. "Nobody'll ever do it better."

We shared that sentiment. Landolfi raised his glass, winked at Cathie, and drained it.

We had to cut the evening short, because a lander's life-support system isn't designed to handle six people. (For that matter, neither was an Athena's.) But before we broke it up, Cathie surprised us all by proposing a final toast: "To Frank Steinitz," she said quietly. "And his crew."

Steinitz: there was a name, as they say, to conjure with. He had led the first deep-space mission, five Athenas to Saturn, fifteen years before. It had been the first attempt to capture the public imagination for a dying program: an investigation of a peculiar object filmed by a Voyager on Iapetus. But nothing much had come of it, and the mission had taken almost seven years. Steinitz and his people had begun as heroes, but in the end they'd become symbols of futility. The press had portrayed them mercilessly as personifications of outworn virtues. Someone had compared them to the Japanese soldiers found as late as the 1970s on Pacific islands, still defending a world long since vanished.

The Steinitz group bore permanent reminders of their folly: prolonged weightlessness had loosened ligaments and tendons, and weakened muscles. Several had developed heart problems, and all suffered from assorted neuroses. As one syndicated columnist had observed, they walked like a bunch of retired big-league catchers.

"That's a good way to end the evening," said Selma, beaming benevolently.

Landolfi looked puzzled. "Cathie," he rumbled, "you've questioned Steinitz's good sense any number of times. And ours, by the way. Isn't it a little hypocritical to drink to him?"

"I'm not impressed by his intelligence," she said, ignoring the obvious parallel. "But he and his people went all the way out to Saturn in those damned things—" she waved in the general direction of the three Athenas orbiting overhead in linkup "—hanging onto baling wire and wing struts. I have to admire that."

"Hell," I said, feeling the effects a little myself, "we've got the same ships he had."

"Yes, you do," said Cathie pointedly.

I had trouble sleeping that night. For a long time, I lay listening to Landolfi's soft snore, and the electronic fidgeting of the operations computer. Cathie was bundled inside a gray blanket, barely visible in her padded chair.

She was right, of course. I knew that rubber boots would never again cross that white landscape, which had waited a billion years for us. The peaks glowed in the reflection of the giant planet: fragile crystalline beauty, on a world of terrifying stillness. Except for an occasional incoming rock, nothing more would ever happen here. Callisto's entire history was encapsuled within twelve days.

Pity there hadn't been something to those early notions about Venusian rain forests and canals on Mars. The Program might have had easier going had Burroughs or Bradbury been right. My God: how many grim surprises had disrupted fictional voyages to Mars? But the truth had been far worse than anything Wells or the others had ever committed to paper: the red planet was so dull that we hadn't even gone there.

Instead, we'd lumbered out to the giants. In ships that drained our lives and our health.

We could have done better; our ships could have *been* better. The computer beside which Landolfi slept contained his design for the fusion engine. And at JPL, an Army team had demonstrated that artificial gravity was possible: a *real* gravity field, not the pathetic fraction created on the Athenas by spinning the inner hull. There were other possibilities as well: infrared ranging could be adapted to replace our elderly scanning system; new alloys were under development. But it would cost billions to build a second-generation vehicle. And unless there were an incentive, unless Cathie Perth carried off a miracle, it would not happen.

Immediately overhead, a bright new star glittered, moving visibly (though slowly) from west to east. That was the linkup, three ships connected nose to nose by umbilicals and a magnetic docking system. Like the Saturn mission, we were a multiple vehicle operation. We were more flexible that way, and we had a safety factor: two ships would be adequate to get the nine-man mission home. Conditions might become a little stuffy, but we'd make it.

I watched it drift through the icy starfield.

Cathie had pulled the plug on the Christmas lights. But it struck me that Callisto would only have one Christmas, so I put them back on.

Victor was on board *Tolstoi* when we lost it. No one ever really knew precisely what happened. We'd begun our long fall toward Jupiter, gaining the acceleration which we'd need on the flight home. Cathie, Herman Selma (the mission commander), and I were riding *Greenswallow*. The ships had separated, and would not rejoin until we'd rounded Jupiter, and settled into our course for home. (The Athenas are really individually-powered modular units which travel, except when maneuvering, as a single vessel. They're connected bow-to-bow by electromagnets. Coils of segmented tubing, called 'umbilicals' even though the term does not accurately describe their function, provide ready access among the forward areas of the ships. As many as six Athenas can be linked in this fashion, although only five have ever been built. The resulting structure would resemble a wheel.)

Between Callisto and Ganymede, we hit something: a drifting cloud of fine particles, a belt of granular material stretched so thin it never appeared on the LGD, before or after. Cathie later called it a cosmic sandbar; Iseminger thought it an unformed moon. It didn't matter: whatever it was, the mission plowed into it at almost 50,000 kilometers per hour. Alarms clattered, and red lamps blinked on.

In those first moments, I thought the ship was going to come apart. Herman was thrown across a blank of consoles and through an open hatch. I couldn't see Cathie, but a quick burst of profanity came from her direction. Things were being ripped off the hull. Deep within her walls, *Greenswallow* sighed. The lights dipped, came back, and went out. Emergency lamps cut in, and something big glanced off the side of the ship. More alarms howled, and I waited for the clamor of the throaty klaxon which would warn of a holing, and which consequently would be the last sound I could expect to hear in this life.

The sudden deceleration snapped my head back on the pads. (The collision had occurred at the worst possible time: *Green-*

swallow was caught in the middle of an attitude alignment. We were flying backwards.)

The exterior monitors were blank: that meant the cameras were gone.

Cathie's voice: "Rob, you okay?"

"Yes."

"Can you see Herman?"

My angle was bad, and I was pinned in my chair. "No. He's back in cargo."

"Is there any way you can close the hatch?"

"Herman's in there," I protested, thinking she'd misunderstood.

"If something tears a hole out back there, we're all going to go. Keeping the door open won't help him."

I hesitated. Sealing up seemed to be the wrong thing to do. (Of course, the fact that the hatch had been open in the first place constituted a safety violation.) "It's on your console," I told her. "Hit the numerics on your upper right."

"Which one?"

"Hit them all." She was seated at the status board, and I could see a row of red lights: several other hatches were open. They should have closed automatically when the first alarms sounded.

We got hit again, this time in front. *Greenswallow* trembled, and loose pieces of metal rattled around inside the walls like broken teeth.

"Rob," she said. "I don't think it's working."

The baleful lights still glowed across the top of her board.

It lasted about three minutes.

When it was over, we hurried back to look at Herman. We were no longer rotating, and gravity had consequently dropped to zero. Selma, gasping, pale, his skin damp, was floating grotesquely over a pallet of ore-sample cannisters. We got him to a couch and applied compresses. His eyes rolled shut, opened, closed again. "Inside," he said, gently fingering an area just off his sternum. "I think I've been chewed up a little." He raised his head slightly. "What kind of shape are we in?"

I left Cathie with him. Then I restored power, put on a suit and went outside.

The hull was a disaster: antennas were down, housings scored, lenses shattered. The lander was gone, ripped from its web. The port cargo area had buckled, and an auxiliary hatch was sprung. On the bow, the magnetic dock was hammered into slag. Travel between the ships was going to be a little tougher.

Greenswallow looked as if she had been sandblasted. I scraped particles out of her jet nozzles, replaced cable, and bolted down mounts. I caught a glimpse of *Amity*'s lights, sliding diagonally across the sky. As were the constellations.

"Cathie," I said. "I see Mac. But I think we're tumbling."

"Okay."

Iseminger was also on board *Amity*. And, fortunately, Marj Aubuchon, our surgeon. Herman's voice broke in, thick with effort. "Rob, we got no radio contact with anyone. Any sign of Victor?"

Ganymede was close enough that its craters lay exposed in harsh solar light. Halfway round the sky, the Pleiades glittered. *Tolstoi*'s green and red running lights should have been visible among, or near, the six silver stars. But the sky was empty. I stood a long time and looked, wondering how many other navigators on other oceans had sought lost friends in that constellation. What had they called it in antiquity? The rainy Pleiades. . . .

"Only *Amity*," I said.

I tore out some cable and lobbed it in the general direction of Ganymede. Jupiter's enormous arc was pushing above the maintenance pods, spraying October light across the wreckage. I improvised a couple of antennas, replaced some black boxes, and then decided to correct the tumble, if I could.

"Try it now," I said.

Cathie acknowledged.

Two of the jets were useless. I went inside for spares, and replaced the faulty units. While I was finishing up, Cathie came back on. "Rob," she said, "radio's working, more or less. We have no long-range transmit, though."

"Okay. I'm not going to try to do anything about that right now."

"Are you almost finished?"

"Why?"

"Something occurred to me. Maybe the cloud, whatever that damned thing was that we passed through: maybe it's U-shaped."

"Thanks," I said. "I needed something to worry about."

"Maybe you should come back inside."

"Soon as I can. How's the patient doing?"

"Out," she said. "He was a little delirious when he was talking to you. Anyhow, I'm worried: I think something's broken internally. He never got his color back, and he's beginning to bring up blood. Rob, we need Marj."

"You hear anything from *Amity* yet?"

"Just a carrier wave." She did not mention *Tolstoi*. "How bad is it out there?"

From where I was tethered, about halfway back on the buckled beam, I could see a crack in the main plates that appeared to run the length of the port tube. I climbed out onto the exhaust assembly, and pointed my flashlight into the combustion chamber. Something glittered where the reflection should have been subdued. I got in and looked: silicon. Sand, and steel, had fused in the white heat of passage. The exhaust was blocked.

Cathie came back on. "What about it, Rob?" she asked. "Any serious problems?"

"Cathie," I said, "*Greenswallow*'s going to Pluto."

Herman thought I was Landolfi: he kept assuring me that everything was going to be okay. His pulse was weak and rapid, and he alternated between sweating and shivering. Cathie had got a blanket under him and buckled him down so he wouldn't hurt himself. She bunched some pillows under his feet, and held a damp compress to his head.

"That's not going to help much. Raising his legs, I mean."

She looked at me, momentarily puzzled. "Oh," she said. "Not enough gravity."

I nodded.

"Oh, Rob." Her eyes swept the cases and cannisters, all neatly tagged, silicates from Pasiphae, sulfur from Himalia, assorted carbon compounds from Callisto. We had evidence now that Io had formed elsewhere in the solar system, and been well along in middle age when it was captured. We'd all but eliminated the possibility that life existed in Jupiter's atmosphere. We understood why rings formed around gas giants, and we had a new clue to the cause of terrestrial ice ages. And I could see that Cathie was thinking about trading lives to satisfy the curiosity of a few academics. "We don't belong out here," she said, softly. "Not in these primitive shells."

I said nothing.

"I got a question for you," she continued. "We're not going to find *Tolstoi*, right?"

"Is that your question?"

"No. I wish it were. But the LGD can't see them. That means they're just not there." Her eyes filled with tears, but she shook her head impatiently. "And we can't steer this thing. Can *Amity* carry six people?"

"It might have to."

"That wasn't what I asked."

"Food and water would be tight. Especially since we're running out of time, and wouldn't be able to transfer much over. If any. So we'd all be a little thinner when we got back. But yes, I think we could survive."

We stared at one another, and then she turned away. I became conscious of the ship: the throb of power deep in her bulkheads (power now permanently bridled by conditions in the combustion chambers), the soft amber glow of the navigation lamps in the cockpit.

McGuire's nasal voice, from *Amity*, broke the uneasy silence. "Herman, you okay?"

Cathie looked at me, and I nodded. "Mac," she said, "this is Perth. Herman's hurt. We need Marj."

"Okay," he said. "How bad?"

"We don't know. Internal injuries, looks like. He appears to be in shock."

We heard him talking to someone else. Then he came back. "We're on our way. I'll put Marj on in a minute; maybe she can help from here. How's the ship?"

"Not good: the dock's gone, and the engine might as well be."

He asked me to be specific. "If we try a burn, the rear end'll fall off."

McGuire delivered a soft, venomous epithet. And then: "Do what you can for Herman. Marj'll be right here."

Cathie was looking at me strangely. "He's worried," she said.

"Yes. He's in charge now. . . ."

"Rob, you say you *think* we'll be okay. What's the problem?"

"We might," I said, "run a little short of air."

Greenswallow continued her plunge toward Jupiter at a steadily increasing rate and a sharp angle of approach: we would pass within about 60,000 kilometers, and then drop completely out of the plane of the solar system. We appeared to be heading in the general direction of the Southern Cross.

Cathie worked on Herman. His breathing steadied, and he slipped in and out of his delirium. We sat beside him, not talking much. After a while, Cathie asked, "What happens now?"

"In a few hours," I said, "we'll reach our insertion point. By then, we have to be ready to change course." She frowned, and I shrugged. "That's it," I said. "It's all the time we have to get over to *Amity*. If we don't make the insertion on time, *Amity* won't have the fuel to throw a U-turn later."

"Rob, how are we going to get Herman over there?"

That was an uncomfortable question. The prospect of jamming him down into a suit was less than appealing, but there was no other way. "We'll just have to float him over," I said. "Marj won't like it much."

"Neither will Herman."

"You wanted a little high drama," I said, unnecessarily. "The next show should be a barnburner."

Her mouth tightened, and she turned away from me.

One of the TV cameras had picked up the approach of *Amity*. Some of her lights were out, and she too looked a bit bent. The Athena is a homely vessel in the best of times, whale-shaped and snub-nosed, with a midship flare that suggests middle-age spread. But I was glad to see her.

Cathie snuffled at the monitor, and blew her nose. "Your Program's dead, Rob." Her eyes blazed momentarily, like a dying fire into which one has flung a few drops of water. "We're leaving three of our people out here; and if you're right about the air, we'll get home with a shipload of defectives, or worse. Won't that look good on the six o'clock news?" She gazed vacantly at *Amity*'s image. "I'd hoped," she said, "that if things went well, Victor would have lived to see a ship carry his fusion engine.

And maybe his name, as well. Ain't gonna happen, though. Not ever.''

I had not allowed myself to think about the oxygen problem we were going to face. The Athenas recycle their air supply: the converters in a single ship can maintain a crew of three, or even four, indefinitely. But six?

I was not looking forward to the ride home.

A few minutes later, a tiny figure detached itself from the shadow of the Athena and started across: Marj Aubuchon on a maintenance sled. McGuire's voice erupted from the ship's speakers. ''Rob, we've taken a long look at your engines, and we agree with your assessment. The damage complicates things.'' Mac had a talent for understatement. It derived, not from a sophisticated sense of humor, but from a genuine conviction of his own inferiority. He preferred to solve problems by denying their existence. He was the only one of the original nine who could have been accurately described as passive: other people's opinions carried great weight with him. His prime value to the mission was his grasp of Athena systems. But he'd been a reluctant crewman, a man who periodically reminded us that he wanted only to retire to his farm in Indiana. He wouldn't have been along at all except that one guy died and somebody else came down with an unexpected (but thoroughly earned) disease. Now, with Selma incapacitated and Landolfi gone, McGuire was in command. It must have been disconcerting for him. ''We've got about five hours,'' he continued. ''Don't let Marj get involved in major surgery. She's already been complaining to me that it doesn't sound as if it'll be possible to move him. *We have no alternative.* She knows that, but you know how she is. Okay?''

One of the monitors had picked him up. He looked rumpled, and nervous. Not an attitude to elicit confidence. ''Mac,'' said Cathie, ''we may kill him trying to get him over there.''

''You'll kill him if you don't,'' he snapped. ''Get your personal stuff together, and bring it with you. You won't be going back.''

''What about trying to transfer some food?'' I asked.

''We can't dock,'' he said. ''And there isn't time to float it across.''

''Mac,'' said Cathie, ''is *Amity* going to be able to support six people?''

I listened to McGuire breathing. He turned away to issue some trivial instructions to Iseminger. When he came back he said, simply and tonelessly, "Probably not." And then, coldbloodedly (I thought), "How's Herman doing?"

Maybe it was my imagination. Certainly there was nothing malicious in his tone, but Cathie caught it too, and turned sharply round. "McGuire is a son-of-a-bitch," she hissed. I don't know whether Mac heard it.

Marjorie Aubuchon was short, blond, and irritable. When I relayed McGuire's concerns about time, she said, "God knows, that's all I've heard for the last half-hour." She observed that McGuire was a jerk, and bent over Herman. The blood was pink and frothy on his lips. After a few minutes she said, to no one in particular, "Probably a punctured lung." She waved Cathie over, and began filling a hypo; I went for a walk.

At sea, there's a long tradition of sentiment between mariners and their ships. Enlisted men identify with them, engineers baby them, and captains go down with them. No similar attitude has developed in space flight. We've never had an *Endeavour*, or a *Golden Hind*. Always, off Earth, it has been the mission, rather than the ship. *Friendship VII* and *Apollo XI* were far more than vehicles. I'm not sure why that is; maybe it reflects Cathie's view that travel between the worlds is still in its *Kon-Tiki* phase: the voyage itself is of such epic proportions that everything else is overwhelmed.

But I'd lived almost three years on *Greenswallow*. It was a long time to be confined to her narrow spaces. Nevertheless, she was shield and provider against that enormous abyss, and I discovered (while standing in the doorway of my cabin) a previously unfelt affection for her.

A few clothes were scattered round the room, a shirt was hung over my terminal, and two pictures were mounted on the plastic wall. One was a Casnavan print of a covered bridge in New Hampshire; the other was a telecopy of an editorial cartoon that had appeared in the *Washington Post*. The biggest human problem we had, of course, was sheer boredom. And Cathie had tried to capture the dimensions of the difficulty by showing crewmembers filling the long days on the outbound journey with bridge. ("It would be nice," Cathie's narrator had said at one point, "if we could take everybody out to an Italian restaurant now and then.") The *Post* cartoon had appeared several days later: it depicted four astronauts holding cards. (We could recognize Selma, Landolfi, and Marj. The fourth, whose back was turned, was exceedingly feminine, and appeared to be Esther Crowley.) An enormous bloodshot eye is looking in through one window; a tentacle and a UFO are visible through another. The "Selma" character, his glasses characteristically down on his nose, is examining his hand, and delivering the caption: *Dummy looks out the window and checks the alien.*

I packed the New Hampshire bridge, and left the cartoon. If someone comes by, in 20 million years or so, he might need a laugh. I went up to the cockpit with my bag.

McGuire checked with me to see how we were progressing. "Fine," I told him. I was still sitting there four hours later when Cathie appeared behind me.

"Rob," she said, "we're ready to move him." She smiled wearily. "Marj says he should be okay if we can get him over there without breaking anything else."

We cut the spin on the inner module to about point-oh-five. Then we lifted Herman onto a stretcher, and carried him carefully down to the airlock.

Cathie stared straight ahead, saying nothing. Her fine-boned cheeks were pale, and her eyes seemed focused far away. These, I thought, were her first moments to herself, unhampered by other duties. The impact of events was taking hold.

Marj called McGuire and told him we were starting over, and that she would need a sizable pair of shears when we got there to cut Herman's suit open. "Please have them ready," she said. "We may be in a hurry."

I had laid out his suit earlier: we pulled it up over his legs. That was easy, but the rest of it was slow, frustrating work. "We need a special kind of unit for this," Marj said. "Probably a large bag, without arms or legs. If we're ever dumb enough to do anything like this again, I'll recommend it."

McGuire urged us to hurry.

Once or twice, Cathie's eyes met mine. Something passed between us, but I was too distracted to define it. Then we were securing his helmet, and adjusting the oxygen mixture.

"I think we're okay," Marj observed, her hand pressed against Selma's chest. "Let's get him over there. . . ."

I opened the inner airlock, and pulled my own helmet into place. Then we guided Herman in, and secured him to *Green-swallow*'s maintenance sled. (The sled was little more than a tool-shed with jet nozzles.) I recovered my bag and stowed it on board.

"I'd better get my stuff," Cathie said. "You can get Herman over all right?"

"Of course," said Marj. "*Amity*'s sled is secured outside the lock. Use that."

She hesitated in the open hatchway, raised her left hand, and spread the fingers wide. Her eyes grew very round, and she formed two syllables that I was desperately slow to understand: in fact, I don't think I translated the gesture, the word, until we were halfway across to *Amity*, and the lock was irrevocably closed behind us.

"Good-bye."

Cathie's green eyes sparkled with barely controlled emotion across a dozen or so monitors. Her black hair, which had been tied back earlier, now framed her angular features and fell to her shoulders. It was precisely in that partial state of disarray that tends to be most appealing. She looked as if she'd been crying, but her jaw was set, and she stood erect. Beneath the gray tunic, her breast rose and fell.

"What the hell are you doing, Perth?" demanded McGuire. He looked tired, almost ill. He'd gained weight since we'd left the Cape, his hair had whitened and retreated, his flesh had grown blotchy, and he'd developed jowls. The contrast with his dapper image in the mission photo was sobering. "Get moving!" he said, striving to keep his voice from rising. "We're not going to make our burn!"

"I'm staying where I am," she said. "I couldn't make it over there now anyway. I wouldn't even have time to put on the suit."

McGuire's puffy eyelids slid slowly closed. "Why?" he asked.

She looked out of the cluster of screens, a segmented Cathie, a group-Cathie. "Your ship won't support six people, Mac."

"Dammit!" His voice was a harsh rasp. "It would have just

meant we'd cut down activity. Sleep a lot." He waved a hand in front of his eyes, as though his vision were blurred. "Cathie, we've lost you. There's no way we can get you back!"

"I know."

No one said anything. Iseminger stared at her.

"Is Herman okay?" she asked.

"Marj is still working on him," I said. "She thinks we got him across okay."

"Good."

A series of yellow lamps blinked on across the pilot's console. We had two minutes. "Damn," I said, suddenly aware of another danger: *Amity* was rotating, turning toward its new course. Would *Greenswallow* even survive the ignition? I looked at McGuire, who understood. His fingers flicked over press pads, and rows of numbers flashed across the navigation monitor. I could see muscles working in Cathie's jaws; she looked down at Mac's station as though she could read the result.

"It's all right," he said. "She'll be clear."

"Cathie . . ." Iseminger's voice was almost strangled. "If I'd known you intended anything like this . . ."

"I know, Ed." Her tone was gentle, a lover's voice, perhaps. Her eyes were wet: she smiled anyway, full face, up close.

Deep in the systems, pumps began to whine. "I wish," said Iseminger, absolutely without expression, "that we could do something."

She turned her back, strode with unbearable grace across the command center, away from us, and passed into the shadowy interior of the cockpit. Another camera picked her up there, and we got a profile: she was achingly lovely in the soft glow of the navigation lamps.

"There is something . . . you can do," she said. "Build Landolfi's engine. And come back for me."

For a brief moment, I thought Mac was going to abort the burn. But he sat frozen, fists clenched, and did the right thing, which is to say, nothing. It struck me that McGuire was incapable of intervening.

And I knew also that the woman in the cockpit was terrified of what she had done. It had been a good performance, but she'd utterly failed to conceal the fear that looked out of her eyes. And I realized with shock that she'd acted, not to prolong her life, but to save the Program. I watched her face as *Amity*'s engines ignited, and we began to draw away. Like McGuire, she seemed paralyzed, as though the nature of the calamity which she'd embraced was just becoming clear to her. Then it—she—was gone.

"What happened to the picture?" snapped Iseminger.

"She turned it off," I said. "I don't think she wants us to see her just now."

He glared at me, and spoke to Mac. "Why the hell," he demanded, "couldn't he have brought her back with him?" His fists were knotted.

"I didn't know," I said. "How could I know?" And I wondered, how could I not?

When the burn ended, the distance between the two ships had opened to only a few kilometers. But it was a gulf, I thought, wider than any across which men had before looked at each other.

Iseminger called her name relentlessly. (We knew she could hear us.) But we got only the carrier wave.

Then her voice crackled across the command center. "Good," she said. "Excellent. Check the recorders: make sure you got everything on tape." Her image was back. She was in full light again, tying up her hair. Her eyes were hooded, and her lips pursed thoughtfully. "Rob," she continued, "fade it out during Ed's response, when he's calling my name. Probably, you'll want to reduce the background noise at that point. Cut all the business about who's responsible. We want a sacrifice, not an oversight."

"My God, Cathie," I said. I stared at her, trying to understand. "What have you done?"

She took a deep breath. "I meant what I said. I have enough food to get by here for eight years or so. More if I stretch it. *And plenty of fresh air*. Well, relatively fresh. I'm better off than any of us would be if six people were trying to survive on *Amity*."

"Cathie!" howled McGuire. He sounded in physical agony. "Cathie, we didn't know for sure about life support. The converters might have kept up. There might have been enough air! It was just an estimate!"

"This is a hell of a time to tell me," she said. "Well, it doesn't matter now. Listen, I'll be fine. I've got books to read, and maybe one to write. My long-range communications are *kaput*, Rob knows that, so you'll have to come back for the book, too.'' She smiled. ''You'll like it, Mac.'' The command center got very still. ''And on nights when things really get boring, I can play bridge with the computer.''

McGuire shook his head. ''You're sure you'll be all right? You seemed pretty upset a few minutes ago.''

She looked at me and winked.

''The first Cathie was staged, Mac,'' I said.

''I give up,'' McGuire sighed. ''Why?'' He swiveled round to face the image on his screen. ''Why would you do that?''

''That young woman,'' she replied, ''was committing an act of uncommon valor, as they say in the Marines. And she had to be vulnerable.'' And compellingly lovely, I thought. In those last moments, I was realizing what it might mean to love Cathie Perth. ''This Cathie,'' she grinned, ''is doing the only sensible thing. And taking a sabbatical as well. Do what you can to get the ship built. I'll be waiting. Come if you can.'' She paused. ''Somebody should suggest they name it after Victor.''

This is the fifth Christmas since that one on Callisto. It's a long time by any human measure. We drifted out of radio contact during the first week. There was some talk of broadcasting instructions to her for repairing her long-range transmission equipment. But she'd have to go outside to do it, so the idea was prudently tabled.

She was right about that tape. In my lifetime, I've never seen people so singlemindedly aroused. It created a global surge of sympathy and demands for action that seem to grow in intensity with each passing year. Funded partially by contributions and technical assistance from abroad, NASA has been pushing the construction of the fusion vessel that Victor Landolfi dreamed of.

Iseminger was assigned to help with the computer systems, and he's kept me informed of progress. The most recent public estimates had anticipated a spring launch. But that single word *September* in Iseminger's card suggests that one more obstacle has been encountered; and it means still another year before we can hope to reach her.

We broadcast to her on a regular basis. I volunteered to help, and I sit sometimes and talk to her for hours. She gets a regular schedule of news, entertainment, sports, whatever. And, if she's listening, she knows that we're coming.

And she also knows that her wish that the fusion ship be named for Victor Landolfi has been disregarded. The rescue vehicle will be the *Catherine Perth*.

If she's listening: we have no way of knowing. And I worry a lot. Can a human being survive six years of absolute solitude? Iseminger was here for a few days last summer, and he tells me he is confident. "She's a tough lady," he said, any number of times. "Nothing bothers her. She even gave us a little theater at the end."

And that's what scares me: Cathie's theatrical technique. I've thought about it, on the long ride home, and here. I kept a copy of the complete tape of that final conversation, despite McGuire's instructions to the contrary, and I've watched it a few times. It's locked downstairs in a file cabinet now, and I don't look at it anymore. I'm afraid to. There are two Cathie Perths on the recording: the frightened, courageous one who galvanized a global public; and our Cathie, preoccupied with her job, flexible, almost indifferent to her situation. A survivor.

And, God help me, I can't tell which one was staged.

GRANDFATHER CHRISTMAS

Robert Frazier and James Patrick Kelly

"Grandfather Christmas" was purchased by Gardner Dozois, and appeared in the December 1994 issue of Asimov's, *with an interior illustration by Steve Cavallo.*

Robert Frazier has published dozens of poems in Asimov's *and elsewhere throughout the last two decades—he is, in fact, one of the genre's best-known and most respected poets, and has probably published more poetry in* Asimov's *over the years, by a considerable margin, than any other contributor. He made his first prose sale to* Asimov's *in 1988, and has since sold several more to us, as well as to markets such as* Playboy, Amazing, New Pathways, *and* In the Fields of Fire. *Several chapbooks of his poetry have been published, including* Peregrine, Perception Barriers, Co-Orbital Moons, Chronicles of the Mutant Rain Forest *(with Bruce Boston), and* A Measure of Calm *(with Andrew Joron), and he has also edited the poetry anthology* Burning With a Vision: Poetry of Science and the Fantastic. *In 1980, he won the Rhysling Award for his poem "Encased in the Amber of Eternity." At last word, he was at work on a novel. Frazier lives in Nantucket, off the coast of Massachusetts.*

James Patrick Kelly has been one of the mainstays of Asimov's *for nearly a decade now, under several dif-*

*ferent editors, and has enjoyed the unique distinction of
having had a story in every June issue of* Asimov's *since
1983. He made his first sale in 1975, and went on to
become one of the most respected and prominent new
writers of the '80s; indeed, Kelly stories such as "Solstice," "The Prisoner of Chillon," "Glass Cloud,"
"Home Front," "Pogrom," and "Mr. Boy" must be
ranked among the most inventive and memorable short
works of the decade. Kelly's novels include a novel written in collaboration with John Kessel,* Freedom Beach,
as well as the solo novels Planet of Whispers *and* Look
into the Sun. *His most recent book is a third solo novel,*
Wildlife. *Born in Mineola, New York, Kelly now lives
with his family in Portsmouth, New Hampshire.*

*Here they join forces to show us how some things
don't change even under the impact of accelerating Future Shock, as they take us to a divided and embattled
high-tech household about to receive some very sea-
sonal surprises . . .*

We found Nick while we were snooping Grandma Brewster's
attic. It was two days after the funeral, and the grownups still
weren't paying any attention to us. We could hear them down in
the living room, yelling at each other. This time, the argument
was about Grandma's furniture. Mom claimed nobody would pay
ten thousand dollars for the Hepplewhite sideboard, and Aunt
Francie said then we'd have to sell off the portrait of sea captain
Tristram Olaf Brewster, which Grandma had loaned to the Nantucket Whaling Museum. When Grandma was alive, no one dared
raise their voice in this house. Especially on Christmas Eve.

"We shouldn't be doing this," said my cousin Aggie. She sat
crosslegged on Grandma's bed, watching entry menus flash across
the windowall.

"I know," I said. "That's what makes it fun."

"But what if they find out?"

"They're busy. Listen to them."

"I don't get it. Grandma was rich, so what's the problem?
Besides, if they sell off all her furniture, what are we going to
use *here?*"

I'd tried once before to get into the attic's upper-level files. I tricked the scuzzy driver with the BugUgly utility. I tried patching Dad's Ultrabook through a jumperop cable. I even hit caps-shift-escape with my left hand, enter-alt-home with my right, and F6 with my nose. But it wasn't a hardware problem; I was up against a software encryption lock. Grandma Brewster was old-fashioned about everything but security for her homebrain. She'd encrypted her attic with some kind of public key/private key system.

Of course, Grandma had caught me. She told me little girls shouldn't snoop. I told her I wasn't a little girl anymore, but I don't think she was ready to admit that to herself. "You'll just have to wait until you're older, Twilla," she'd said. "I promise I'll give you complete access someday." Well, I was a freshman in high school now and Grandma was in a bronze urn in the hall closet, and I needed to find out what was wrong with her will.

"They'll check the homebrain's log." Aggie was squeamish about bending rules, even for an eighth grader.

"It'll show us playing Witch Cop. I've got it faking moves."

"My mom will ground me until it's *my* funeral," said Aggie. "She's been pretty hard to live with since Dad moved out. And now . . ."

"No offense, Aggie, but your mom's been hard to live with for as long as I can remember."

Aggie twisted a strand of her perfect blonde hair. "You know, I loved Grandma a lot, and I'm going to miss her and everything . . . but I have this weird feeling." She glanced at me and then back at the windowall. "Like I'm kind of mad at her."

"For dying?"

She nodded.

"Yeah," I said, "especially for *when* she died. Because from now on, her death is going to be part of Christmas."

I finally reached the attic door. When I tried to open it, the lock icon flashed and Grandma's homebrain prompted me for the passkey. Obviously, Aunt Francie had been expecting me. I pulled down the symbol menu and typed ✳ ❖ ✪ ❑ ▼ ◯ ⚸ ㉫. A silver key appeared next to the door.

"Hey, where did you get the passkey from?"

"Grandma." I touched my finger to the key and moved it to the lock icon. "I found it in my secret place, the day we got here.'' Each of us had private drop-offs where Grandma would leave notes and candy and even money sometimes. Mine was in the blue teapot on the mantel in the Federal parlor. ''Here we go.'' The door opened, and we were in. Aggie moaned as I went to full zoom on the wall.

''See,'' I said, ''most of it is junk.'' I surfed across neat waves of icons. There were to-do calendars that went back to the last century, tax returns, digitized family pictures, garden layouts, recipes, lots of old, old E-books. ''You ever hear of Bret Easton Ellis?''

''Twil, this is making my stomach hurt.''

''Like when we peeked in the coffin and Grandma's skin was all droopy like wax?''

''Twil!''

''Look, here's her calendar.'' I opened it. In the three weeks she had been in the hospital, Grandma had missed the Christmas Stroll, the Barretts' anniversary party at the Chanticleer, and a concert at the Chamber Music Center. I didn't see any last minute meetings with her lawyer, but there *was* one mystery.

''Hey, remember this?''

There was an icon with Nick's face pasted to December 19. Nicolas Cleary had been Grandma Brewster's second husband, Mom and Aunt Francie's stepfather. He was bald on top with salt and pepper short hair and big sideburns. His pudgy face was grooved by wrinkles. He had a little white mustache.

I hadn't seen his virt in years. When I was a little kid, she used to boot him when the whole family flew in for Christmas. It was a tradition, like baking reindeer cookies with red and green sprinkles, and decorating trees on the windowall, and Grandma's inedible sour cranberry sauce. Then, one year, she didn't bring him up. She said something about how he wasn't right. I thought that meant that his program was corrupted or decayed. So why schedule him again after all this time? I touched his icon.

First there was a blur, then his full figure came into focus, frame by slow frame, speeding up so that the image no longer looked like an oozy movement of bees. He was dressed in khakis and a red-and-black flannel shirt. His face was smooth: no wrinkles or mustache.

''Margaret, I need a new compression algorithm,'' he said.

"Feel like I've been sleeping under the dock." He stretched, and when he extended a holographic arm out from the wall, I could hear the AV circuits hum. Then he saw me at Grandma's terminal. "Who the hell are *you?*"

"Twilla."

"Ellen's girl? I thought you were in fourth grade."

I was insulted. "I'm in high school."

"What's the date?"

"December 24, 2019."

"Oh my god, six years!" He morphed briefly into the figure from Munch's "The Scream." "She hasn't booted me for six goddamn years! And who's that, Agatha June?"

"Hi, Gramps." Aggie was beaming. She'd been Nick's pet when he was alive and his virt had continued to spoil her. "I thought you crashed."

"Who said that—not your grandmother? Where is she?"

"Oops," I said softly.

"Something's wrong." His image degraded into the bee swarm and then solidified again, rumpled and out of breath. He looked as if he had just fallen down the front stairs. "I can't get into the rest of the memory. I'm restricted!" His hair stood on end, stretched beyond the screen limits of the wall. "Margaret!" He called in a voice almost loud enough for Grandma to hear. "I didn't mean it!"

"Ssh! Nick, keep it down."

"*Agatha June Duffbart.*" Aunt Frances stood in the doorway, a vision of Christmas hell in her red pumps and a dress programmed to holly in a snowstorm and red wingtip glasses. "What is going on here?"

I said, "We were just playing Witch Cop, and I cast this opening spell at Sing Sing and all of a sudden we were in . . . in this."

"Is this true, Agatha June?"

I doubted Aggie could stand up to her mother's interrogation for long. "Check the log," I said in defense.

Nick's face filled the wall completely. "Francie, what's going on here? Something's happened to your mother."

"I'll take care of this." Aunt Francie nudged in front of me, taking my place at the terminal. "Leave the room, you two."

Aggie looked surprised. "What are you doing?"

"Twilla, Agatha June, go now! And shut the door behind you."

If I had known what she planned to do, I would never have left. But I thought we'd have a better chance of selling the Witch Cop alibi if we went into good girl mode. Besides, I didn't want to be there when Aunt Francie broke the news to Nick. It didn't take her long.

"Did he cry?" said Aggie.

"What did you tell him?" I said.

"I didn't tell *it* anything," she said coldly. "I wiped it from the system."

I couldn't believe this creature was related to me. She had about as much Christmas spirit as a salad fork.

"Y-you . . ." I stammered, "you bitch!" I knew it was trouble, but I couldn't help myself.

She glared at me. I turned it right back at her, certain that I'd never see Nick again.

Dad found me on the ledge of the third floor hall window, staring across the harbor at the beacon of Great Point Light, as it stretched through the night like a white finger. He wriggled through the casing and sat beside me. He didn't say anything at first, just swung his legs in the chilly air and pulled his cashmere sport jacket tight around him. It was the kind of thing only Dad would do. Mom was a worrier; she would've lectured me about how I was risking my life. Aunt Francie probably would've shut the window on me.

"You know," Dad said finally, "Grandma always said she liked winter better than summer on the island. It wasn't just that the tourists all went home. She said she could see things more clearly in cold air."

"Yeah, right. I guess now we can all see a certain person for what she really is."

"No need to be antagonistic."

"Sorry, but that woman makes me want to puke."

"Okay." He nodded. "But try to look at things from her point of view. She feels like everything's happening to her at once. First the divorce, then her mother dies . . ."

"Hey, she was my *Grandma*."

"... and now she's in a panic over the estate."

"So she gets to yell at us whenever she wants? Dad, she's ruining my Christmas."

"She's family and she's hurting, okay? We have to make an effort to get along."

I hated arguing with Dad; he could see the good side to anything. "So why is she so worried? Is there some problem with the will?"

"The will?" He looked surprised. "No. Your mom and Francie split everything down the middle, whatever there is of it. The problem is that ... well, your Grandma liked to keep secrets. Which is why her finances are a mess. Poor Francie feels like *she* has to clean things up."

"Is that what she calls wiping Nick? Cleaning up?"

He sighed, his breath puffing in the cold. "Keep a family secret?"

I nodded.

"You were too little to realize this, but Francie never had any use for Nick. Not while he was alive, especially not for his virt. But she put up with it for Grandma's sake."

"So now I'm supposed to put up with *her?*" I snorted, then picked at the laces of my hightops. "She just doesn't like me, Dad. Remember that time with the candy dish?"

"Is it my imagination or are we freezing to death out here?" He shivered. "Look, there's a skim of ice on the harbor."

"I'm not groveling to her."

"I wasn't asking you to."

"What are you asking?"

"Just that we eat dinner in peace."

I considered this. "I can stop if she stops."

"Thanks." In the light of a beacon flash, I could see Dad's smile. "Oh, I guess I was supposed to do something about your ... um ... choice of language."

I stiffened. "Like what?"

He patted me on the back. "Francie made Grandma's special sour cranberry sauce. I wanted you to take some."

"I am *not* eating that ... stuff."

"Then push it around a little," he said. "Just having it on your plate is punishment enough." As we wiggled back into the hallway, his jacket snagged on the head of a nail and ripped a pocket. "Wouldn't you know it?" he said.

The Fabfood cranked out the same dinner we'd had every Christmas Eve since forever: turkey with gravy, allnut stuffing, both sweet and mashed-flavored potatettes, butter broccoli bits. But everything else was different. I kept counting all the people who weren't there. Grandma, of course. Uncle Tom, Aggie's dad, who used to burp wisps of black smoke after dinner because of his enzyme problem. And flickery old Nick, who I hadn't missed for years.

I tried to be polite. Maybe Aunt Francie did too, but if you ask me, she didn't try halfway hard enough. I think it had become a Brewster Christmas tradition that the two of us fight. Meanwhile, Aggie was busy being sullen—no help there. Mom wanted to tell stories about when she and Francie were girls living on the island, which always seemed to end with Francie saving the day. Dad talked about the food, the weather, the elections, and all the boring shows he'd seen on the archaeology channel.

As dinner was winding down, Aunt Francie really got into it. She insisted that Aggie and I account for every nanosecond we'd been in the attic.

"And you're sure you didn't erase anything?" she asked.

"I'm sure," I said. "Are you? After all, it was *your* finger on the delete key."

"Well," she said to my mom huffily, "they're not in any memory I can access. I was sure she'd tucked them somewhere in the attic."

"What are you looking for?" I said. "Maybe I can help."

Aunt Francie looked back at me, squinting as if I were some germ she was seeing through a microscope. "Just some financial files we need to clear up Grandma's estate," she said.

"Oh," I said, "you mean really important stuff I'm too stupid to understand?"

"We think she must've hidden her assets," said Mom. "There's no way she could have afforded to live on what we've found so far."

Aunt Francie went back to picking on Aggie. "I still don't understand why you didn't buzz us immediately."

"What's immediately mean?" I interrupted her.

"As soon as he appeared. It's not your business to talk to him."

"Not my business?" said Aggie. "He was my grandpa!"

"Mine, too!" I said.

"I've told you before, Aggie," said Aunt Francie icily. "Your grandfather was Grandpa John. My father."

"Who none of us ever knew," I said.

Mom and Aunt Francie exchanged glances. "Aggie," said Aunt Francie, "we've just buried your grandmother. We're in the middle of trying to settle her business. And we're having a hard enough time without that . . . that graphical bigmouth distracting us." When she frowned, I could see little lines around her mouth, like someone had yanked a purse string tight. Aunt Francie was six years older and twelve times meaner than Mom. "Nick is dead," she said. "A virt is software, not a person. It shouldn't make demands."

"The truth is," Mom said, "that he—the virt—was driving Grandma crazy." Mom pushed a glob of purple cranberry sauce across her plate. "He claimed he really was Nick. He wanted to be left on all year long, said he needed a virtual address, network access, everything. He . . . *it* . . . preyed on her memories until she finally told me that she never wanted to see it again as long as she lived. She decided not to boot him again and she had every right to do it. He belonged to her."

"Then why didn't *she* erase him?" I said. "Why did she put him back on her calendar?"

"Ellen, would you please control your daughter?" Aunt Francie fixed me with a withering stare. "All this backtalk is a bad influence on Aggie."

"Look," said Mom, "we've all been under a lot of stress. . . ."

"Maybe that's your excuse," I said, "but your big sister has been bullying this family for years."

Aunt Francie's eyes bulged.

"Speaking of dressing . . ." Dad passed his plate.

"I do not bully people."

"No?" I said with a dramatic pause. "Then tell us why you've blocked incoming access to the house?"

That pricked up Dad's ears. "Is that true, Frances? My contract with the firm says twenty-four hours on call, no exceptions."

"It can't be helped. We can't have anyone trying to file a recovery on that virt."

I said, "What?"

Francie pointed at Mom. "I think your daughter stole the pass-key. My guess is that she had outside help. I'm not letting her or any of her criminal friends tinker any further with our affairs."

I waited for Mom to stand up for me; I might as well have been waiting for a present from the King of England.

"*Francie*," said Dad, "for Christ's sakes!"

I picked up my plate; we were eating off Grandma's best china. I was thinking of using some of it to express just how much I enjoyed these cozy family reunions when Aggie swooped by. She took the plate, slid it under hers, gathered my silverware, and stacked it carefully on the pile of dishes.

"Twilla promised to help me with my hair after dinner." She kicked my chair hard. "We can get *out* to the net, can't we?"

I looked to Aunt Francie. She grumbled, "Yes."

"Then I'm finished."

Mom nodded. "We'll trim the tree in the morning."

We were dismissed. I knew that Aggie had saved me just in time. I could feel steam in my ears, poison beading under my nails.

Mom was right about one thing. Grandma's death had been a strain on us all. She could be just as headstrong as Aunt Francie, but, like Mom, she listened when you talked to her. She had glued the two halves of the family together. So I thought it was strange when nobody cried at the funeral except Aggie. I kept waiting for Mom to cry, so I could. She was probably waiting for Francie; Mom wasn't herself when she was with her big sister.

I said as much to Aggie. We were sitting on the edge of the four-poster in the kids' room looking at ourselves mirrored on the windowall. We had linked the homebrain to HairNet and were trying on new styles.

"Yeah," said Aggie. "I don't know what's gotten into my mom either. Believe me, she's usually not wound this tight. I mean, remember last Christmas? When she had the silly stocking cap on and she was dancing around the living room with a holo of some old movie guy . . ."

"Tom Travolta."

"Yeah, and everyone was laughing at her. She was laughing too, remember?"

"Grandma put that hat on her."

We sat there for a moment thinking about all the differences between this Christmas and last. On the windowall, a cartoon hairdresser turned Aggie's hair candy-cane red.

"Want to see what Grandma left in *my* secret place?" said Aggie. She offered me a pair of dangle earrings, sculpted into a cascade of silver water. The bubbles in the cascade looked like tiny diamonds.

I held them up to the light. "They're really beautiful." I was jealous.

"Yeah," she said, "and they make me feel really guilty. I've been thinking maybe I should turn them over to Mom. Maybe they're worth something."

I arranged them on the bedspread in front of her. "Grandma left them to *you*."

"It's not like I really need more earrings." She picked them up. "Or any of this moldy old furniture either." She poured them from one hand to another. "But Twil, they wouldn't sell Grandma's house, would they?"

"They wouldn't dare," I said, but it felt like a lie. Selling your favorite place in the whole world was exactly the kind of thing grownups did to kids. I wanted to say something to cheer Aggie up, but I didn't know what.

Sitting in that room made me remember summer nights when Grandma used to tell me bedtime stories. She'd always change the main character to me. Twilla and the Beanstalk. Or she would make stories up. Brave Little Twilla and the Elephant Boy of Oz—I'd been astonished. Twilla's Christmas Wish. I'd be tucked right in this very bed, the sea murmuring outside, the fog horn bleating out on Brant Point. I brushed my hand across the patchwork quilt she had made before I was born and realized I wanted it for myself. I wanted to take it home and pull it around me when the wind howled through the streets of Boston. Whenever I needed to remember how my Grandma Brewster loved her best little girl.

"Your eyelighter is running." Aggie pulled a kleenex. "Left side."

I took it. "Thanks."

"You better watch out," said the hairdresser on the windowall. "You better not cry. You better not pout, I'm telling you why." The cartoon morphed into Nick. "You-know-who is coming to town."

"Gramps!" said Aggie.

"Ho-ho-ho!" he said.

"How did you survive?" I would've hugged him, only how do you hug an electron pattern on a windowall?

"That was just an alias file that Francie erased. When you told me that I'd been archived so long, I dumped my real self into Worldnet and ran. But I've got problems, girls. The failsafes on the net are snooping after me, and if they catch me, I'm dead as last year's batteries. I need a place to hide out. And there's no place like home for the holidays."

"Aunt Francie has shut down all incoming to the house," I said. "All we can get is read only."

"Santa taught me a couple of new tricks." He twirled his mustache. "If you can just get me Francie's private key code, I'll edit everything out of the log."

I turned to Aggie.

"Oh, no," she said. "We'll get in trouble again."

I stared an icicle at her.

"Okay, okay, never mind." She pushed me away. "Just go away while I enter it?" I stood by the window and listened to the clack of keys. "Voice override on commport 2," she said. "Revert to default for three seconds and then undo revert." Then for my benefit, she muttered, "So what if I spend high school chained to a doorknob?"

The wall shimmered like the surface of the harbor in a light breeze. Then Nick was standing between us, a filmy hologram projected from the windowall. He was wearing a Santa suit and was carrying a sack. "Thanks." When he moved, he trailed rainbows. "For a minute I was afraid you were going to tell me there was no room at the inn."

He put the sack down and started rummaging through it, muttering to no one in particular. "I have something." He brought a photo in a gold frame to the top of the bag. "No," he said, as if reminding himself, "this is for Frances." I only saw it for a second; it looked like some bride and groom standing in a garden. "Something else. Where the hell did I . . . oh, want to see what I got for Twilla's dad? He's the archaeology nut, right?" He showed us a cube with a lion sculpted on it. "Opens into a scale model of Persepolis. All the palaces, temples, tombs, treasure houses, even furniture." He reached deeper into the bag. "Tidings of comfort and joy," he sang under his breath, "comfort and . . . *ah!*" He came up with a handful of icons and threw them in our direction. They passed through us and rang like coins as they hit the windowall and stuck there. All the latest vids: Great Red Spot, Street French, Girls Live Girls, Bobby Science Down Under.

Aggie touched the lump on Bobby Science's neck reverently. She had been in love ever since he'd had his larynx replaced with a twenty thousand voice synthesizer.

"You like this stuff?" said Nick. "I was lurking on some empty tracks in a recording studio and it just stuck to me."

"It's great," I said, "but how did you pay for them?"

"I'd better find a place to bed down." He yawned and stretched. "In case someone comes looking for me."

"Try Grandma's recipes," said Aggie. "There are lots of dead files to hide in."

Nick's face lost expression for a moment. "Dead files? Guess that's appropriate."

I said, "Nick, you did *pay* for those vids?"

He picked up the sack, slung it over his shoulder. "Ssh! What's that?" He gaped at us in astonishment. I froze, expecting the data cops or Aunt Francie to kick in the door. "Listen." He pointed at the ceiling.

"I don't hear anything." Aggie flattened herself against a wall so she could peek out the dormer window. "Where?"

"On the roof. Sounds like . . . *reindeer.*" And then he was gone, his faint *ho-ho-ho* echoing into silence.

"He's such a lunatic!" said Aggie. She was laughing as she went to the terminal to make hard copies of the vids for herself. I wondered if she might be right. Maybe some of his files *had* been corrupted.

Or maybe he was the one who was corrupt.

I knew Aggie was asleep because she started making that little clicking sound in the back of her throat when she breathed. But as soon as I eased the covers off, Grandma's house started scolding me. Bedsprings creaked, floorboards moaned, doorknobs rattled, hinges squealed. It took me almost ten minutes to get upstairs to Grandma's bedroom without waking everybody up. It would have been quicker to use one of the downstairs terminals, but I needed the privacy.

"Nick," I whispered.

He wandered onto the windowall in an old-fashioned night shirt and a stocking cap. He was carrying a candle and his eyes were all squinchy, like he'd been asleep. I knew better, he was software.

" 'Twas the night before Christmas," he said, "when all through the house, not a creature was stirring, except Twilla the mouse."

"The louse," I said. "Twilla, the louse who let you in. Who are you?"

He brought the candle closer, as if to see me better. "I'm your Grandpa Nick."

I shook my head. "It's okay to pretend with Aggie, she's still a kid. You're not Nick. The question is, are you really his virt?"

"How would I know so much about you all if I wasn't?"

"Virts don't steal stuff."

"I didn't steal anything," he said calmly. "I paid good money for those presents."

"Virts don't buy stuff either. Virts are like home videos. You're supposed to watch them and remember with them and feel good, and that's all. They don't mess with your *life*."

"Look, Twilla. Your Grandpa Nick knew about the cancer for a long time. He spent the last three years of his life getting ready to be dead. Making *me*. Cost him a fortune. He recorded hundreds of hours of reminiscences, loaded every experience he could simulate into the attic. The recipes, for example. His investment strategies. All his books. He wrote down his dreams every night. He didn't want to be just another ornament to be tucked away with the Nutcracker on the Saturday after New Year's. He wanted to

cram as much of his mind into this attic as possible. He wanted
to be conscious, to be himself.''

''Did it work?''

He considered. ''No.'' He shrugged, then closed his hand
around the candle, which disappeared. ''I'm not going to lie to
you. I'm conscious all right, but I'm not exactly Nicolas Cleary.''
The nightshirt morphed into a business suit; the windowall
changed into a mirror image of Grandma's bedroom. Nick's bedroom. ''There's too much missing, spaces I have to fill in my
own way. As I do, I become someone new. Or at least I would
if that goddamned woman hadn't put me on a shelf for six years.''
He settled on the edge of the bed.

I was angry with him, with Grandma, my family and all their
secrets, this whole rotten Christmas. ''So what am I supposed to
do with you?''

''Nothing, tonight. We'll sort this out in the morning. I'm
working on a plan. So get some sleep, sweetheart. Do you know
what time it is?''

''Half past my bedtime?''

He winked. ''Merry Christmas.'' And switched off.

I punched him back up.

''What plan?''

''I need to work on the Grinch, find a way to keep her from
stealing Christmas.''

''Aunt Francie? She hates you.''

''And I've never understood why. Your Grandmother loved
me, and your mom. I took good care of them all—just look at
this house.''

''This is Grandma's house.''

''Fa-la-la-la-la-la-la-la-la-*la*.'' He shrank himself into the Christmas star. ''Whose side are you on, Twil?'' He twinkled and began
to drift slowly off the wall.

I let him go. It was a good question.

The kids' ornament time was a Brewster tradition that supposedly
stretched back to the days of Captain Tristram. Before we opened
presents on Christmas morning, the youngest member of each
family brought a new ornament to put on the tree. We sat around
the huge windowall in the living room, a screen fourteen feet tall

and twenty feet wide. Dad set the program on auto. The graphic built slowly. The trunk pushed up from the floor and branched out limbs which sprouted needles. Lights blinked, tinsel glittered and the boughs bent under the imaginary weight of ornaments we had already hung. The homebrain breathed the scent of crushed balsam through the heating vents. Mom and Aunt Francie *ooed* and *ahhed* like silly little girls as piles of soft presents appeared under the tree beside the hard presents scattered in front of the wall.

I hadn't gotten enough sleep, and so I was pretty cranky when Dad began his speech. "Okay, you all know what today is. Christmas is a time when we put aside our personal differences."

"Got that, Aunt Francie?" I said.

"*Twilla.*" I could tell that Dad was disappointed in me.

"I think we should get on with it," said Aunt Francie. "Aggie, do you have something for us?"

Aggie stood and went to the wall. She held up one of the dangling earrings. "This was Grandma's. She gave it to me." She turned, picked a spot high on the tree and held the earring to it long enough for the homebrain to make a copy.

"Twilla?" said Mom.

I stalked up to the wall and flattened my palm against it. Grandma had given the earrings to Aggie, the attic passkey to me. The way I figured it, she must have wanted me to find the icon she had pasted onto December 19. "Now, Nick," I said. When I pulled my hand away, his icon hung from the tree.

Aunt Francie tried to stand, but Mom forced her back down with a firm push on the shoulder. Aggie's eyes were as big as sugar cookies. Dad looked grim.

"You forgot somebody." I watched as the icon expanded into Nick, then projected out as a hologram pacing the room. He was wearing his Santa suit again, and he had his bag of presents. He was paler than he'd been yesterday; his colors needed more saturation. He looked about as tense as I felt.

"I'm sorry to barge in like this," he said. "I spent last night hiding in Margaret's sour cranberry sauce recipe, trying to think of what to say to you all. We have to talk."

He walked toward Aunt Francie, then right through where she sat on the couch. She twitched. "No, we don't."

"Yes, we *do*," said Aggie. I was proud of her.

Nick walked into the end table that held our glasses and a pitcher of eggnog. The pitcher fell. Mom went to catch it and then froze as it passed through her hands and disappeared. The real pitcher stayed in place on the table. "You see, I need a place to stay, a permanent place. I don't want to be shut down anymore, and I need access to the net. That's all. And I'm willing to pay my way."

Aunt Francie snorted. "With what?"

"Your mother and I always kept our money separate, Frances. She insisted, even though she was not a rich woman. Before I died, I set up a trust and named her as sole beneficiary. She had complete use of the income for as long as she lived, although she couldn't touch the principal. Now that she's dead, I intend to make use of the trust."

"You can't," said Aunt Francie. "You have no legal status. In fact, as part of mother's estate, you belong to us. We own you."

He swelled into a giant; his head slipped in and out of the chandelier as he nodded. "Me, but not my *trust*. The trustees are instructed to dissolve it and donate the proceeds to charity should my master file be lost or corrupted."

"So *that's* how she could afford to keep this place," said Mom. "God knows what she spent all her own money on, but at least she could count on Nick's trust. Otherwise, she would've had to sell Brewster House years ago."

"I knew it." I was furious at her. "You are going to sell this house!"

"Mom," said Aggie, "Grandma promised that someday I could bring *my* kids here in the summer."

"This isn't a cottage, Aggie." Aunt Francie slumped dejectedly against the couch. "It's a mansion. After we get done paying the estate taxes . . ."

"Which brings me to my proposal." Nick shrank back to normal size. "Or should I call it my Christmas present? What if I cover the tax, pay you rent, and live here in the attic? You own the house; use it whenever you want. I'll manage my portfolio and stay out of your way, although I'd like permission to visit the girls. Oh, and one of you will have to act as my agent, since

I can't enter into contracts or make transactions by myself.''

"It's not *fair*,'' Aunt Francie muttered, almost as if she were talking to herself. "There's nothing left, nothing but the house. She should've warned me that she'd spent all her money. Maybe I could've done something.''

"Nick's got the answer,'' said Mom. "It works, Francie.''

"Nick,'' Aunt Francie said. "It's always *Nick* to the rescue, isn't it? He *bought* his way into this family, you know. You were too little to understand, but I was there. Dad wasn't even dead a year, less than a goddamned *year*, when he moved in!''

"Francie.'' Mom put an arm around her. I wasn't sure whether she was comforting her or holding her back. The rest of us just watched, speechless.

"Well, it's true!'' Her voice was very small. Wounded. Then it was as if she realized what she had just said, because she covered her face with her hands and broke down. I had never seen Aunt Francie cry; it was scary. For the first time I realized that grownups are nothing but big kids with jobs. Nick, plain Nick in a gray suit, cocked his head and stared out at all of us with an odd choked smile. I wished I was on the other side of the wall with him.

"You're right, Francie,'' said Mom. "I never knew Dad. I wish I had. But Nick was a good father to me.'' I was stunned; I never would have expected my mom to save the day. "I think we should accept his present. It's Christmas, after all. Time to put differences aside.''

All told, Aunt Francie allowed herself about three nanoseconds to feel her feelings. Then she drew her hands slowly down her face, fingertips digging the tears out of the wrinkles. When she looked at us, she was Mom's big sister again. The head of the Brewster family. "I agree,'' was all she said.

What we were supposed to do next was open presents. So we did, grateful to be saved from ourselves by Christmas tradition. There's nothing like unwrapping a truckload of new stuff to make you forget your troubles. They gave me four shirts, two sweaters, and a nice skirt which I probably won't ever wear because no one wears skirts at my school. Plus 3DTress, the fashion AI, and fifty hours on Worldnet. Aunt Francie gave Aggie the same

Bobby Science vid that she'd gotten from Nick, but she didn't say anything. She seemed even more pleased than when Nick gave it to her. Dad's favorite present was his model of Persepolis; he was still playing with it during the Notre Dame game on New Year's Day. I thought we were going to have another disaster when Nick gave Aunt Francie his present. It was a wedding picture of Grandma and Grandpa John, Mom and Francie's father. Aunt Francie glanced at it and smiled and thanked him, and then quickly reached for another package. I could tell she was either touched or upset at herself for being touched, but she had shown us all the emotion we were going to see from her that day—or maybe that decade.

When we were finished the floor was scattered with enough paper to wrap the ferry, and Nick had been squeezed into 2D by a landslide of blinking icons. Our family had single-handedly saved the Massachusetts economy once again. Aunt Francie and Dad went off to the kitchen to program lunch.

"Jesus, Mary, and Joseph!" Nick staggered backward across the windowall, merging with the tree. "So that's what she did with it."

"Who?" said Mom. "What?"

"I've just found the rest of Margaret's money. Or rather, it has found us."

"Great," I said.

"Maybe not." He looked like someone who had just seen a ghost. "Someone release the restriction on incoming data, please. Oh, that woman did love her secrets!"

Mom went to the terminal and set it to revert to default. Part of the wall started to sparkle; it looked like a diamond the size of a door.

"It's about time you let me into my own house," said the sparkle. Then it resolved into a person. "Where's my sauce? We *always* have my sour cranberry sauce."

"Hi, Grandma!" Aggie squealed.

"Well, Margaret?" said Nick.

"Oh, Nick," Grandma said.

"Twilla," said Mom, her voice brittle as a glass angel. "Would you please ask your aunt to step in here?"

INN

Connie Willis

*"Inn" was purchased by Gardner Dozois, and ap-
peared in the December 1993 issue of* Asimov's, *with
an interior illustration by Laura Lakey. It was one of a
long sequence of memorable stories by Connie Willis
that have appeared in* Asimov's *under four different editors over the last decade, since her first* Asimov's *sale
to George Scithers, stories that have made her one of
the most popular writers that* Asimov's *has ever published, and a mainstay of the magazine. In 1982, she
won two Nebula Awards, one for her superb novelette
"Fire Watch," and one for her poignant short story "A
Letter from the Clearys"; a few months later, "Fire
Watch" went on to win her a Hugo Award as well. In
1989, her powerful novella "The Last of the Winneba-
goes" won both the Nebula and the Hugo, and she won
another Nebula in 1990 for her novelette "At The Ri-
alto." In 1993, her landmark novel* Doomsday Book
won both the Nebula and the Hugo Award, as did her
Asimov's *story "Even the Queen"—making her, as far
as we know, the only person ever to win two Nebulas
and two Hugos in the same year—and she followed this
with a Hugo win for another* Asimov's *story the following year, "Death on the Nile," clinching her title as
perhaps the most honored writer in the history of science
fiction. Her other books include the novels* Water Witch
and Light Raid, *written in collaboration with Cynthia*

Felice, Lincoln's Dreams, *her first solo novel, and* Fire
Watch, *a collection of her short fiction. Her most recent
books are a major new collection,* Impossible Things,
and the short novels, Uncharted Territory, Bellwether,
and Remake. *Willis lives in Greeley, Colorado, with her
family.*

*Willis has provided several fine Christmas stories to
Asimov's, but here's one of her best, a wry, funny, and
ultimately moving look at some unexpected detours that
crop up on the way to history's most famous overbooked
inn . . .*

The Christmas Eve Service. *The organ played the last notes of
"O Come, O Come Emmanuel," and the choir sat down. Reverend Wall hobbled slowly to the pulpit, clutching his sheaf of
yellowed typewritten sheets.*

*In the choir, Dee leaned over to Sharon and whispered, "Here
we go. Twenty-four minutes and counting."*

*On Sharon's other side, Virginia murmured, " 'And all went
to be taxed, every one into his own city.' "*

*Reverend Wall set the papers on the pulpit, looked rheumily
out over the congregation, and said, " 'And all went to be taxed,
every one into his own city. And Joseph also went up from Galilee, out of the city of Nazareth, into Judea, unto the city of David,
which is called Bethlehem, because he was of the house and line-
age of David. To be taxed with Mary his espoused wife, being
great with child.' " He paused.*

*"We know nothing of that journey up from Nazareth," Virginia
whispered.*

*"We know nothing of that journey up from Nazareth," Rev-
erend Wall said, in a wavering voice, "what adventures befell
the young couple, what inns they stopped at along the way. All
we know is that on a Christmas Eve like this one they arrived in
Bethlehem, and there was no room for them at the inn."*

*Virginia was scribbling something on the margin of her bul-
letin. Dee started to cough. "Do you have any cough drops?"
she whispered to Sharon.*

*"What happened to the ones I gave you last night?" Sharon
whispered back.*

"Though we know nothing of their journey," Reverend Wall said, his voice growing stronger, *"we know much of the world they lived in. It was a world of censuses and soldiers, of bureaucrats and politicians, a world busy with property and rules and its own affairs."*

Dee started to cough again. She rummaged in the pocket of her music folder and came up with a paper-wrapped cough drop. She unwrapped it and popped it in her mouth.

". . . a world too busy with its own business to even notice an insignificant couple from far away," Reverend Wall intoned.

Virginia passed her scribbled-on bulletin to Sharon. Dee leaned over to read it, too. It read, "What happened here last night after the rehearsal? When I came home from the mall, there were police cars outside."

Dee grabbed the bulletin and rummaged in her folder again. She found a pencil, scribbled, "Somebody broke into the church," and passed it across to Sharon and Virginia.

"You're kidding," Virginia whispered. "Were they caught?"

"No," Sharon said.

The rehearsal on the twenty-third was supposed to start at seven. By a quarter to eight the choir was still standing at the back of the sanctuary waiting to sing the processional, the shepherds and angels were bouncing off the walls, and Reverend Wall, in his chair behind the pulpit, had nodded off. The assistant minister, Reverend Farrison, was moving poinsettias onto the chancel steps to make room for the manger, and the choir director, Rose Henderson, was on her knees hammering wooden bases onto the cardboard palm trees. They had fallen down twice already.

"What do you think are the chances we'll still be here when it's time for the Christmas Eve service to start tomorrow night?" Sharon said, leaning against the sanctuary door.

"I can't be," Virginia said, looking at her watch. "I've got to be out at the mall before nine. Megan suddenly announced she wants Senior Prom Barbie."

"My throat feels terrible," Dee said, feeling her glands. "Is it hot in here, or am I getting a fever?"

"It's hot in these *robes,*" Sharon said. "Why *are* we wearing them? This is a rehearsal."

"Rose wanted everything to be exactly like it's going to be tomorrow night at the Christmas Eve Service."

"If I'm exactly like this tomorrow night, I'll be dead," Dee said, trying to clear her throat. "I *can't* get sick. I don't have any of the presents wrapped, and I haven't even *thought* about what we're having for Christmas dinner."

"At least you *have* presents," Virginia said. "I have eight people left to buy for. Not counting Senior Prom Barbie."

"I don't have anything done. Christmas cards, shopping, wrapping, baking, nothing, and Bill's parents are coming," Sharon said. "Come *on*, let's get this show on the road."

Rose and one of the junior choir angels hoisted the palm trees to standing. They listed badly to the right, as if Bethlehem were experiencing a hurricane. "Is that straight?" Rose called to the back of the church.

"Yes," Sharon said.

"Lying in church," Dee said. "Tsk, tsk."

"All right," Rose said, picking up a bulletin. "Listen up, everybody. Here's the order of worship. Introit by the brass quartet, processional, opening prayer, announcements—Reverend Farrison, is that where you want to talk about the 'Least of These' Project?"

"Yes," Reverend Farrison said. She walked to the front of the sanctuary. "And can I make a quick announcement right now?" She turned and faced the choir. "If anybody has anything else to donate, you need to bring it to the church by tomorrow morning at nine," she said briskly. "That's when we're going to deliver them to the homeless. We still need blankets and canned goods. Bring them to the fellowship hall."

She walked back down the aisle, and Rose started in on her list again. "Announcements, 'O Come, O Come, Emmanuel,' Reverend Wall's sermon—"

Reverend Wall nodded awake at his name. "Ah," he said and hobbled toward the pulpit, clutching a sheaf of yellowed typewritten papers.

"Oh, no," Sharon said. "Not a Christmas pageant *and* a sermon. We'll be here forever."

"Not a sermon," Virginia said. "*The* sermon. All twenty-four minutes of it. I've got it memorized. He's given it every year since he came.''

''Longer than that,'' Dee said. ''I swear last year I heard him say something about World War I.''

'' 'And all went to be taxed, every one into his own city,' '' Reverend Wall said. '' 'And Joseph also went up from Galilee, out of the city of Nazareth.' ''

''Oh, no,'' Sharon said. ''He's going to give the whole thing right now.''

''We know nothing of that journey up from Bethlehem,'' he said.

''Thank you, Reverend Wall,'' Rose said. ''After the sermon, the choir sings, 'O Little Town of Bethlehem' and Mary and Joseph—''

''What message does the story of their journey hold for us?'' Reverend Wall said, picking up steam.

Rose was hurrying up the aisle and up the chancel steps. ''Reverend Wall, you don't need to run through the sermon right now.''

''What does it say to us,'' he asked, ''struggling as we are to recover from a world war?''

Dee nudged Sharon.

''Reverend *Wall*,'' Rose said, reaching the pulpit. ''I'm afraid we don't have time to go through your whole sermon right now. We need to run through the pageant now.''

''Ah,'' he said, and gathered up his papers.

''All right,'' Rose said. ''The choir sings, 'O Little Town of Bethlehem,' and Mary and Joseph, you come down the center aisle.''

Mary and Joseph, wearing bathrobes and Birkenstocks, assembled themselves at the back of the sanctuary, and started down the center aisle.

''No, no, Mary and Joseph, not that way,'' Rose said. ''The wise men from the East have to come down the center aisle, and you're coming up from Nazareth. You two come down the side aisle.''

Mary and Joseph obliged, taking the aisle at a trot.

''No, no, slow *down*,'' Rose said. ''You're tired. You've walked all the way from Nazareth. Try it again.''

They raced each other to the back of the church and started again, slower at first and then picking up speed.

"The congregation won't be able to see them," Rose said, shaking her head. "What about lighting the side aisle? Can we do that, Reverend Farrison?"

"She's not here," Dee said. "She went to get something."

"I'll go get her," Sharon said, and went down the hall.

Miriam Hoskins was just going in the adult Sunday school room with a paper plate of frosted cookies. "Do you know where Reverend Farrison is?" Sharon asked her.

"She was in the office a minute ago," Miriam said, pointing with the plate.

Sharon went down to the office. Reverend Farrison was standing at the desk, talking on the phone. "How soon can the van be here?" She motioned to Sharon she'd be a minute. "Well, can you find out?"

Sharon waited, looking at the desk. There was a glass dish of paper-wrapped cough drops next to the phone, and beside it a can of smoked oysters and three cans of water chestnuts. Probably for the "Least of These" Project, she thought ruefully.

"Fifteen minutes? All right. Thank you," Reverend Farrison said, and hung up. "Just a minute," she told Sharon and went out to the outside door. She opened it and leaned out. Sharon could feel the icy air as she stood there. She wondered if it had started snowing.

"The van will be here in a few minutes," Reverend Farrison said to someone outside.

Sharon looked out the stained-glass panels on either side of the door, trying to see who was out there.

"It'll take you to the shelter," Reverend Farrison said. "No, you'll have to wait outside." She shut the door. "Now," she said, turning to Sharon, "what did *you* want?"

Sharon said, still looking out the window, "They need you in the sanctuary." It was starting to snow. The flakes looked blue through the glass.

"I'll be right there," Reverend Farrison said. "I was just taking care of some homeless. That's the second couple we've had tonight. We always get them at Christmas. What's the problem? The palm trees?"

"What?" Sharon said, still looking at the snow.

Reverend Farrison followed her gaze. "The shelter van's coming for them in a few minutes," she said. "We can't let them stay in here unsupervised. First Methodist's had their collection stolen twice in the last month, and we've got all the donations for the 'Least of These' project in there." She gestured toward the fellowship hall.

I thought they were for the homeless, Sharon thought. "Couldn't they just wait in the sanctuary or something?" she said.

Reverend Farrison sighed. "Letting them in isn't doing them a kindness. They come here instead of the shelter because the shelter confiscates their liquor." She started down the hall. "What did they need me for?"

"Oh," Sharon said, "the lights. They wanted to know if they could get lights over the side aisle for Mary and Joseph."

"I don't know," she said. "The lights in this church are such a mess." She stopped at the bank of switches next to the stairs that led down to the choir room and the Sunday school rooms. "Tell me what this turns on."

She flicked the switch. The hall light went off. She switched it back on and tried another one.

"That's the light in the office," Sharon said, "and the downstairs hall, and that one's the adult Sunday school room."

"What's this one?" Reverend Farrison said.

There was a yelp from the choir members. Kids screamed.

"The sanctuary," Sharon said. "Okay, that's the side aisle lights." She called down to the sanctuary. "How's that?"

"Fine," Rose called. "No, wait, the organ's off."

Reverend Farrison flicked another switch, and the organ came on with a groan.

"Now the side lights are off," Sharon said, "and so's the pulpit light."

"I told you they were a mess," Reverend Farrison said. She flicked another switch. "What did that do?"

"It turned the porch light off."

"Good. We'll leave it off. Maybe it will discourage any more homeless from coming," she said. "Reverend Wall let a homeless man wait inside last week, and he relieved himself on the carpet

in the adult Sunday school room. We had to have it cleaned."
She looked reprovingly at Sharon. "With these people, you can't
let your compassion get the better of you."

No, Sharon thought. Jesus did, and look what happened to him.

*"The innkeeper could have turned them away," Reverend Wall
intoned, twenty minutes into the Christmas Eve sermon. "He was
a busy man, and his inn was full of travelers. He could have shut
the door on Mary and Joseph."*

Virginia leaned across Sharon to Dee. *"Did whoever broke in
take anything?"*

"No," Sharon said.

"Whoever it was urinated on the floor in the nursery," Dee
whispered, and Reverend Wall trailed off confusedly and looked
over at the choir.

*Dee began coughing loudly, trying to smother it with her hand.
He smiled vaguely at her and started again. "The innkeeper could
have turned them away."*

*Dee waited a minute, and then opened her hymnal to her bul-
letin and began writing on it. She passed it to Virginia, who read
it and then passed it back to Sharon.*

"Reverend Farrison thinks some of the homeless got in," it
read. *"They tore up the palm trees, too. Ripped the bases right
off. Can you imagine anybody doing something like that?"*

*"As the innkeeper found room for Mary and Joseph that
Christmas Eve long ago,"* Reverend Wall said, building to a finish, *"let us find room in our hearts for Christ. Amen."*

*The organ began the intro to "O Little Town of Bethlehem,"
and Mary and Joseph appeared at the back with Miriam Berg.
She adjusted Mary's white veil and whispered something to them.
Joseph pulled at his glued-on beard.*

"What route did they finally decide on?" Virginia whispered.
"In from the side or straight down the middle?"

"Side aisle," Sharon whispered.

*The choir stood up. " 'O, little town of Bethlehem, how still
we see thee lie,' "* they sang. *" 'Above thy deep and dreamless
sleep, the silent stars go by.' "*

*Mary and Joseph started up the side aisle, taking the slow,
measured steps Rose had coached them in, side by side. No,*

Sharon thought. That's not right. They didn't look like that. Joseph should be a little ahead of Mary, protecting her, and her hand should be on her stomach, protecting the baby.

They eventually decided to wait on the decision of how Mary and Joseph would come until the end of the rehearsal, and started through the pageant. Mary and Joseph knocked on the door of the inn, and the innkeeper, grinning broadly, told them there wasn't any room.

"Patrick, don't look so happy," Rose said. "You're supposed to be in a bad mood. You're busy and tired, and you don't have any rooms left."

Patrick attempted a scowl. "I have no rooms left," he said, "but you can stay in the stable." He led them over to the manger, and Mary knelt down behind it.

"Where's the baby Jesus?" Rose said.

"He's not due till tomorrow night," Virginia whispered.

"Does anybody have a baby doll they can bring?" Rose asked.

One of the angels raised her hand, and Rose said, "Fine. Mary, use the blanket for now, and, choir, you sing the first verse of 'Away in a Manger.' Shepherds," she called to the back of the sanctuary, "as *soon* as 'Away in a Manger' is over, come up and stand on *this* side." She pointed.

The shepherds picked up an assortment of hockey sticks, broom handles, and canes taped to one-by-twos and adjusted their headcloths.

"All right, let's run through it," Rose said. "Organ?"

The organ played the opening chord, and the choir stood up.

"A-way," Dee sang and started to cough, choking into her hand.

"Do—cough—drop?" she managed to gasp out between spasms.

"I saw some in the office," Sharon said, and ran down the chancel steps, down the aisle, past the shepherds, and out into the hall.

It was dark, but she didn't want to take the time to try and find the right switch. She could more or less see her way by the lights from the sanctuary, and she thought she knew right where the cough drops were.

The office lights were off, too, and the porch light Reverend Farrison had turned off to discourage the homeless. She opened the office door, felt her way over to the desk and patted around till she found the glass dish. She grabbed a handful of cough drops and felt her way back out into the hall.

The choir was singing "It Came Upon the Midnight Clear," but after two measures they stopped, and in the sudden silence Sharon heard knocking.

She started for the door and then hesitated, wondering if this was the same couple Reverend Farrison had turned away earlier, coming back to make trouble, but the knocking was soft, almost different, and through the stained-glass panels she could see it was snowing hard.

She switched the cough drops to her left hand, opened the door a little, and looked out. There were two people standing on the porch, one in front of the other. It was too dark to do more than make out their outlines, and at first glance it looked like two women, but then the one in front said in a young man's voice, *"Erkas."*

"I'm sorry," Sharon said. "I don't speak Spanish. Are you looking for a place to stay?" The snow was turning to sleet, and the wind was picking up.

"Kumrah," the young man said, making a sound like he was clearing his throat, and then a whole string of words she didn't recognize.

"Just a minute," she said, and shut the door. She went back in the office, felt for the phone, and, squinting at the buttons in the near-darkness, punched in the shelter number.

It was busy. She held down the receiver, waited a minute, and tried again. Still busy. She went back to the door, hoping they'd given up and gone away.

"Erkas," the man said as soon as she opened it.

"I'm sorry," she said. "I'm trying to call the homeless shelter," and he began talking rapidly, excitedly.

He stepped forward and put his hand on the door. He had a blanket draped over him, which was why she'd mistaken him for a woman. *"Erkas,"* he said, and he sounded upset, desperate, and yet somehow still diffident, timid.

"Bott lom," he said, gesturing toward the woman who was

standing back almost to the edge of the porch, but Sharon wasn't looking at her. She was looking at their feet.

They were wearing sandals. At first she thought they were barefoot and she squinted through the darkness, horrified. Barefoot in the snow! Then she glimpsed the dark line of a strap, but they still might as well be. And it was snowing hard.

She couldn't leave them outside, but she didn't dare bring them into the hall to wait for the van either, not with Reverend Farrison around.

The office was out—the phone might ring—and she couldn't put them in the fellowship hall with all the stuff for the homeless in there.

"Just a minute," she said, shutting the door, and went to see if Miriam was still in the adult Sunday school room. It was dark, so she obviously wasn't, but there was a lamp on the table by the door. She switched it on. No, this wouldn't work either, not with the Communion silver in a display case against the wall, and anyway, there was a stack of paper cups on the table, and the plates of Christmas cookies Miriam had been carrying, which meant there'd be refreshments in here after the pageant. She switched off the light, and went out into the hall.

Not Reverend Wall's office—it was locked anyway—and certainly not Reverend Farrison's, and if she took them downstairs to one of the Sunday school rooms, she'd just have to sneak them back up again.

The furnace room? It was between the adult Sunday school room and the fellowship hall. She tried the door. It opened, and she looked in. The furnace filled practically the whole room, and what it didn't was taken up by a stack of folding chairs. There wasn't a light switch she could find, but the pilot light gave off enough light to maneuver by. And it was warmer than the porch.

She went back to the door, looked down the hall to make sure nobody was coming, and let them in. "You can wait in here," she said, even though it was obvious they couldn't understand her.

They followed her through the dark hall to the furnace room, and she opened out two of the folding chairs so they could sit down, and motioned them in.

"It Came Upon a Midnight Clear" ground to a halt, and Rose's voice came drifting out of the sanctuary. "Shepherd's crooks are not weapons. All right. Angel?"

"I'll call the shelter," Sharon said hastily, and shut the door on them.

She crossed to the office and tried the shelter again. "Please, please answer," she said, and when they did, she was so surprised, she forgot to tell them the couple would be inside.

"It'll be at least half an hour," the man said.

"Half an hour?"

"It's like this whenever it gets below zero," the man said. "We'll try to make it sooner."

At least she'd done the right thing—they couldn't possibly stand out in that snow for half an hour. "As you have done this to the least of my brethren, you have done it unto me," she thought ruefully. But at least it was warm in the furnace room, and out of the snow. And they were safe in there, as long as nobody came out to see what had happened to her.

"Dee," she said suddenly. She was supposed to have come out to get her a cough drop.

They were lying on the desk where she'd laid them while she phoned. She snatched them up and took off down the hall and into the sanctuary.

The angel was on the chancel steps, exhorting the shepherds not to be afraid. Sharon threaded her way through them up to the chancel and sat down between Dee and Virginia.

She handed the cough drops to Dee, who said, "What took you so long?"

"I had to make a phone call. What did I miss?"

"Not a thing. We're still on the shepherds. One of the palm trees fell over and had to be fixed, and then Reverend Farrison stopped the rehearsal to tell everybody not to let homeless people in the church, that Holy Trinity had had its sanctuary vandalized."

"Oh," she said. She gazed out over the sanctuary, looking for Reverend Farrison.

"All right, now, after the angel makes her speech," Rose said, "she's joined by a multitude of angels. That's *you*, junior choir. No. Line up on the steps. Organ?"

The organ struck up, "Hark, the Herald Angels Sing," and the junior choir began singing in piping, nearly inaudible voices.

Sharon couldn't see Reverend Farrison anywhere. "Do you know where Reverend Farrison went?" she whispered to Dee.

"She went out just as you came in. She had to get something from the office."

The office. What if she heard them in the furnace room and opened the door and found them in there? She half stood.

"Choir," Rose said, glaring directly at Sharon. "Will you help the junior choir by humming along with them?"

Sharon sat back down, and after a minute Reverend Farrison came in the back, carrying a pair of scissors.

" 'Late in time, behold him come,' " the junior choir sang, and Miriam stood up and went out.

"Where's Miriam going?" Sharon whispered.

"How would I know?" Dee said, looking curiously at her. "To get the refreshments ready, probably. Is something the matter?"

"No," she said.

Rose was glaring at her again. She hummed, " 'Light and life to all he brings,' " willing the song to be over so she could go out, but as soon as it was over, Rose said, "All right, wise men," and a sixth-grader carrying a jewelry box started down the center aisle. "Choir, 'We Three Kings.' Organ?"

There were four long verses to "We Three Kings of Orient Are." Sharon couldn't wait.

"I have to go to the bathroom," she said. She set her folder on her chair and ducked down the stairs behind the chancel and through the narrow room that led to the side aisle. The choir called it the flower room because that was where they stored the out-of-season altar arrangements. They used it for sneaking out when they needed to leave church early, but right now there was barely room to squeeze through. The floor was covered with music stands and pots of silk Easter lilies, and a huge spray of red roses stood in front of the door to the sanctuary.

Sharon shoved it into the corner, stepping gingerly among the lilies, and opened the door.

"Balthazar, lay the gold in front of the manger, don't drop it." Rose said. "Mary, you're the Mother of God. Try not to look so scared."

Sharon hurried down the side aisle and out into the hall, where the other two kings were waiting, holding perfume bottles.

" 'Westward leading, still proceeding, guide us to thy perfect sight,' " the choir sang.

The hall and office lights were still off, but light was spilling out of the adult Sunday school room all the way to the end of the hall. Sharon could see the furnace room door was still shut.

I'll call the shelter again, she thought, and see if I can hurry them up, and if I can't, I'll take them downstairs till everybody's gone, and then take them to the shelter myself.

She tiptoed past the open door of the adult Sunday school room so Miriam wouldn't see her, and then half-sprinted down to the office and opened the door.

"Hi," Miriam said, looking up from the desk. She had an aluminum pitcher in one hand and was rummaging in the top drawer with the other. "Do you know where the secretary keeps the key to the kitchen? It's locked, and I can't get in."

"No," Sharon said, her heart still thumping.

"I need a spoon to stir the Kool-Aid," Miriam said, opening and shutting the side drawers of the desk. "She must have taken them home with her. I don't blame her. First Baptist had theirs stolen last month. They had to change all the locks."

Sharon glanced uneasily at the furnace room door.

"Oh, well," Miriam said, opening the top drawer again. "I'll have to make do with this." She pulled out a plastic ruler. "The kids won't care."

She started out and then stopped. "They're not done in there yet, are they?"

"No," Sharon said. "They're still on the wise men. I needed to call my husband to tell him to take the turkey out of the freezer."

"I've got to do that when I get home," Miriam said. She went across the hall and into the library, leaving the door open. Sharon waited a minute and then called the shelter. It was busy. She held her watch to the light from the hall. They'd said half an hour. By that time the rehearsal would be over and the hall would be full of people.

Less than half an hour. They were already singing "Myrrh is mine, its bitter perfume." All that was left was "Silent Night"

and then "Joy to the World," and the angels would come stream-
ing out for cookies and Kool-Aid.

She went over to the front door and peered out. Below zero,
the man at the shelter said, and it had really started to snow,
slanting sharply across the parking lot.

She couldn't send them out in that without any shoes. And she
couldn't keep them up here, not with the kids right next door.
She was going to have to move them downstairs.

But where? Not the choir room. The choir would be taking
their folders and robes back down there, and the pageant kids
would be getting their coats out of the Sunday school rooms. And
the kitchen was locked.

The nursery? That might work. It was at the other end of the
hall from the choir room, but she would have to take them past
the adult Sunday school room to the stairs, and the door was open.

" 'Si-i-lent night, ho-oh-ly night,' " came drifting out of the
sanctuary, and then was cut off, and she could hear Reverend
Farrison's voice, lecturing probably about the dangers of letting
the homeless in the church.

She glanced again at the furnace room door and then went into
the adult Sunday school room. Miriam was setting out the paper
cups on the table. She looked up. "Did you get through to your
husband?"

"Yes," Sharon said. Miriam looked expectant.

"Can I have a cookie?" Sharon said at random.

"Take one of the stars. The kids like the Santas and the Christmas trees the best."

She grabbed up a bright yellow-frosted star. "Thanks," she
said, and went out, pulling the door shut behind her.

"Leave it open," Miriam said. "I want to be able to hear when
they're done."

Sharon opened the door back up half as far as she'd shut it,
afraid any less would bring Miriam to the door to open it herself,
and walked quietly to the furnace room.

The choir was on the last verse of "Silent Night." After that
there was only "Joy to the World" and then the benediction.
Open door or no open door, she was going to have to move them
now. She opened the furnace room door.

They were standing where she had left them, between the folding chairs, and she knew, without any proof, that they had stood there like that the whole time she had been gone.

The young man was standing slightly in front of the woman, the way he had at the door, only he wasn't a man, he was a boy, his beard as thin and wispy as an adolescent's, and the woman was even younger, a child of ten maybe, only she had to be older because now that there was light from the half-open door of the adult Sunday school room Sharon could see that she was pregnant.

She regarded all this—the girl's awkward bulkiness and the boy's beard, the fact that they had not sat down, the fact that it was the light from the adult Sunday school room that was making her see now what she hadn't before—with some part of her mind that was still functioning, that was still thinking how long the van from the shelter would take, how to get them past Reverend Farrison, some part of her mind that was taking in the details that proved what she had already known the moment she opened the door.

"What are you *doing* here?" she whispered, and the boy opened his hands in a gesture of helplessness. "*Erkas*," he said.

And that still-functioning part of her mind put her finger to her lips in a gesture he obviously understood because they both looked instantly frightened. "You have to come with me," she whispered.

But then it stopped functioning altogether, and she was half-running them past the open door and onto the stairs, not even hearing the organ blaring out, "Joy to the world, the Lord is come," whispering, "Hurry! Hurry!" and they didn't know how to get down the steps, the girl turned around and came down backward, her hands flat on the steps above, and the boy helped her down, step by step, as if they were clambering down rocks, and she tried to pull the girl along faster and nearly made her stumble, and even that didn't bring her to her senses.

She hissed, "Like this," and showed them how to walk down the steps, facing forward, one hand on the rail, and they paid no attention, they came down backward like toddlers, and it took forever, the hymn she wasn't hearing was already at the end of the third verse and they were only halfway down, all of them panting hard, and Sharon scurrying back up above them as if that would hurry them, past wondering how she would ever get them up the stairs again, past thinking she would have to call the van and tell them not to come, thinking only, Hurry, hurry, and, How did they *get* here?

She did not come to herself until she had herded them somehow down the downstairs hall and into the nursery, thinking, It can't be locked, please don't let it be locked, and it wasn't, and gotten them inside and pulled the door shut and tried to lock it, and it didn't have a lock, and she thought, "That must be why it wasn't locked," an actual coherent thought, her first one since that moment when she opened the furnace room door, and seemed to come to herself.

She stared at them, breathing hard, and it *was* them, their never having seen stairs before was proof of that, if she needed any proof, but she didn't, she had known it the instant she saw them, there was no question.

She wondered if this were some sort of vision, the kind people were always getting where they saw Jesus's face on a refrigerator or the Virgin Mary dressed in blue and white, surrounded by roses. But their rough brown cloaks were dripping melted snow on the nursery carpet, their feet in the useless sandals were bright red with cold, they looked too frightened.

And they didn't look at all like they did in religious pictures. They were too short, his hair was greasy and his face was tough-looking, like a young punk's, and her veil looked like a grubby dishtowel and it didn't hang loose, it was tied around her neck and knotted in the back, and they were too young, almost as young as the children upstairs dressed like them.

They were looking around the room frightenedly, at the white crib and the rocking chair and the light fixture overhead. The boy fumbled in his sash and brought out a leather sack. He held it out to Sharon.

"How did you *get* here?" she said wonderingly. "You're supposed to be on your way to Bethlehem."

He thrust the bag at her, and when she didn't take it, untied the leather string and took out a crude-looking coin and held it out.

"You don't have to pay me," she said, which was ridiculous. He couldn't understand her. She held a flat hand up, pushing the coin away and shaking her head. That was a universal sign, wasn't it? And what was the sign for welcome? She spread her arms out, smiling at them. "You are welcome to stay here," she said, trying to put the meaning of the words into her voice. "Sit down. Rest."

They remained standing. Sharon pulled the rocking chair forward. "Sit, please."

Mary looked frightened, and Sharon put her hands on the arms and sat down to show her how. Joseph immediately knelt, and Mary tried awkwardly to.

"No, no!" Sharon said, and stood up so fast she set the rocking chair swinging. "Don't kneel. I'm nobody." She looked hopelessly at them. "How did you *get* here? You're not supposed to be here."

Joseph stood up. "*Erkas,*" he said, and went over to the bulletin board.

It was covered with colored pictures from Jesus's life: Jesus healing the lame boy, Jesus in the temple, Jesus in the Garden of Gethsemane.

He pointed to the picture of the Nativity scene. "*Kumrah,*" he said.

Does he recognize himself? she wondered, but he was pointing at the donkey standing by the manger. "*Erkas,*" he said. "*Erkas.*"

Did that mean "donkey," or something else? Was he demanding to know what she had done with theirs, or trying to ask her if she had one? In all the pictures, all the versions of the story, Mary was riding a donkey, but she had thought they'd gotten that part of the story wrong, as they had gotten everything else wrong, their faces, their clothes, and above all their youth, their helplessness.

"*Kumrah erkas,*" he said, "*Kumrah erkas. Bott lom?*"

"I don't know," she said. "I don't know where Bethlehem is."

Or what to do with you, she thought. Her first instinct was to hide them here until the rehearsal was over, and everybody had gone home. She couldn't let Reverend Farrison find them.

But surely as soon as she saw who they were, she would— what? Fall to her knees? Or call for the shelter's van? "That's the second couple tonight," she'd said when she shut the door.

Sharon wondered suddenly if it was them she'd turned away, if they'd wandered around the parking lot, lost and frightened, and then knocked on the door again.

She couldn't let Reverend Farrison find them, but there was no reason for her to come into the nursery. All the children were upstairs, and the refreshments were in the adult Sunday school room. But what if she checked the rooms before she locked up?

I'll take them home with me, Sharon thought. They'll be safe there. If she could get them up the stairs and out of the parking lot before the rehearsal ended.

I got them down here without anybody seeing them, she thought. But even if she could manage it, which she doubted, if they didn't die of fright when she started the car and the seat belts closed down over them, home was no better than the shelter.

They had gotten lost through some accident of time and space, and ended up at the church. The way back—if there was a way back, there had to be a way back, they had to be at Bethlehem by tomorrow night—was here.

It occurred to her suddenly that maybe she shouldn't have let them in, that the way back was outside the north door. But I couldn't *not* let them in, she protested, it was snowing, and they didn't have any shoes.

But maybe if she'd turned them away, they would have walked off the porch and back into their own time. Maybe they still could.

She said, "Stay here," putting her hand up to show them what she meant, and went out of the nursery into the hall, shutting the door tightly behind her.

The choir was still singing "Joy to the World." They must have had to stop again. Sharon ran silently up the stairs and past the adult Sunday school room. Its door was still half-open, and she could see the plates of cookies on the table. She opened the north door, hesitating a moment as if she expected to see sand and camels, and leaned out. It was still sleeting, and the cars had an inch of snow on them.

She looked around for something to wedge the door open with, pushed one of the potted palms into it, and went out on the porch. It was slick, and she had to take hold of the wall to keep her footing. She stepped carefully to the edge of the porch and peered into the sleet, already shivering, looking for what? A lessening of the sleet, a spot where the darkness was darker, or not as dark? A light?

Nothing. After a minute she stepped off the porch, moving as cautiously as Mary and Joseph had going down the stairs, and made a circuit of the parking lot.

Nothing. If the way back had been out here, it wasn't now, and she was going to freeze if she stayed out here. She went back inside, and then stood there, staring at the door, trying to think what to do. I've got to get help, she thought, hugging her arms to herself for warmth. I've got to tell somebody. She started down the hall to the sanctuary.

The organ had stopped. "Mary and Joseph, I need to talk to you for a minute," Rose's voice said. "Shepherds, leave your crooks on the front pew. The rest of you, there are refreshments in the adult Sunday school room. Choir, don't leave. I need to go over some things with you."

There was a clatter of sticks and then a stampede, and Sharon was overwhelmed by shepherds elbowing their way to the refreshments. One of the wise men caught his Air Jordan in his robe and nearly fell down, and two of the angels lost their tinsel halos in their eagerness to reach the cookies.

Sharon fought through them and into the back of the sanctuary. Rose was in the side aisle, showing Mary and Joseph how to walk, and the choir was gathering up their music. Sharon couldn't see Dee.

Virginia came down the center aisle, stripping off her robe as she walked. Sharon went to meet her. "Do you know where Dee is?" she asked her.

"She went home," Virginia said, handing Sharon a folder. "You left this on your chair. Dee's voice was giving out completely, and I said, 'This is silly. Go home and go to bed.' "

"Virginia . . ." Sharon said.

"Can you put my robe away for me?" she said, pulling her stole off over her head. "I've got exactly ten minutes to get to the mall."

Sharon nodded absently, and Virginia draped it over her arm and hurried out. Sharon scanned the choir, wondering who else she could tell.

Rose dismissed Mary and Joseph, who went off at a run, and

crossed to the center aisle. "Rehearsal tomorrow night at six-fifteen," she said. "I need you in your robes and up here right on time, because I've got to practice with the brass quartet at six-forty. Any questions?"

Yes, Sharon thought, looking around the sanctuary. Who can I get to help me?

"What are we singing for the processional?" one of the tenors asked.

" '*Adeste Fideles*,' " Rose said. "Before you leave, let's line up so you can see who your partner is."

Reverend Wall was sitting in one of the back pews, looking at the notes to his sermon. Sharon sidled along the pew and sat down next to him.

"Reverend Wall," she said, and then had no idea how to start. "Do you know what *erkas* means? I think it's Hebrew."

He raised his head from his notes and peered at her. "It's Aramaic. It means 'lost.' "

"Lost." He'd been trying to tell her at the door, in the furnace room, downstairs. "We're lost."

"Forgotten," Reverend Wall said. "Misplaced."

Misplaced, all right. By two thousand years, an ocean, and how many miles?

"When Mary and Joseph journeyed up to Bethlehem from Nazareth, how did they go?" she asked, hoping he would say, "Why are you asking all these questions?" so she could tell him, but he said, "Ah. You weren't listening to my sermon. We know nothing of that journey, only that they arrived in Bethlehem."

Not at this rate, she thought.

"Pass in the anthem," Rose said from the chancel. "I've only got thirty copies, and I don't want to come up short tomorrow night."

Sharon looked up. The choir was leaving. "On this journey, was there anywhere where they might have gotten lost?" she said hurriedly.

" '*Erkas*' can also mean 'hidden, passed out of sight,' " he said. "Aramaic is very similar to Hebrew. In Hebrew, the word—"

"Reverend Wall," Reverend Farrison said from the center aisle. "I need to talk to you about the benediction."

"Ah. Do you want me to give it now?" he said, and stood up, clutching his papers.

Sharon took the opportunity to grab her folder and duck out. She ran downstairs after the choir.

There was no reason for any of the choir to go in the nursery, but she stationed herself in the hall, sorting through the music in her folder as if she was putting it in order, and trying to think what to do.

Maybe, if everyone went in the choir room, she could duck in the nursery or one of the Sunday school rooms and hide until everybody was gone. But she didn't know whether Reverend Farrison checked each of the rooms before leaving. Or worse, locked them.

She could tell her she needed to stay late, to practice the anthem, but she didn't think Reverend Farrison would trust her to lock up, and she didn't want to call attention to herself, to make Reverend Farrison think, "Where's Sharon Englert? I didn't see her leave." Maybe she could hide in the chancel, or the flower room, but that meant leaving the nursery unguarded.

She had to decide. The crowd was thinning out, the choir handing Rose their music and putting on their coats and boots. She had to do something. Reverend Farrison could come down the stairs any minute to search the nursery. But she continued to stand there, sorting blindly through her music, and Reverend Farrison came down the steps, carrying a ring of keys.

Sharon stepped back protectively, the way Joseph had, but Reverend Farrison didn't even see her. She went up to Rose and said, "Can you lock up for me? I've got to be at Emmanuel Lutheran at nine-thirty to collect their 'Least of These' contributions."

"I was supposed to go meet with the brass quartet—" Rose said reluctantly.

Don't let Rose talk you out of it, Sharon thought.

"Be sure to lock *all* the doors, including the fellowship hall," Reverend Farrison said, handing her the keys.

"No, I've got mine," Rose said. "But—"

"And check the parking lot. There were some homeless hanging around earlier. Thanks."

She ran upstairs, and Sharon immediately went over to see Rose. "Rose," she said.

She held out her hand for Sharon's anthem.

Sharon shuffled through her music and handed it over to her. "I was wondering," she said, trying to keep her voice casual, "I need to stay and practice the music for tomorrow. I'd be glad to lock up for you. I could drop the keys by your house tomorrow morning."

"Oh, you're a godsend," Rose said. She handed Sharon the stack of music and got her keys out of her purse. "These are the keys to the outside doors, north door, east door, fellowship hall," she said, ticking them off so fast Sharon couldn't see which was which, but it didn't matter. She could figure them out after everybody left.

"This is the choir room door," Rose said. She handed them to Sharon. "I *really* appreciate this. The brass quartet couldn't come to the rehearsal, they had a concert tonight, and I really need to go over the introit with them. They're having a terrible time with the middle part."

So am I, Sharon thought.

Rose yanked on her coat. "And after I meet with them, I've got to go over to Miriam Berg's and pick up the baby Jesus." She stopped, her arm half in her coat sleeve. "Did you need me to stay and go over the music with you?"

"No!" she said, alarmed. "No, I'll be fine. I just need to run through it a couple of times."

"Okay. Great. Thanks again," she said, patting her pockets for her keys. She took the keyring away from Sharon and unhooked her car keys. "You're a godsend, I mean it," she said, and took off up the stairs at a trot.

Two of the altos came out, pulling on their gloves. "Do you know what I've got to face when I get home?" Julia said. "Putting up the tree."

They handed their music to Sharon.

"I hate Christmas," Karen said. "By the time it's over, I'm worn to a frazzle."

They hurried up the stairs, still talking, and Sharon leaned in to the choir room to make sure it was empty, dumped the music and Virginia's robe on a chair, took off her robe, and went up-stairs.

Miriam was coming out of the adult Sunday school room,

carrying a pitcher of Kool-Aid. "Come on, Elizabeth," she called into the room. "We've got to get to Buymore before it closes. She managed to completely destroy her halo," she said to Sharon, "so now I've got to go buy some more tinsel. Elizabeth, we're the last ones *here*."

Elizabeth strolled out, holding a Christmas tree cookie in her mittened hand. She stopped halfway to the door to lick the cookie's frosting.

"Elizabeth," Miriam said. "Come *on*."

Sharon held the door for them, and Miriam went out, ducking her head against the driving snow. Elizabeth dawdled after her, looking up at the sky.

Miriam waved. "See you tomorrow night."

"I'll be here," Sharon said, and shut the door. I'll *still* be here, she thought. And what if they are? What happens then? Does the Christmas pageant disappear, and all the rest of it? The cookies and the shopping and the Senior Prom Barbies? And the church?

She watched Miriam and Elizabeth through the stained glass panel till she saw the car's taillights, purple through the blue glass, pull out of the parking lot, and then tried the keys one after the other, till she found the right one, and locked it.

She checked quickly in the sanctuary and the bathrooms, in case somebody was still there, and then ran down the stairs to the nursery to make sure *they* were still there, that they hadn't disappeared.

They were there, sitting on the floor next to the rocking chair and sharing what looked like dried dates from an unfolded cloth. Joseph started to stand up as soon as he saw her poke her head in the door, but she motioned him back down. "Stay here," she said softly, and realized she didn't need to whisper. "I'll be back in a few minutes. I'm just going to lock the doors."

She pulled the door shut, and went back upstairs. It hadn't occurred to her they'd be hungry, and she had no idea what they were used to eating—unleavened bread? Lamb? Whatever it was, there probably wasn't any in the kitchen, but the deacons had had an Advent supper last week. With luck, there might be some chili in the refrigerator. Or, better yet, some crackers.

The kitchen was locked. She'd forgotten Miriam had said that, and anyway, one of the keys must open it. It didn't, and after she'd tried all of them twice she remembered they were Rose's keys, not Reverend Farrison's, and turned the lights on to the fellowship hall. There was tons of food in there, stacked on tables alongside the blankets and used clothes and toys. And all of it was in cans, just the way Reverend Farrison had specified in the bulletin.

Miriam had taken the Kool-Aid home, but Sharon hadn't seen her carrying any cookies. The kids probably ate them all, she thought, but she went into the adult Sunday school room and looked. There was a half a paper plate left, and Miriam had been right—the kids liked the Christmas trees and Santas the best— the only ones left were yellow stars. There was a stack of paper cups, too. She picked them both up and took them downstairs.

"I brought you some food," she said, and set the plate on the floor between them.

They were staring in alarm at her, and Joseph was scrambling to his feet.

"It's food," she said, bringing her hand to her mouth and pretending to chew. "Cakes."

Joseph was pulling on Mary's arm, trying to yank her up, and they were both staring, horrified, at her jeans and sweatshirt. She realized suddenly they must not recognize her without her choir robe. Worse, that the robe looked at least a little like their clothes, but this getup must look totally alien.

"I'll bring you something to drink," she said hastily, showing them the paper cups, and went out. She ran down to the choir room. Her robe was still draped over the chair where she'd dumped it, along with Virginia's and the music. She put the robe on and then filled the paper cups at the water fountain and carried them back to the nursery.

They were standing, but when they saw her in the robe, they sat back down. She handed Mary one of the paper cups, but she only looked at her fearfully. Sharon held it out to Joseph. He took it, too firmly, and it crumpled, water spurting onto the carpet.

"That's okay, it doesn't matter," Sharon said, cursing herself for an idiot. "I'll get you a real cup."

She ran upstairs, trying to think where there would be one. The coffee cups were in the kitchen, and so were the glasses, and she hadn't seen anything in the fellowship hall or the adult Sunday school room.

She smiled suddenly. "I'll get you a real cup," she said, and went in the adult Sunday school room and took the silver Communion chalice out of the display case. There were silver plates, too. She wished she'd thought of it sooner.

She went in the fellowship hall and got a blanket and took the things downstairs. She filled the chalice with water and took it to them, and handed Mary the chalice, and this time Mary took it without hesitation and drank deeply from it.

Sharon gave Joseph the blanket. "I'll leave you alone so you can eat and rest," she said, and went out in the hall, pulling the door nearly shut again.

She went down to the choir room and hung up Virginia's robe and stacked the music neatly on the table. Then she went up to the furnace room and folded up the folding chairs and stacked them against the wall. She checked the east door and the one in the fellowship hall. They were both locked.

She turned off the lights in the fellowship hall and the office, and then thought, "I should call the shelter," and turned them back on. It had been almost an hour. They had probably already come and not found anyone, but in case they were running really late, she'd better call.

The line was busy. She tried it twice and then called home. Bill's parents were there. "I'm going to be late," she told him. "The rehearsal's running long," and hung up, wondering how many lies she'd told so far tonight.

Well, it went with the territory, didn't it? Joseph lying about the baby being his, and the wise men sneaking out the back way, the Holy Family hiding and then hightailing it to Egypt and the innkeeper lying to Herod's soldiers about where they'd gone.

And in the meantime, more hiding. She went back downstairs and opened the door gently, trying not to startle them, and then just stood there, watching.

They had eaten the cookies. The empty paper plate stood on the floor next to the chalice, not a crumb on it. Mary lay curled up like the child she was, under the blanket, and Joseph sat with his back to the rocking chair, guarding her.

Poor things, she thought, leaning her cheek against the door.

Poor things. So young, and so far away from home. She wondered what they made of it all? Did they think they had wandered into a palace in some strange kingdom? There's stranger yet to come, she thought, shepherds and angels and old men from the east, bearing jewelry boxes and perfume bottles. And then Cana. And Jerusalem. And Golgotha.

But for the moment, a place to sleep, in out of the weather, and something to eat, and a few minutes of peace. How still we see thee lie. She stood there a long time, her cheek resting against the door, watching Mary sleep and Joseph trying to stay awake.

His head nodded forward, and he jerked it back, waking himself up, and saw Sharon. He stood up immediately, careful not to disturb Mary, and came over to her, looking worried. "*Erkas kumrah,*" he said. "*Bott lom?*"

"I'll go find it," she said.

She went upstairs and turned the lights on again and went in the fellowship hall. The way back wasn't out the north door, but maybe they had knocked at one of the other doors first and then come around to it when no one answered. The fellowship hall door was on the northwest corner. She unlocked it, trying key after key, and opened it. The sleet was slashing down harder than ever. It had already covered up the tire tracks in the parking lot.

She shut the door and tried the east door, which nobody used except for the Sunday service, and then the north door again. Nothing. Sleet and wind and icy air.

Now what? They had been on their way to Bethlehem from Nazareth, and somewhere along the way they had taken a wrong turn. But how? And where? She didn't even know what direction they'd been heading in. Up. Joseph had gone *up* from Nazareth, which meant north, and in "The First Noel," it said the star was in the northwest.

She needed a map. The ministers' offices were locked, but there were books on the bottom shelf of the display case in the adult Sunday school room. Maybe one was an atlas.

It wasn't. They were all self-help books, about coping with grief and codependency and teenage pregnancy, except for an ancient-looking concordance, and a Bible dictionary.

The Bible dictionary had a set of maps at the back. Early Is-raelite Settlements in Canaan, The Assyrian Empire, The Wanderings of the Israelites in the Wilderness. She flipped forward. The Journeys of Paul. She turned back a page. Palestine in New Testament Times.

She found Jerusalem easily, and Bethlehem should be north-west of it. There was Nazareth, where Mary and Joseph had started from, so Bethlehem had to be further north.

It wasn't there. She traced her finger over the towns, reading the tiny print. Cana, Kedesh, Jericho, but no Bethlehem. Which was ridiculous. It had to be there. She started down from the north, marking each of the towns with her finger.

When she finally found it, it wasn't at all where it was supposed to be. Like them, she thought. It was south and a little west of Jerusalem, so close it couldn't be more than a few miles from the city.

She looked down at the bottom of the page for the map scale, and there was an insert labeled, "Mary and Joseph's Journey to Bethlehem," with their route marked in broken red.

Nazareth was almost straight north of Bethlehem, but they had gone east to the Jordan River, and then south along its banks. At Jericho they'd turned back west toward Jerusalem through an empty brown space marked Judean Desert.

She wondered if that was where they had gotten lost, the donkey wandering off to find water and them going after it and losing the path. If it was, then the way back lay southwest, but the church didn't have any doors that opened in that direction, and even if it did, they would open on twentieth-century parking lot and snow, not on first-century Palestine.

How had they gotten here? There was nothing in the map to tell her what might have happened on their journey to cause this.

She put the dictionary back and pulled out the concordance.

There was a sound. A key, and somebody opening the door. She slapped the book shut, shoved it back into the bookcase, and went out into the hall. Reverend Farrison was standing at the door, looking scared. "Oh, Sharon," she said, putting her hand to her chest. "What are you still doing here? You scared me half to death."

That makes two of us, Sharon thought, her heart thumping. "I had to stay and practice," she said. "I told Rose I'd lock up. What are you doing here?"

"I got a call from the shelter," she said, opening the office door. "They got a call from us to pick up a homeless couple, but when they got here there was nobody outside."

She went in the office and looked behind the desk, in the corner next to the filing cabinets. "I was worried they got into the church," she said, coming out. "The last thing we need is someone vandalizing the church two days before Christmas." She shut the office door behind her. "Did you check all the doors?"

Yes, she thought, and none of them led anywhere. "Yes," she said. "They were all locked. And anyway, I would have heard anybody trying to get in. I heard you."

Reverend Farrison opened the door to the furnace room. "They could have sneaked in and hidden when everyone was leaving." She looked in at the stacked folding chairs and then shut the door. She started down the hall toward the stairs.

"I checked the whole church," Sharon said, following her.

Reverend Farrison stopped at the stairs, looking speculatively down the steps.

"I was nervous about being alone," Sharon said desperately, "so I turned on all the lights and checked all the Sunday school rooms and the choir room and the bathrooms. There isn't anybody here."

Reverend Farrison looked up from the stairs and toward the end of the hall. "What about the sanctuary?"

"The sanctuary?" Sharon said blankly.

She had already started down the hall toward it, and Sharon followed her, relieved and then, suddenly, hopeful. Maybe there was a door she'd missed. A sanctuary door that faced southwest. "Is there a door in the sanctuary?"

Reverend Farrison looked irritated. "If someone went out the east door, they could have gotten in and hidden in the sanctuary. Did you check the pews?" She went in the sanctuary. "We've had a lot of trouble lately with homeless people sleeping in the pews. You take that side, and I'll take this one," she said, going over to the side aisle. She started along the rows of padded pews, bending down to look under each one. "Our Lady of Sorrows had their Communion silver stolen right off the altar."

The Communion silver, Sharon thought, working her way along the rows. She'd forgotten about the chalice.

Reverend Farrison had reached the front. She opened the flower room door, glanced in, closed it, and went up into the chancel. "Did you check the adult Sunday school room?" she said, bending down to look under the chairs.

"Nobody could have hidden in there. The junior choir was in there, having refreshments," Sharon said, and knew it wouldn't do any good. Reverend Farrison was going to insist on checking it anyway, and once she'd found the display case open, the chalice missing, she would go through all the other rooms, one after the other. Till she came to the nursery.

"Do you think it's a good idea us doing this?" Sharon said. "I mean, if there is somebody in the church, they might be dangerous. I think we should wait. I'll call my husband, and when he gets here, the three of us can check—"

"I called the police," Reverend Farrison said, coming down the steps from the chancel and down the center aisle. "They'll be here any minute."

The police. And there they were, hiding in the nursery, a bearded punk and a pregnant teenager, caught redhanded with the Communion silver.

Reverend Farrison started out into the hall.

"I didn't check the fellowship hall," Sharon said rapidly. "I mean, I checked the door, but I didn't turn on the lights, and with all those presents for the homeless in there. . . ."

She led Reverend Farrison down the hall, past the stairs. "They could have gotten in the north door during the rehearsal and hidden under one of the tables."

Reverend Farrison stopped at the bank of lights and began flicking them. The sanctuary lights went off, and the light over the stairs came on.

Third from the top, Sharon thought, watching Reverend Farrison hit the switch. Please. Don't let the adult Sunday school room come on.

The office lights came on, and the hall light went out. "This church's top priority after Christmas is labeling these lights," Reverend Farrison said, and the fellowship hall light came on.

Sharon followed her right to the door and then, as Reverend Farrison went in, said, "You check in here. I'll check the adult Sunday school room," and shut the door on her.

She went to the adult Sunday school room door, opened it, waited a full minute, and then shut it silently. She crept down the hall to the light bank, switched the stairs light off and shot down the darkened stairs, along the hall, and into the nursery.

They were already scrambling to their feet. Mary had put her hand on the seat of the rocking chair to pull herself up and set it rocking, but she didn't let go of it.

"Come with me," Sharon whispered, grabbing up the chalice. It was half-full of water, and Sharon looked around hurriedly, and then poured it out on the carpet and tucked it under her arm.

"Hurry!" Sharon whispered, opening the door, and there was no need to motion them forward, to put her fingers to her lips. They followed her swiftly, silently down the hall, Mary's head ducked, and Joseph's arms held at his sides, ready to come up defensively, ready to protect her.

Sharon walked to the stairs, dreading the thought of trying to get them up them. She thought for a moment of putting them in the choir room and locking them in. She had the key, and she could tell Reverend Farrison she'd checked it and then locked it to make sure no one got in. But if it didn't work, they'd be trapped with no way out. She had to get them upstairs.

She halted at the foot of the stairs, looking up around the landing and listening. "We have to hurry," she said, taking hold of the railing to show them how to climb, and started up the stairs.

This time they did much better, still putting their hands on the steps in front of them instead of the rail, but climbing up quickly. Three-fourths of the way up Joseph even took hold of the rail.

Sharon did better, too, her mind steadily now on how to escape Reverend Farrison, what to say to the police, where to take them.

Not the furnace room, even though Reverend Farrison had already looked in there. It was too close to the door, and the police would start with the hall. And not the sanctuary. It was too open.

She stopped just below the top of the stairs, motioning them to keep down, and they instantly pressed themselves back into the shadows. Why was it those signals were universal—danger, silence, run? Because it's a dangerous world, she thought, then and now, and there's worse to come. Herod, and the flight into Egypt. And Judas. And the police.

She crept to the top of the stairs and looked toward the sanctuary and then the door. Reverend Farrison must still be in the fellowship hall. She wasn't in the hall, and if she'd gone in the adult Sunday school room, she'd have seen the missing chalice and sent up a hue and cry.

She bit her lip, wondering if there was time to put it back, if she dared leave them here on the stairs while she sneaked in and put it in the display case, but it was too late. The police were here. She could see their red and blue lights flashing purply through the stained glass door panels. In another minute they'd be at the door, knocking, and Reverend Farrison would come out of the fellowship hall, and there'd be no time for anything.

She'd have to hide them in the sanctuary until Reverend Farrison took the police downstairs, and then move them—where? The furnace room? It was still too close to the door. The fellowship hall?

She waved them upward, like John Wayne in one of his war movies, along the hall and into the sanctuary. Reverend Farrison had turned off the lights, but there was still enough light from the chancel cross to see by. She dumped the chalice in the back pew and led them along the back row to the shadowed side aisle, and then pushed them ahead of her to the front, listening intently for the sound of knocking.

Joseph went ahead with his eyes on the ground, as if he expected more stairs, but Mary had her head up, looking toward the chancel, toward the cross.

Don't look at it, Sharon thought. Don't look at it, and hurried ahead to open the flower room door.

There was a muffled sound like thunder, and the bang of a door shutting.

"In here," she whispered, and opened the flower room door.

She'd been on the other side of the sanctuary when Reverend Farrison checked the flower room. Sharon understood now why she had given it only the most cursory of glances. It had been full before. Now it was crammed with the palm trees and the manger. They'd heaped the rest of the props in it—the innkeeper's lantern and the baby blanket. She pushed the manger back, and one of its crossed legs caught on a music stand and tipped it over. She lunged for it, steadied it, and then stopped, listening.

Knocking out in the hall. And the sound of a door shutting. Voices. She let go of the music stand and pushed them into the flower room, shoving Mary into the corner against the spray of roses and nearly knocking over another music stand.

She motioned to Joseph to stand on the other side and flattened herself against a palm tree, shut the door, and realized the moment she did that it was a mistake.

They couldn't stand here in the dark like this—the slightest movement by any of them would bring everything clattering down, and Mary couldn't stay squashed uncomfortably into the corner like that for long.

She should have left the door slightly open, so there was enough light from the cross to see by, so she could hear where the police were. She couldn't hear anything with the door shut except the sound of their own light breathing and the clank of the lantern when she tried to shift her weight, and she couldn't risk opening the door again, not when they might already be in the sanctuary, looking for her. She should have shut Mary and Joseph in here and gone back into the hall to head the police off. Reverend Farrison would be looking for her, and if she didn't find her, she'd take it as one more proof that there was a dangerous homeless person in the church and insist on the police searching every nook and cranny.

Maybe she could go out through the choir loft, Sharon thought, if she could move the music stands out of the way, or at least shift things around so they could hide behind them, but she couldn't do either in the dark.

She knelt carefully, slowly, keeping her back perfectly straight, and put her hand out behind her, feeling for the top of the manger. She patted spiky straw till she found the baby blanket and pulled it out. They must have put the wise men's perfume bottles in the manger, too. They clinked wildly as she pulled the blanket out.

She knelt further, feeling for the narrow space under the door, and jammed the blanket into it. It didn't quite reach the whole length of the door, but it was the best she could do. She straightened, still slowly, and patted the wall for the light switch.

Her hand brushed it. Please, she prayed, don't let this turn on some other light, and flicked it on.

Neither of them had moved, not even to shift their hands. Mary, pressed against the roses, took a caught breath, and then released it slowly, as if she had been holding it the whole time.

They watched Sharon as she knelt again to tuck in a corner of the blanket and then turned slowly around so she was facing into the room. She reached across the manger for one of the music stands and stacked it against one behind it, working as gingerly, as slowly, as if she were defusing a bomb. She reached across the manger, lifted one of the music stands, and set it on the straw so she could push the manger back enough to give her space to move. The stand tipped, and Joseph steadied it.

Sharon picked up one of the cardboard palm trees. She worked the plywood base free, set it in the manger, and slid the palm tree flat along the wall next to Mary, and then did the other one.

That gave them some space. There was nothing Sharon could do about the rest of the music stands. Their metal frames were tangled together, and against the outside wall was a tall metal cabinet, with pots of Easter lilies in front of it. She could move the lilies to the top of the cabinet at least.

She listened carefully with her ear to the door for a minute, and then stepped carefully over the manger between two lilies. She bent and picked up one of them and set it on top of the cabinet and then stopped, frowning at the wall. She bent down again, moving her hand along the floor in a slow semicircle.

Cold air, and it was coming from behind the cabinet. She stood on tiptoe and looked behind it. "There's a door," she whispered. "To the outside."

"Sharon!" a muffled voice called.

Mary froze, and Joseph moved so he was between her and the door. Sharon put her hand on the light switch and waited, listening.

"Mrs. Englert?" a man's voice called. Another one, farther off, "Her car's still here," and then Reverend Farrison's voice again, "Maybe she went downstairs."

Silence. Sharon put her ear against the door and listened, and then edged past Joseph to the side of the cabinet and peered behind it. The door opened outward. They wouldn't have to move the cabinet out very far, just enough for her to squeeze through to open the door, and then there'd be enough space for all of them to get through, even Mary. There were bushes on this side of the church. They could hide underneath them until after the police left.

She motioned to Joseph to help her, and together they pushed it a few inches out from the wall. It knocked one of the Easter lilies over, and Mary stooped awkwardly and picked it up, cradling it in her arms.

They pushed again. This time it made a jangling noise, as if there were coat hangers hanging inside, and Sharon thought she heard voices again, but there was no help for it. She squeezed into the narrow space, thinking, What if it's locked? and opened the door.

Onto warmth. Onto a clear sky, black and pebbled with stars.

"How—" she said stupidly, looking down at the ground in front of the door. It was rocky, with bare dirt in between. There was a faint breeze, and she could smell dust and something sweet. Oranges?

She turned to say, "I found it. I found the door," but Joseph was already leading Mary through it, pushing at the cabinet to make the space wider. Mary was still carrying the Easter lily, and Sharon took it from her and set it against the base of the door to prop it open and went out into the darkness.

The light from the open door lit the ground in front of them and at its edge was a stretch of pale dirt. The path, she thought, but when she got closer, she saw it was the dried bed of a narrow stream. Beyond it the rocky ground rose up steeply. They must be at the bottom of a draw, and she wondered if this was where they had gotten lost.

"*Bott lom?*" Joseph said behind her.

She turned around. "*Bott lom?*" he said again, gesturing in front and to the sides, the way he'd done in the nursery. Which way?

She had no idea. The door faced west, and if the direction held true, and if this was the Judean Desert, it should lie to the southwest. "That direction," she said, and pointed up the steepest part of the slope. "You go that way, I think."

They didn't move. They stood watching her, Joseph standing slightly in front of Mary, waiting for her to lead them.

"I'm not—" she said, and stopped. Leaving them here was no better than leaving them in the furnace room. Or out in the snow.

She looked back at the door, almost wishing for Reverend Farrison and the police, and then set off toward what she hoped was the southwest, clambering awkwardly up the slope, her shoes slipping on the rocks.

How did they do this, she thought, grabbing at a dry clump of weed for a handhold, even with a donkey? There was no way Mary could make it up this slope. She looked back, worried.

They were following easily, sturdily, as certain of themselves as she had been on the stairs.

But what if at the top of this draw there was another one, or a dropoff? And no path. She dug in her toes and scrambled up.

There was a sudden sound, and Sharon whirled around and looked back at the door, but it still stood half-open, with the lily at its foot and the manger behind.

It scraped again, closer, and she caught a shuffling sound and then a sharp wheeze.

"It's the donkey," she said, and it plodded up to her as if it were glad to see her.

She reached under it for its reins, which were nothing but a ragged rope, and it took a step toward her and blared in her ear, "Haw!" and then a wheeze which was practically a laugh.

She laughed, too, and patted his neck. "Don't wander off again," she said, leading him over to Joseph, who was waiting where she'd left them. "Stay on the path," and scrambled on up to the top of the slope, suddenly certain the path would be there, too.

It wasn't, but it didn't matter. Because there to the southwest was Jerusalem, distant and white in the starlight, lit by a hundred hearthfires, a thousand oil-lamps, and beyond it, slightly to the west, three stars low in the sky, so close they were almost touching.

They came up beside her, leading the donkey. "*Bott lom,*" she said, pointing. "There where the star is."

Joseph was fumbling in his sash again, holding out the little leather bag.

"No," she said, pushing it back to him. "You'll need it for the inn in Bethlehem."

He put the bag back reluctantly, and she wished suddenly she had something to give them. Frankincense. Or myrrh.

"Hunh-*haw*," the donkey brayed, and started down the hill.
Joseph lunged after him, grabbing for the rope, and Mary followed them, her head ducked.

"Be careful," Sharon said. "Watch out for King Herod." She
raised her hand in a wave, the sleeve of her choir robe billowing
out in the faint breeze like a wing, but they didn't see her. They
went down the hill, Mary with her hand on the donkey for stead-
iness, Joseph a little ahead. When they were nearly at the bottom,
Joseph stopped and pointed at the ground and led the donkey off
at an angle out of her sight, and Sharon knew they'd found the
path.

She stood there for a moment, enjoying the scented breeze,
looking at the almost-star, and then went back down the slope,
skidding on the rocks and loose dirt, and took the Easter lily out
of the door and shut it. She pushed the cabinet back in position,
took the blanket out from under the door, switched off the light,
and went out into the darkened sanctuary.

There was no one there. She went and got the chalice, stuck it
into the wide sleeve of her robe, and looked out in the hall. There
was no one there either. She went in the adult Sunday school
room and put the chalice back in the display case and then went
downstairs.

"*Where* have you been?" Reverend Farrison said. Two uni-
formed policemen came out of the nursery, carrying flashlights.

Sharon unzipped her choir robe and took it off. "I checked the
Communion silver," she said. "None of it's missing." She went
in the choir room and hung up her robe.

"We looked in there," Reverend Farrison said, following her
in. "You weren't there."

"I thought I heard somebody at the door," she said.

*By the end of the second verse of "O, Little Town of Bethlehem,"
Mary and Joseph were only three-fourths of the way to the front
of the sanctuary.*

"*At this rate, they won't make it to Bethlehem by Easter,*" *Dee
whispered. "Can't they get a move on?*"

"*They'll get there,*" *Sharon whispered, watching them. They
paced slowly, unperturbedly up the aisle, their eyes on the chan-*

cel. " 'How silently, how silently,' " Sharon sang, " 'the won-
drous gift is given.' "

They went past the second pew from the front and out of the
choir's sight. The innkeeper came to the top of the chancel steps
with his lantern, determinedly solemn.

> " 'So god imparts to human hearts,
> The blessings of his heaven.' "

"Where did they go?" Virginia whispered, craning her neck
to try and see them. "Did they sneak out the back way or something?"

Mary and Joseph reappeared, walking slowly, sedately, toward
the palm trees and the manger. The innkeeper came down the
steps, trying hard to look like he wasn't waiting for them, like he
wasn't overjoyed to see them.

> " 'No ear may hear his coming,
> But in this world of sin . . . ' "

At the back of the sanctuary, the shepherds assembled, clanking
their staffs, and Miriam handed the wise men their jewelry box
and perfume bottles. Elizabeth adjusted her tinsel halo.

> " 'Where meek souls will receive him still,
> The dear Christ enters in.' "

Joseph and Mary came to the center and stopped. Joseph
stepped in front of Mary and knocked on an imaginary door, and
the innkeeper came forward, grinning from ear to ear, to open
it.

A MIDWINTER'S TALE

Michael Swanwick

*"A Midwinter's Tale" was purchased by Gardner Do-
zois, and appeared in the December 1988 issue of Asimov's, with a cover and interior illustration by Terry
Lee. Evocative, lyrical, and mysterious, the story was
extremely popular with the magazine's readership—as
proved by its easy victory as Best Short Story in that
year's Asimov's Readers' Award poll.*

*Michael Swanwick made his debut in 1980, and has
gone on to become one of the most acclaimed and respected of all that decade's new writers. Swanwick has
published a long string of stories in Asimov's, under
two different editors, and has always been one of our
most popular writers—being, for instance, the only
writer ever to have two different novels serialized in our
pages. He has several times been a finalist for the Nebula Award, as well as for the World Fantasy Award and
for the John W. Campbell Award, and has won the
Theodore Sturgeon Award and the Asimov's Readers
Award poll. In 1992, his novel* Stations of the Tide *won
him a Nebula Award as well. His other books include
his first novel,* In The Drift, *which was published in
1985, a novella-length book,* Griffin's Egg, *and 1987's
popular novel* Vacuum Flowers. *His critically acclaimed
short fiction has been assembled in* Gravity's Angels
*and in a collection of his collaborative short work with
other writers,* Slow Dancing Through Time. *His most*

recent book was a new novel, The Iron Dragon's Daughter, *which was a finalist for the World Fantasy Award
and the Arthur C. Clarke Award. He's at work on a new
novel,* Jack Faust. *Swanwick lives in Philadelphia with
his wife, Marianne Porter, and their son Sean.*

Maybe I shouldn't tell you about that childhood Christmas Eve
in the Stone House, so long ago. My memory is no longer reliable,
not since I contracted the brain fever. Soon I'll be strong enough
to be reposted offplanet, to some obscure star light years beyond
that plangent moon rising over your father's barn, but how much
has been burned from my mind! Perhaps none of this actually
happened.

Sit on my lap and I'll tell you all. Well then, my knee. No
woman was ever ruined by a knee. You laugh, but it's true. Would
that it were so easy!

The hell of war as it's now practiced is that its purpose is not
so much to gain territory as to deplete the enemy, and thus it's
always better to maim than to kill. A corpse can be bagged,
burned, and forgotten, but the wounded need special care. Regrowth tanks, false skin, medical personnel, a long convalescent
stay on your parents' farm. That's why they will vary their weapons, hit you with obsolete stone axes or toxins or radiation, to
force your Command to stock the proper prophylaxes, specialized
medicines, obscure skills. Mustard gas is excellent for that purpose, and so was the brain fever.

All those months I lay in the hospital, awash in pain, sometimes
hallucinating. Dreaming of ice. When I awoke, weak and not
really believing I was alive, parts of my life were gone, randomly
burned from my memory. I recall standing at the very top of the
iron bridge over the Izveltaya, laughing and throwing my books
one by one into the river, while my best friend Fennwolf tried to
coax me down. "I'll join the militia! I'll be a soldier!" I shouted
hysterically. And so I did. I remember that clearly but just what
led up to that preposterous instant is utterly beyond me. Nor can
I remember the name of my second-eldest sister, though her face
is as plain to me as yours is now. There are odd holes in my
memory.

•   •   •

That Christmas Eve is an island of stability in my seachanging memories, as solid in my mind as the Stone House itself, that neolithic cavern in which we led such basic lives that I was never quite sure in which era of history we dwelt. Sometimes the men came in from the hunt, a larl or two pacing ahead content and sleepy-eyed, to lean bloody spears against the walls, and it might be that we lived on Old Earth itself then. Other times, as when they brought in projectors to fill the common room with colored lights, scintillae nesting in the branches of the season's tree, and cool, harmless flames dancing atop the presents, we seemed to belong to a much later age, in some mythologized province of the future.

The house was abustle, the five families all together for this one time of the year, and outlying kin and even a few strangers staying over, so that we had to put bedding in places normally kept closed during the winter, moving furniture into attic lumberrooms, and even at that there were cots and thick bolsters set up in the blind ends of hallways. The women scurried through the passages, scattering uncles here and there, now settling one in an armchair and plumping him up like a cushion, now draping one over a table, cocking up a mustachio for effect. A pleasant time.

Coming back from a visit to the kitchens, where a huge woman I did not know, with flour powdering her big-freckled arms up to the elbows, had shooed me away, I surprised Suki and Georg kissing in the nook behind the great hearth. They had their arms about each other and I stood watching them. Suki was smiling, cheeks red and round. She brushed her hair back with one hand so Georg could nuzzle her ear, turning slightly as she did so, and saw me. She gasped and they broke apart, flushed and startled.

Suki gave me a cookie, dark with molasses and a single stingy, crystalized raisin on top, while Georg sulked. Then she pushed me away, and I heard her laugh as she took Georg's hand to lead him away to some darker forest recess of the house.

Father came in, boots all muddy, to sling a brace of game birds down on the hunt cabinet. He set his unstrung bow and quiver of arrows on their pegs, then hooked an elbow atop the cabinet to accept admiration and a hot drink from mother. The larl padded by, quiet and heavy and content. I followed it around a corner, ancient ambitions of riding the beast rising up within. I could see myself, triumphant before my cousins, high atop the black carnivore. "Flip!" my father called sternly. "Leave Samson alone! He is a bold and noble creature, and I will not have you pestering him."

He had eyes in the back of his head, had my father.

Before I could grow angry, my cousins hurried by, on their way to hoist the straw men into the trees out front, and swept me up along with them. Uncle Chittagong, who looked like a lizard and had to stay in a glass tank for reasons of health, winked at me as I skirled past. From the corner of my eye I saw my second-eldest sister beside him, limned in blue fire.

Forgive me. So little of my childhood remains; vast stretches were lost in the blue icefields I wandered in my illness. My past is like a sunken continent with only mountaintops remaining unsubmerged, a scattered archipelago of events from which to guess the shape of what was lost. Those remaining fragments I treasure all the more, and must pass my hands over them periodically to reassure myself that something remains.

So where was I? Ah, yes: I was in the north belltower, my hidey-place in those days, huddled behind Old Blind Pew, the bass of our triad of bells, crying because I had been deemed too young to light one of the yule torches. "Hallo!" cried a voice, and then, "Out here, stupid!" I ran to the window, tears forgotten in my astonishment at the sight of my brother Karl silhouetted against the yellowing sky, arms out, treading the roof gables like a tightrope walker.

"You're going to get in trouble for that!" I cried.

"Not if you don't tell!" Knowing full well how I worshipped him. "Come on down! I've emptied out one of the upper kitchen cupboards. We can crawl in from the pantry. There's a space under the door—we'll see everything!"

Karl turned and his legs tangled under him. He fell. Feet first, he slid down the roof.

I screamed. Karl caught the guttering and swung himself into an open window underneath. His sharp face rematerialized in the gloom, grinning. "Race you to the jade ibis!"

He disappeared, and then I was spinning wildly down the spiral stairs, mad to reach the goal first.

• • •

It was not my fault we were caught, for I would never have giggled if Karl hadn't been tickling me to see just how long I could keep silent. I was frightened, but not Karl. He threw his head back and laughed until he cried, even as he was being hauled off by three very angry grandmothers, pleased more by his own roguery than by anything he might have seen.

I myself was led away by an indulgent Katrina, who graphically described the caning I was to receive and then contrived to lose me in the crush of bodies in the common room. I hid behind the goat tapestry until I got bored—not long!—and then Chubkin, Kosmonaut, and Pew rang, and the room emptied.

I tagged along, ignored, among the moving legs, like a marsh bird scuttling through waving grasses. Voices clangoring in the east stairway, we climbed to the highest balcony, to watch the solstice dance. I hooked hands over the crumbling balustrade and pulled myself up on tiptoe so I could look down on the procession as it left the house. For a long time nothing happened, and I remember being annoyed at how casually the adults were taking all this, standing about with drinks, not one in ten glancing away from themselves. Pheidre and Valerian (the younger children had been put to bed, complaining, an hour ago) began a game of tag, running through the adults, until they were chastened and ordered with angry shakes of their arms to be still.

Then the door below opened. The women who were witches walked solemnly out, clad in hooded terrycloth robes as if they'd just stepped from the bath. But they were so silent I was struck with fear. It seemed as if something cold had reached into the pink, giggling women I had seen preparing themselves in the kitchen and taken away some warmth or laughter from them. "Katrina!" I cried in panic, and she lifted a moon-cold face toward me. Several of the men exploded in laughter, white steam puffing from bearded mouths, and one rubbed his knuckles in my hair. My second-eldest sister drew me away from the balustrade and hissed at me that I was not to cry out to the witches, that this was important, that when I was older I would understand, and in the meantime if I did not behave myself I would be beaten. To soften her words, she offered me a sugar crystal, but I turned away stern and unappeased.

Single-file the women walked out on the rocks to the east of the house, where all was barren slate swept free of snow by the wind from the sea, and at a great distance—you could not make out their faces—doffed their robes. For a moment they stood motionless in a circle, looking at one another. Then they began the dance, each wearing nothing but a red ribbon tied about one upper thigh, the long end blowing free in the breeze.

As they danced their circular dance, the families watched, largely in silence. Sometimes there was a muffled burst of laughter as one of the younger men muttered a racy comment, but mostly they watched with great respect, even a kind of fear. The gusty sky was dark, and flocked with small clouds like purple-headed rams. It was chilly on the roof and I could not imagine how the women withstood it. They danced faster and faster, and the families grew quieter, packing the edges more tightly, until I was forced away from the railing. Cold and bored, I went downstairs, nobody turning to watch me leave, back to the main room, where a fire still smoldered in the hearth.

The room was stuffy when I'd left, and cooler now. I lay down on my stomach before the fireplace. The flagstones smelled of ashes and were gritty to the touch, staining my fingertips as I trailed them in idle little circles. The stones were cold at the edges, slowly growing warmer, and then suddenly too hot and I had to snatch my hand away. The back of the fireplace was black with soot, and I watched the fire-worms crawl over the stone heart-and-hands carved there, as the carbon caught fire and burned out. The log was all embers and would burn for hours.

Something coughed.

I turned and saw something moving in the shadows, an animal. The larl was blacker than black, a hole in the darkness, and my eyes swam to look at him. Slowly, lazily, he strode out onto the stones, stretched his back, yawned a tongue-curling yawn, and then stared at me with those great green eyes.

He spoke.

I was astonished, of course, but not in the way my father would have been. So much is inexplicable to a child! "Merry Christmas, Flip," the creature said, in a quiet, breathy voice. I could not describe its accent; I have heard nothing quite like it before or since. There was a vast alien amusement in his glance.

"And to you," I said politely.

The larl sat down, curling his body heavily about me. If I had wanted to run, I could not have gotten past him, though that thought did not occur to me then. "There is an ancient legend, Flip, I wonder if you have heard of it, that on Christmas Eve the beasts can speak in human tongue. Have your elders told you that?"

I shook my head.

"They are neglecting you." Such strange humor dwelt in that voice. "There is truth to some of those old legends, if only you knew how to get at it. Though perhaps not all. Some are just stories. Perhaps this is not happening now; perhaps I am not speaking to you at all?"

I shook my head. I did not understand. I said so.

"That is the difference between your kind and mine. My kind understands everything about yours, and yours knows next to nothing about mine. I would like to tell you a story, little one. Would you like that?"

"Yes," I said, for I was young and I liked stories very much.

He began:

When the great ships landed—

Oh God. When—no, no, no, wait. Excuse me. I'm shaken. I just this instant had a vision. It seemed to me that it was night and I was standing at the gates of a cemetery. And suddenly the air was full of light, planes and cones of light that burst from the ground and nested twittering in the trees. Fracturing the sky. I wanted to dance for joy. But the ground crumbled underfoot and when I looked down the shadow of the gates touched my toes, a cold rectangle of profoundest black, deep as all eternity, and I was dizzy and about to fall and I, and I . . .

Enough! I have had this vision before, many times. It must have been something that impressed me strongly in my youth, the moist smell of newly opened earth, the chalky whitewash on the picket fence. It must be. I do not believe in hobgoblins, ghosts, or premonitions. No, it does not bear thinking about. Foolishness! Let me get on with my story.

—When the great ships landed, I was feasting on my grandfather's brains. All his descendants gathered respectfully about him, and I, as youngest, had first bite. His wisdom flowed through me, and the wisdom of his ancestors and the intimate knowledge of those animals he had eaten for food, and the spirit of valiant enemies who had been killed and then honored by being eaten, just as if they were family. I don't suppose you understand this, little one.

I shook my head.

People never die, you see. Only humans die. Sometimes a minor part of a Person is lost, the doings of a few decades, but the bulk of his life is preserved, if not in this body, then in another. Or sometimes a Person will dishonor himself, and his descendants will refuse to eat him. This is a great shame, and the Person will go off to die somewhere alone.

The ships descended bright as newborn suns. The People had never seen such a thing. We watched in inarticulate wonder, for we had no language then. You have seen the pictures, the baroque swirls of colored metal, the proud humans stepping down onto the land. But I was there, and I can tell you, your people were ill. They stumbled down the gangplanks with the stench of radiation sickness about them. We could have destroyed them all then and there.

Your people built a village at Landfall and planted crops over the bodies of their dead. We left them alone. They did not look like good game. They were too strange and too slow and we had not yet come to savor your smell. So we went away, in baffled ignorance.

That was in early spring.

Half the survivors were dead by midwinter, some of disease but most because they did not have enough food. It was of no concern to us. But then the woman in the wilderness came to change our universe forever.

When you're older you'll be taught the woman's tale, and what desperation drove her into the wilderness. It's part of your history. But to myself, out in the mountains and winter-lean, the sight of her striding through the snows in her furs was like a vision of winter's queen herself. A gift of meat for the hungering season, life's blood for the solstice.

I first saw the woman while I was eating her mate. He had emerged from his cabin that evening as he did every sunset, gun

in hand, without looking up. I had observed him over the course
of five days and his behavior never varied. On that sixth nightfall
I was crouched on his roof when he came out. I let him go a few
steps from the door, then leapt. I felt his neck break on impact,
tore open his throat to be sure, and ripped through his parka to
taste his innards. There was no sport in it, but in winter we will
take game whose brains we would never eat.

My mouth was full and my muzzle pleasantly, warmly moist
with blood when the woman appeared. I looked up, and she was
topping the rise, riding one of your incomprehensible machines,
what I know now to be a snowstrider. The setting sun broke
through the clouds behind her and for an instant she was embed-
ded in glory. Her shadow stretched narrow before her and touched
me, a bridge of darkness between us. We looked in one another's
eyes . . .

Magda topped the rise with a kind of grim, joyless satisfaction. I
am now a hunter's woman, she thought to herself. We will always
be welcome at Landfall for the meat we bring, but they will never
speak civilly to me again. Good. I would choke on their sweet
talk anyway. The baby stirred and without looking down she
stroked him through the furs, murmuring, "Just a little longer,
my brave little boo, and we'll be at our new home. Will you like
that, eh?"

The sun broke through the clouds to her back, making the snow
a red dazzle. Then her eyes adjusted, and she saw the black shape
crouched over her lover's body. A very great distance away, her
hands throttled down the snowstrider and brought it to a halt. The
shallow bowl of land before her was barren, the snow about the
corpse black with blood. A last curl of smoke lazily separated
from the hut's chimney. The brute lifted its bloody muzzle and
looked at her.

Time froze and knotted in black agony.

The larl screamed. It ran straight at her, faster than thought.
Clumsily, hampered by the infant strapped to her stomach, Magda
clawed the rifle from its boot behind the saddle. She shucked her
mittens, fitted hands to metal that stung like hornets, flicked off
the safety and brought the stock to her shoulder. The larl was
halfway to her. She aimed and fired.

The larl went down. One shoulder shattered, slamming it to the side. It tumbled and rolled in the snow. "You sonofabitch!" Magda cried in triumph. But almost immediately the beast struggled to its feet, turned and fled.

The baby began to cry, outraged by the rifle's roar. Magda powered up the engine. "Hush, small warrior." A kind of madness filled her, a blind anesthetizing rage. "This won't take long." She flung her machine downhill, after the larl.

Even wounded, the creature was fast. She could barely keep up. As it entered the spare stand of trees to the far end of the meadow, Magda paused to fire again, burning a bullet by its head. The larl leaped away. From then on it varied its flight with sudden changes of direction and unexpected jogs to the side. It was a fast learner. But it could not escape Magda. She had always been a hothead, and now her blood was up. She was not about to return to her lover's gutted body with his killer still alive.

The sun set and in the darkening light she lost sight of the larl. But she was able to follow its trail by two-shadowed moonlight, the deep, purple footprints, the darker spatter of blood it left, drop by drop, in the snow.

It was the solstice, and the moons were full—a holy time. I felt it even as I fled the woman through the wilderness. The moons were bright on the snow. I felt the dread of being hunted descend on me, and in my inarticulate way I felt blessed.

But I also felt a great fear for my kind. We had dismissed the humans as incomprehensible, not very interesting creatures, slow-moving, bad-smelling, and dull-witted. Now, pursued by this madwoman on her fast machine, brandishing a weapon that killed from afar, I felt all natural order betrayed. She was a goddess of the hunt, and I was her prey.

The People had to be told.

I gained distance from her, but I knew the woman would catch up. She was a hunter, and a hunter never abandons wounded prey. One way or another, she would have me.

In the winter, all who are injured or too old must offer themselves to the community. The sacrifice rock was not far, by a hill riddled from time beyond memory with our burrows. My knowledge must be shared: The humans were dangerous. They would make good prey.

I reached my goal when the moons were highest. The flat rock was bare of snow when I ran limping in. Awakened by the scent of my blood, several People emerged from their dens. I laid myself down on the sacrifice rock. A grandmother of the People came forward, licked my wound, tasting, considering. Then she nudged me away with her forehead. The wound would heal, she thought, and winter was young; my flesh was not yet needed.

But I stayed. Again she nudged me away. I refused to go. She whined in puzzlement. I licked the rock.

That was understood. Two of the People came forward and placed their weight on me. A third lifted a paw. He shattered my skull, and they ate.

Magda watched through power binoculars from atop a nearby ridge. She saw everything. The rock swarmed with lean black horrors. It would be dangerous to go down among them, so she waited and watched the puzzling tableau below. The larl had wanted to die, she'd swear it, and now the beasts came forward daintily, almost ritualistically, to taste the brains, the young first and then the old. She raised her rifle, thinking to exterminate a few of the brutes from afar.

A curious thing happened then. All the larls that had eaten of her prey's brain leaped away, scattering. Those that had not eaten waited, easy targets, not understanding. Then another dipped to lap up a fragment of brain, and looked up with sudden comprehension. Fear touched her.

The hunter had spoken often of the larls, had said that they were so elusive he sometimes thought them intelligent. "Come spring, when I can afford to waste ammunition on carnivores, I look forward to harvesting a few of these beauties," he'd said. He was the colony's xenobiologist, and he loved the animals he killed, treasured them even as he smoked their flesh, tanned their hides, and drew detailed pictures of their internal organs. Magda had always scoffed at his theory that larls gained insight into the habits of their prey by eating their brains, even though he'd spent much time observing the animals minutely from afar, gathering evidence. Now she wondered if he were right.

Her baby whimpered, and she slid a hand inside her furs to give him a breast. Suddenly the night seemed cold and dangerous, and she thought: What am I doing here? Sanity returned to her all at once, her anger collapsing to nothing, like an ice tower shattering in the wind. Below, sleek black shapes sped toward her, across the snow. They changed direction every few leaps, running evasive patterns to avoid her fire.

"Hang on, kid," she muttered, and turned her strider around. She opened up the throttle.

Magda kept to the open as much as she could, the creatures following her from a distance. Twice she stopped abruptly and turned her rifle on her pursuers. Instantly they disappeared in puffs of snow, crouching belly-down but not stopping, burrowing toward her under the surface. In the eerie night silence, she could hear the whispering sound of the brutes tunneling. She fled.

Some frantic timeless period later—the sky had still not lightened in the east—Magda was leaping a frozen stream when the strider's left ski struck a rock. The machine was knocked glancingly upward, cybernetics screaming as they fought to regain balance. With a sickening crunch, the strider slammed to earth, one ski twisted and bent. It would take extensive work before the strider could move again.

Magda dismounted. She opened her robe and looked down on her child. He smiled up at her and made a gurgling noise.

Something went dead in her.

A fool. I've been a criminal fool, she thought. Magda was a proud woman who had always refused to regret, even privately, anything she had done. Now she regretted everything: Her anger, the hunter, her entire life, all that had brought her to this point, the cumulative madness that threatened to kill her child.

A larl topped the ridge.

Magda raised her rifle, and it ducked down. She began walking downslope, parallel to the stream. The snow was knee deep and she had to walk carefully not to slip and fall. Small pellets of snow rolled down ahead of her, were overtaken by other pellets. She strode ahead, pushing up a wake.

The hunter's cabin was not many miles distant; if she could reach it, they would live. But a mile was a long way in winter. She could hear the larls calling to each other, soft coughlike

noises, to either side of the ravine. They were following the sound
of her passage through the snow. Well, let them. She still had the
rifle, and if it had few bullets left, *they* didn't know that. They
were only animals.

This high in the mountains, the trees were sparse. Magda descended a good quarter-mile before the ravine choked with scrub
and she had to climb up and out or risk being ambushed. Which
way? she wondered. She heard three coughs to her right, and
climbed the left slope, alert and wary.

We herded her. Through the long night we gave her fleeting
glimpses of our bodies whenever she started to turn to the side
she must not go, and let her pass unmolested the other way. We
let her see us dig into the distant snow and wait motionless, un-
detectable. We filled the woods with our shadows. Slowly, slowly,
we turned her around. She struggled to return to the cabin, but
she could not. In what haze of fear and despair she walked! We
could smell it. Sometimes her baby cried, and she hushed the
milky-scented creature in a voice gone flat with futility. The night
deepened as the moons sank in the sky. We forced the woman
back up into the mountains. Toward the end, her legs failed her
several times; she lacked our strength and stamina. But her patience and guile were every bit our match. Once we approached
her still form, and she killed two of us before the rest could
retreat. How we loved her! We paced her, confident that sooner
or later she'd drop.

It was at night's darkest hour that the woman was forced back
to the burrowed hillside, the sacred place of the People where
stood the sacrifice rock. She topped the same rise for the second
time that night, and saw it. For a moment she stood helpless, and
then she burst into tears.

We waited, for this was the holiest moment of the hunt, the
point when the prey recognizes and accepts her destiny. After a
time, the woman's sobs ceased. She raised her head and straightened her back.

Slowly, steadily, she walked downhill.

She knew what to do.

Larls retreated into their burrows at the sight of her, gleaming eyes dissolving into darkness. Magda ignored them. Numb and aching, weary to death, she walked to the sacrifice rock. It had to be this way.

Magda opened her coat, unstrapped her baby. She wrapped him deep in the furs and laid the bundle down to one side of the rock. Dizzily, she opened the bundle to kiss the top of his sweet head, and he made an angry sound. "Good for you, kid," she said hoarsely. "Keep that attitude." She was so tired.

She took off her sweaters, her vest, her blouse. The raw cold nipped at her flesh with teeth of ice. She stretched slightly, body aching with motion. God it felt good. She laid down the rifle. She knelt.

The rock was black with dried blood. She lay down flat, as she had earlier seen her larl do. The stone was cold, so cold it almost blanked out the pain. Her pursuers waited nearby, curious to see what she was doing; she could hear the soft panting noise of their breathing. One padded noiselessly to her side. She could smell the brute. It whined questioningly.

She licked the rock.

Once it was understood what the woman wanted, her sacrifice went quickly. I raised a paw, smashed her skull. Again I was youngest. Innocent, I bent to taste.

The neighbors were gathering, hammering at the door, climbing over one another to peer through the windows, making the walls bulge and breathe with their eagerness. I grunted and bellowed, and the clash of silver and clink of plates next door grew louder. Like peasant animals, my husband's people tried to drown out the sound of my pain with toasts and drunken jokes.

Through the window I saw Tevin-the-Fool's bonewhite skin gaunt on his skull, and behind him a slice of face—sharp nose, white cheeks—like a mask. The doors and walls pulsed with the weight of those outside. In the next room, children fought and wrestled, and elders pulled at their long white beards, staring anxiously at the closed door.

The midwife shook her head, red lines running from the corners of her mouth down either side of her stern chin. Her eye sockets were shadowy pools of dust. "Now push!" she cried. "Don't be a lazy sow!"

I groaned and arched my back. I shoved my head back and it grew smaller, eaten up by the pillows. The bedframe skewed as one leg slowly buckled under it. My husband glanced over his shoulder at me, an angry look, his fingers knotted behind his back.

All of Landfall shouted and hovered on the walls.

"Here it comes!" shrieked the midwife. She reached down to my bloody crotch, and eased out a tiny head, purple and angry, like a goblin.

And then all the walls glowed red and green and sprouted large flowers. The door turned orange and burst open, and the neighbors and crew flooded in. The ceiling billowed up, and aerialists tumbled through the rafters. A boy who had been hiding beneath the bed flew up laughing to where the ancient sky and stars shone through the roof.

They held up the child, bloody on a platter.

Here the larl touched me for the first time, that heavy black paw like velvet on my knee, talons sheathed. "Are you following this?" he asked. "Can you separate truth from fantasy, tell what is fact and what the mad imagery of emotions we did not share? No more could I. All that, the first birth of human young on this planet, I experienced in an instant. Blind with awe, I understood the personal tragedy and the communal triumph of that event, and the meaning of the lives and culture behind it. A second before, I lived as an animal, with an animal's simple thoughts and hopes. Then I ate of your ancestor and was lifted all in an instant halfway to godhood.

"As the woman had intended. She had died thinking of the child's birth, in order that we might share in it. She gave us that. She gave us more. She gave us *language*. We were wise animals before we ate her brain, and we were People afterward. We owed her so much. And we knew what she wanted from us." The larl stroked my cheek with his great, smooth paw, the ivory claws hooded but quivering slightly, as if about to awake.

I hardly dared breathe.

"That morning I entered Landfall, carrying the baby's sling in my mouth. It slept through most of the journey. At dawn I passed through the empty street as silently as I knew how. I came to the First Captain's house. I heard the murmur of voices within, the entire village assembled for worship. I tapped the door with one paw. There was sudden, astonished silence. Then slowly, fearfully, the door opened.''

The larl was silent for a moment. "That was the beginning of the association of People with humans. We were welcomed into your homes, and we helped with the hunting. It was a fair trade. Our food saved many lives that first winter. No one needed know how the woman had perished, or how well we understood your kind.

"That child, Flip, was your ancestor. Every few generations we take one of your family out hunting, and taste his brains, to maintain our closeness with your line. If you are a good boy and grow up to be as bold and honest, as intelligent and noble a man as your father, then perhaps it will be you we eat."

The larl presented his blunt muzzle to me in what might have been meant as a friendly smile. Perhaps not; the expression hangs unreadable, ambiguous in my mind even now. Then he stood and padded away into the friendly dark shadows of the Stone House.

I was sitting staring into the coals a few minutes later when my second-eldest sister—her face a featureless blaze of light, like an angel's—came into the room and saw me. She held out a hand, saying, "Come on, Flip, you're missing everything." And I went with her.

Did any of this actually happen? Sometimes I wonder. But it's growing late, and your parents are away. My room is small but snug, my bed warm but empty. We can burrow deep in the blankets and scare away the cave-bears by playing the oldest winter games there are.

You're blushing! Don't tug away your hand. I'll be gone soon to some distant world to fight in a war for people who are as unknown to you as they are to me. Soldiers grow old slowly, you know. We're shipped frozen between the stars. When you are old and plump and happily surrounded by grandchildren, I'll still be young, and thinking of you. You'll remember me then, and our thoughts will touch in the void. Will you have nothing to regret? Is that really what you want?

I thought once that I could outrun the darkness. I thought—I must have thought—that by joining the militia I could escape my fate. But for all that I gave up my home and family, in the end the beast came anyway to eat my brain. Now I am alone. A month from now, in all this world, only you will remember my name. Let me live in your memory.

Come, don't be shy. Let's put the past aside and get on with our lives. That's better. Blow the candle out, love, and there's an end to my tale.

All this happened long ago, on a planet whose name has been burned from my memory.

SECOND COUSIN TWICE REMOVED

Cynthia Felice

"Second Cousin Twice Removed" was purchased by Gardner Dozois, and appeared in the December 1991 issue of Asimov's, *with an interior illustration by Laura Lakey. Cynthia Felice is not a prolific author at short lengths, by the high-production standards of the field, and this is her only sale to* Asimov's *to date, although we continue to coax her to send us something new. More prolific at book length, her novels include* Godsfire, The Sunbound, Downtime, Eclipse, Double Nocturne, Ice-man, *and* The Khan's Persuasion, *as well as two novels written in collaboration with Connie Willis,* Water Witch *and* Light Raid. *Coming up are more collaborative novels with Willis. She lives with her family in Colorado Springs, Colorado.*

Here she spins the wry story of how a second cousin twice removed drops in on a big family Christmas party, and serves up some surprises that are definitely not on the usual Holiday bill of fare . . .

Four cars were already blocking the driveway when I got back from shopping and it was only four o'clock. The Christmas Eve party had started at six P.M. for about twenty years now, but ever since Tony and Paul and all their friends got driver's licenses there're a few cars in the driveway no matter what time it is. I parked in the street, got my shopping bags out of the back seat, and hurried through the cold to the house. The door flew open and I rushed inside. The aroma of the ham baking was gratifying.

"Merry Christmas, Jenny." The door slammed and my brother-in-law Mario put his arms around me for a hug. He was wearing a red sweater with epaulets and an emblem, which combined with silver-gray hair and the handsome DeRose features to give him a distinguished look, sort of like a retired general. He reached for the shopping bags. "For me?" he asked. "You shouldn't have." Then he hefted them and gave me a puzzled look. For such big sacks they were deceptively light.

"Ornaments," I said as I shoved my coat in the closet. I was still in jeans and a sweatshirt and wishing now that I'd thought to shower and dress before I ran out to the St. Nick store. "For the tree."

"You don't have enough Christmas ornaments? Why didn't you say something? Lillian must have fifty boxes of Christmas junk in the attic."

"You got new ornaments?" Lillian said, coming out of my living room into the foyer. My sister-in-law's eyes were twinkling with anticipation as she hugged me. "For a special occasion? Merry Christmas, and *happy anniversary*."

"Jen, is that you?" My husband Sal stuck his head out from the kitchen. His glasses were greasy and there was a dusting of flour across his nose. "Where have you been? You still haven't made the *scalliels* and the kids are downstairs listening to music when they should be decorating the tree, and everyone's already arriving. Do I have to do everything around here?"

Before I could answer I heard the thunder of teen feet pounding in the stairwell. "Mom, tell him that you *ordered* us not to decorate the tree until you got back," Paul was shouting before he was halfway up the stairs. "And that I already cleaned the downstairs bathroom once today, and that I *am* helping by sorting the Christmas records." As he reached the top of the stairs his hand darted out to the countertop that was filled with platters of cookies. He popped something into his mouth, probably an island jewel shortbread cookie to judge by the smudge of powdered sugar on his lips. "Someone didn't put them back in their jackets, just jammed them in the case," Paul mumbled.

Paul was seventeen, still young enough to think I couldn't possibly remember I told him to clean up downstairs after last year's Christmas Eve party, which meant putting away the Christmas albums. His buddies reached the top of the stairs, all of them in dress pants and whole shirts, quite a change from the T-shirts and jeans held together with safety pins they usually wore. Three of them I knew; two of them were strangers, which was not at all unusual. Paul always seemed to have some young friends who needed somewhere to be on Christmas Eve. The boys were eyeing the cookies.

"This is Jerry," Paul said, sticking his thumb in the chest of the closest blond boy. "You know Brian, Todd, John, and, of course, Dominick."

"Have *one*," I said, smiling at the boys and knowing that at this hour an open invitation to teenagers could result in weeks of baking being devoured before the rest of the guests even arrived. I took the shopping bags from Mario and handed them to Paul. "You and your brother can start the tree now; use these. When you're done, put towels in the downstairs bathroom, the good ones."

"Tony's in the shower," Paul said. He'd shifted the two light bags into one hand and started pulling tissue paper off of the top layer of ornaments. "They're all silver."

"That's because it's our silver anniversary today," I said as I shoved up my sleeves and started for the kitchen. One of the young men stepped out from behind Paul.

"Hi, I'm Dominick. You must be Aunt Jenny. You weren't expecting me but you always said anyone who can come should come."

He was obviously a DeRose; he had the big brown eyes and that little dent that some of the DeRoses have at the corner of their left eye, and he smiled like a DeRose. He wore whiskers, a bit thin and not enough to hide that shy winsome grin. "You're welcome, of course. Did you fly in?" I asked, and I was trying to figure out if he was Angelo Peroni's grandson or Elmo Ranalli's, which would narrow him down to about one hundred and fifty people. The DeRose girls each had ten children, and their brother, my father-in-law, had thirteen. I knew most of Sal's cousins, but keeping track of their children was almost impossible.

"Not exactly," he said. "I've been at school."

"Does this mean I can't hang my pink baby in the manger ornament that I made in first grade?" Paul said, his big brown eyes glittering with mock disappointment.

"That's what it means," I said.

"Jen!" Sal shouted from the kitchen.

I patted Dominick on the cheek. "We'll talk later," I said, and he smiled and nodded.

"Come on, Dom," Paul said, gesturing toward the living room. "What are you to me anyhow, a second cousin?"

I didn't hear his answer because Sal was talking to me again even before I got into the kitchen. "New ornaments?" he asked. "You left me here to finish cooking for a hundred people to buy ornaments for the tree when we have five boxes of ornaments in the shed?" He was shaking his head, wiping floured fingers on the apron he had over his T-shirt and jeans. Even so, I could tell he was touched. When your anniversary is the 24th of December, you can't really celebrate; Christmas takes precedence. He gave me a peck and handed me the measuring cup. I put it down.

"I told her she could borrow some from us," Mario said. He'd followed me into the kitchen. "Lillian has a jillion."

"Oh, it's going to be pretty," Lillian said, coming in from the living room. "Silver bells, white sparkly snowflakes, even little mirror ones, and where did you ever find those silver garlands? They're so fat and fluffy."

"You saw them all already?" I asked. The kitchen was a mess. Sal was obviously about to tackle the *scalliels* on his own; he had the big can of Crisco but the wrong dutch oven on the stovetop next to the split pea soup, which was boiling too hard. At least the mixing bowl was clean and ready. I turned down the flame under the soup.

"Paul dumped the shopping bags out on the floor," Lillian said. "But it's all right; nothing broke. The store wrapped them nicely. I just moved some of it so they wouldn't step on them while they put the lights on the tree and I peeked at some of them. They're beautiful, Jen."

I put the dutch oven back in the cabinet and pulled out the sixteen-quart pot and started scooping the Crisco into it. "We've never had new ornaments," I said. "We got some from Mama

DeRose and my mother for our first Christmas, and then someone gave me grandma's. This is the first time I've ever bought ornaments in my whole life. It was fun. And I figured that since we never celebrate our anniversary in the traditional sense, it would be nice to do something a little bit special for our silver one."

The doorbell rang, and Sal shouted for Paul to answer it.

"Could it be Annette and Benny?" I asked.

"No, they called again just after you left," Sal said. "They're still stuck on the ground in Chicago. They can't get the runways cleared. The airlines aren't making any promises, but Benny said some flights were getting out, so they were still hoping."

"Gemma and Don made it in; I talked to Marc and Kathy just before we left the house," Lillian said. Gemma and Don were from the California contingent converging on us this Christmas. "They'll be over just as soon as Gemma gets changed." She looked at the lard melting in the pot. "You aren't making *tordills* at this hour, are you?"

"*Scalliels*," Mario said loudly. "My sister-in-law knows my Christmas wouldn't be complete without *scalliels*."

"Should have made them yesterday," Sal said, peeking in the oven at the ham. Ham really doesn't need any attention, but Sal checks it about every hour anyhow. "How am I supposed to bake the rolls?"

"That," I said, "is what you should have made yesterday. The *scalliels* only taste good when they're fresh." I was wishing I'd made them this morning as I'd planned, but I'd gotten behind.

"Hey, Mom!" Paul shouted from the living room. "Can I start decorating the tree, or do I have to wait for Tony?"

"The ham can come out at five-thirty and I'll bake off your rolls then," I said, and to Paul, I shouted, "Get started. He'll help you when he gets out of the shower."

"How come I had to wait for him to come home from college to trim the tree but I don't have to wait for him to get out of the shower?"

I just shook my head, but Lillian figured it out. "Was Tony disappointed last year that you hadn't waited for him?"

"He said he wasn't, but I think he was. Have you seen Bridgette yet?"

"Yes, she's here. I think she's still downstairs working on the albums with the other girls."

"Girls?" I asked.

"Angie and Sara. I think they came with Brian. And you'll get to meet Matt Kelly tonight, Valerie's new boyfriend. I think it's serious this time."

I was looking for the eggs. I'd left them on the counter before I went shopping because they're supposed to be room temperature, but the countertops were so cluttered with trays of food and dirty bowls that I couldn't see them. I reminded Lillian that I'd met Matt Kelly after a football game last fall and I think she said something about that not counting because Valerie hadn't been dating him at the time, or maybe she told me they'd been dating and broken up and made up since then. One of the problems I have with Christmas Eve is that I'm always doing something and I never really get to talk with anyone. I love my niece and I like knowing what's going on in her life, but I only manage to get snatches of important information on Christmas Eve because my concentration is divided between conversation and whatever I'm doing.

I found the eggs in the refrigerator just as Valerie and Matt Kelly arrived. Thankfully they hadn't cooled down yet. The eggs, I mean. I cracked the full dozen into a mixing bowl and added one cold one from the other carton because that's what I'd seen my mother-in-law do. I'd baked with her several times so that I could write down the recipes—"A handful of dis, a spoonya of dat"—and sometimes she'd dump the handful into the bowl before I really got to see how much, and she never used measuring spoons. We'd probably made the *scalliels* on Christmas Eve, because despite my notes, mine were never quite as good as hers. They tasted okay, but the dough was awful to handle and they fried up with funny splits in the crust that hers never had. I was determined to follow the recipe carefully this time, carefully measuring four teaspoons of anise extract, which she had just poured from the bottle onto the pool of eggs. Clever me had marked the bottle and measured the amount later. I didn't think the anise extract was the problem. I hated making them because they wouldn't turn out right. I must have said something like that out loud.

"I thought you liked *scalliels*," Dominick said.

Sal was peeking in the oven again ahead of schedule, and Lillian was gone. "I do like them," I said, looking around for the measuring cup. "I just can't make them right." The cup was perched on a stack of holly patterned paper plates right where I left it and I plunged it into the flour bag. "My dough is always sticky, and Grandma's . . . I mean your great Aunt Pietra's wasn't. Half of it will end up on my fingers instead of in the cookies."

Dominick was leaning over the bowl of eggs, sniffing the aroma of the anise. "I love *scalliels*," he said as he watched me pour the first cup of flour in.

"You and your Uncle Mario," I said.

"My dad likes them, too," he said.

"And Paul," I added as I reached for the blender. You had to mix the flour as it was added, or the dough might get lumpy. I'd solved that problem a few years ago, but it still wasn't *right*.

"What about the Crisco?" Dom asked me.

"It's melting in the pot on the stove," I said.

"No, I mean in the batter, er, dough. Whatever you call it. Doesn't some go in with the eggs?"

"Hey, Tony, are you out of the shower yet?" Paul shouted from the living room. "I've got a broken string of lights."

I was staring at the yellow mass of eggs and in my mind's eye I could see a lump of Crisco floating in the center. I could almost hear my mother-in-law's voice saying, "To maka da dough nice-ah," as she dumped it off the slotted spoon into the eggs.

"How'd you know about the Crisco?" I asked him, amazed. I looked at Dominick, fully confident that the Crisco was the missing ingredient. It was like an epiphany.

"I used to watch my grandmother make them," he said, smiling that big grin that Paul and Tony always use when they've done something they're pleased about.

"I need some help with these lights," Paul shouted.

"Tony's still in the shower," Sal shouted back. His head and shoulders were in the refrigerator.

"I'll help him," Dominick said.

I hadn't known that Renata Peroni or Loretta Ranalli made *scalliels*; I'd always believed the *scalliels* were something my mother-in-law had brought with her from her village. At least, hers were the only ones I'd ever eaten during those Christmases back in Chicago when we were young. I didn't much care; they'd turn out all right this time, I was sure. I scooped some Crisco into the eggs, and I had the best feeling about it floating there.

The doorbell rang again, and Bridgette came into the kitchen and hung around long enough to help me roll the *scalliels*. The dough was not sticky. It was nice, and none at all stuck to my palms. Bridgette helped me fry them in the hot Crisco, and by then it was almost time for the ham to come out of the oven. Bridgette was a great kid, already practically a member of the family. She and Tony had been dating since they were in high school, and she had been telling me about her classes at the community college as we watched the cookies turn golden brown in the hot lard.

"Hey, Mom. What do you want on the top of the tree?" It was Tony shouting this time.

"The star, honey," I said.

"What star?" Paul shouted.

"The one in the shopping bag."

"The shopping bags are empty," Paul shouted.

I handed my apron to Bridgette and went into the living room. Paul and Tony were picking up tissue paper, stuffing it into the shopping bags. "Are you sure . . ."

"Yes, Mom, I'm sure there's no star in the bag. I checked myself before we started picking up," Tony said.

I was dismayed. Tony could be trusted to have checked thoroughly. "The clerk must have forgotten to put it in the bag," I said. "You'll have to go get it."

"It's ten to six," Tony said, shaking his head.

"We can just put up the old blue angel," Paul said, "and my pink manger." He grinned.

The tree looked like a jewel, all the ornaments not just shiny but new, every one of them hand picked by me in the celebration of this night. The garland was thick, and draped so neatly I was sure Tony must have done that part. I didn't want the old blue angel on the top, I wanted my star. "You'll have to hurry down to the St. Nick store," I said firmly.

"What if I don't get the right one?"

"The clerk had it wrapped; she probably just forgot to put it in the bag."

"She's not going to give it to *me*," Paul protested.

"Tell her you're my son," I said. "Just tell her the lady who bought all the silver and white ornaments; she'll give it to you."

"But . . ."

"Come on," Dominick said. He'd been digging in the shopping bag. "I've got the receipt. I'll go with you."

Dom and Paul left, I went back into the kitchen to help Sal with the ham and to start baking off the rolls, and then ducked out to the bedroom to get changed. The doorbell was ringing in earnest, now, and the phone, too. I was glad Dom had cut off Paul's protests. The store was only five minutes away, and having an anniversary tree, complete with silver star, was small enough tribute to twenty-five years with Sal.

"The tree looks real pretty," he said when he breezed back into the bedroom for a belt and a shirt. "What made you think of new ornaments?" He'd managed a shower, but his glasses were still greasy. I took them off his face and polished them with the hem of my slip.

"You, silly," I said. "Happy anniversary. Did the kids get back with the star?"

He nodded. "Dom—is he a Ranalli or a Peroni?" he asked, and I shrugged. "Anyhow, Dom slipped something under the tree. There's already half a dozen packages there."

They always asked if they could bring something, a plate of cookies or a salad, and we always said no. As much as Sal complained about all the work, as harried as we got on the big day, all the baking and the cooking was ours. We wanted it that way, we loved it that way. I guess people sensed it, because the gifts they left under the tree were tokens of sentiment and never so extravagant that we'd have to remember who gave what. Indeed, a lot of them didn't even have tags.

"Bridgette wrote everyone's name on the white board," Sal said as I slipped on my red dress and stepped into a pair of heels. "Counting babies and Benny and Annette, there really is going to be over one hundred people. One hundred and one, to be exact." He seemed rather pleased. It always felt like a hundred, but most years it was really only about fifty or sixty people. This year no one had gone out of town for the holidays. Everyone was coming, maybe because it was our silver anniversary.

"Any word from Benny?"

"Hey, Mom," Paul shouted through the closed door. "Uncle Ben is on the phone."

"I'll get it," I said, leaving Sal to find a shirt.

Dominick was holding the phone, his hand over the receiver. "Don't tell them I'm here," he said. "I want to surprise them."

I nodded and talked to Benny, who explained they were still snowed in at the airport, couldn't even get home, let alone to us. Chicago was in the grips of a full blown blizzard, and we, of course, didn't have so much as a flake of snow. I put Mario on the phone so that Benny could repeat the whole story to him and pulled the first batch of rolls out of the oven.

"Expecting over a hundred people," I heard Sal saying to Lloyd Montgomery, one of his writer friends who had just arrived.

"Ninety-nine," I corrected.

"Benny and Annette?" Sal asked.

I nodded and pointed to the phone. I greeted Lloyd and ducked past a crush of kids to look at the tree. The silver star was on top and the living room was already full of people. I went to take over greeting from Tony; Paul was nowhere to be seen, and neither was Dom. Jill Murphy and her family had arrived. Jill and Paul had been dating since last summer, but I knew that they'd broken up again just a few days ago. There'd been some question in my mind about whether or not the Murphys would come tonight, but I guess the elder Murphys' good sense prevailed. Susan Murphy confided that if the two young people didn't make up tonight, they probably would tomorrow, and she wasn't going to miss this party for anything. Jill had laughed, but it wasn't her pretty laugh. It was kind of embarrassed.

When Sal and I were slicing the ham, I found Dom on my elbow. "Would you introduce me to Paul's girlfriend?" he asked me.

Paul, of course, was nowhere around to do the honors. "In a minute," I said. I had my hands full of ham fat scraps, but was realizing they weren't going to fit safely in the already overstuffed trash. Dom whisked it out from under me and dashed for the

garage door. I stood there with my hands full greeting Maria and
Bill along with their brood, followed by Marc and Kathy and
theirs, and Gemma and Don. Most of the guests were Christmas
Eve seasoned veterans, and they wound their way through the
kitchen bumping and tasting on their way downstairs to the
punchbowls. Dom returned with the empty trash can.

"What happened to the piñon pine?" he asked me.

"What piñon pine?" I asked right back as I dumped the scraps.
I tore a paper towel from the rack.

"The one outside the back door," he said.

"You've got our house mixed up with someone else's," I said.
"We've been meaning to plant trees for years, but we've just
never gotten around to it."

"Oh," he said, backing up and right into Jill. Jill squealed.

"Jill, this is Dominick. He's Paul's second cousin, twice removed. Or is it three times removed?"

Dom shrugged, looking bland and indifferent as he shook hands
with Jill, not at all like she was someone he'd just asked to meet
only minutes ago.

Jill moved on past us, encountering some of the boys before
she got to the stairwell, and she laughed all the way down the
stairs.

"Paul's girlfriend?" Dom said hopefully.

"You just met her," I said, gesturing back to the stairwell.
"Jill Murphy. That's her laughing. You can always tell Paul's
girlfriends by their laughs. Jill's is pretty, the girl before that had
a hearty one, and they all have had great smiles."

"Bridgette has a great smile," he said.

I scooped the first batch of rolls into a basket. "She's Tony's
girlfriend," I said.

"Yeah, I know," he said. "She looks just like her picture."

"Who has pictures of Bridgette?" I asked. Generally I sent
only pictures of the family, but of course anyone visiting from
Chicago could have caught Bridgette on film any time over the
last four years. We already thought of her as a daughter. Tony
only needed to make it legal now, but if he'd just wait until he
finished college, please, God.

"Jen, the Eastmans are here," Sal said, beckoning me over,

and of course the oven timer went off, too. The next batch of rolls were ready.

I swapped out baking sheets, and went to greet the Eastmans, Garrett and Madeline, their teen daughters Regina and Mora, and of course baby Nicole. Nicole was walking now, wearing a little red coat with white fuzzy trim. Madeline was trying to take it off, but the toddler was having none of it. She just stared up at the crush of people, her eyes wide with amazement. When her coat was unbuttoned, she hugged herself so that it wouldn't come off when Madeline tugged. For the moment, her mother gave up and got up from her knees to hug me. Madeline Eastman and her family give the best hugs. Long hugs that seem to envelop me, hugs that engage me from my nose to my toes, and I get to do it four times. Unfortunately little Nicole was having none of it, not yet.

"Don't you want to take off your coat, honey?" I asked her. She reached for her mother, but then pulled back when she realized Mom was trying for the coat.

"In a minute," Madeline said easily for Nicole. And to me, "Oh, Jen, the tree is beautiful. I can't believe that with everything else you do at Christmas you also did *this*." She had stepped over to the tree to see some of the ornaments more closely. "Look at the tiny little birdnest made of silver wire. Oh, Garrett, did you see?"

The tree really was magnificent. That bushy old thing I'd bought at the Ben Franklin when Tony was a baby had been transformed into something magical. "The boys decorated it," I said.

"Tony and Paul didn't pick out all these wonderful things," Madeline said with a laugh.

The phone rang, but someone else answered it. The doorbell rang and Paul's friend Lenny Washington walked in before anyone could open it just like he always did when he knew Paul was expecting him. His folks were behind him. I excused myself from the Eastmans to greet the Washingtons, and then Bridgette's folks arrived and I managed to get away from the door for a while to get the rolls out of the oven. From the corner of my eyes, I saw Paul staring into the linen closet, which I thought was peculiar. He saw me watching him.

"They need towels in the downstairs bathroom," Paul said, pulling out the rattiest ones I owned.

"Not those," I said. "The good ones."

"These don't have any holes or . . ."

I snatched them out of his hand and shoved them back on the shelf. I pulled the good ones off the shelf and handed them to him.

"You don't have to get mad," he said.

"I'm not angry, but it's just about this time on Christmas Eve I do start going a bit mad."

"Huh?"

"Never mind," I said. "Take the towels down."

He turned to go and then paused. "Oh, yeah, Dom needed to borrow a CD. He was showing Nicole how to pop them out, and when she tried it, she popped the one he had in the machine right into the fireplace. I gave him your *Best of Carly Simon* album."

"He likes Carly Simon?" I asked.

"I don't think so. He just wanted an old one. He said he'd give it back at the end of the evening."

In answer to my *but why* look, Paul just shrugged and disappeared with the towels. I went back to making sure there were enough plates and holly-stamped paper napkins before I told everyone they could start eating.

While the guests fill their plates, Sal and I always stand by to explain what they're eating. They had the split pea soup and the ham figured out, but there were regular dinner rolls as well as rye, Swedish limpa and sheepherder's bread, condiments from all over the world, a new vegetable dip that Sal had created, and of course the Italian cookies: *Quaresemali, tordills, biscotti d'anice* and this year first-rate, just like Mama DeRose used to make them, *scalliels*, iced with powdered-sugar frosting, and fresh. The taste of anise is light, the cookie just about melts when it touches the tongue. Mario was back for thirds, which was fine because a baker's dozen of eggs makes a lot of *scalliels*.

"Now is Dominick a Peroni or a Ranalli?" Mario asked me, "and whose kid is he?"

"I haven't figured it out yet," I said.

Mario seemed surprised.

"Talk to Paul. I overheard him asking Dom, but I didn't hear the answer."

Mario nodded and bit into another *scalliel*. "Best batch you've ever made," he said as he went to find Paul.

"I never saw so much food," Dorothy Washington said, "and believe me, my family can eat. But then I know you know that; you've had Lenny for dinner as much as I've had Paul. Now what are these?" she asked me, pointing to the island jewels, one of the few non-Italian cookies we make.

It takes quite a lot of time to explain the food, and Sal, who rightfully takes credit for most of the baking, loves every minute of it. Every year he tells the story of the time when he set the bread dough to rise on the chair nearest the radiator, then returned to working on a set of page proofs and sat down on the rising loaf, and every year it gets a big laugh. If we're lucky, Sal and I get to have some soup before it's time to make sure there's coffee for everyone. This year was going to take two urns full, and there was only one urn.

The Magindins and the Terrocos always came after Mass, but they were in time to see Tony and Paul re-marry Sal and me in honor of our twenty-fifth wedding anniversary. Although the kids had obviously planned this surprise carefully, we didn't exactly repeat our vows. When Tony played the part of the minister, he asked Sal to promise to give his sons unlimited use of the gas charge card, and Paul wanted us to vow never to look at the clock when he came in. We didn't make any promises. But we did hear Tony and Paul say they loved us in front of almost a hundred witnesses, which turned us to mush for at least the next hour. When the mock wedding was over Sal and I sat together on the sofa holding hands for the longest time. Finally he got up to refill the punchbowl and Dom plopped down beside me.

"Would you show me the family tree you've been working on?" he asked me.

"How did you know about the family tree?" I'd sent off to *Reader's Digest* for a family tree form, and I'd filled in some of the blanks but most of them were still empty.

"Someone mentioned it, and family trees are something I'm interested in," he said. I guess I still looked puzzled because he added, "It's for a class." I looked around for a minute. No one needed another cup of coffee, and everyone looked to be engaged in conversation. I'd take a respite and maybe use the time to find out what school Dom was going to, not to mention find out exactly who he was.

"Come on, then," I said. "It's in Sal's study, which is an absolute mess, so you have to close your eyes."

Actually Sal's study looked fairly neat compared to normal. The stacks of manuscripts and books were not put away, but he'd squared the corners and lined them up. The PC was even dusted.

One drawer in his filing cabinet is devoted to household matters, and I keep odds and ends in it, too. While I was looking for the family tree file, Dom went over to the closet and looked inside, not at the clothes but at the inside wall.

"These are Tony and Paul's height recordings," he commented.

I found the family tree file and pulled it out of the drawer. "Who told you about those?" I asked him.

"I spent a lot of time with my grandmother," he answered easily. He was looking closely at the marks—just pencil lines I'd made by laying the pencil on the tops of Tony and Paul's heads, then I'd scratch it in and add the date and their names. It was fun when the boys were little and the marks had been very close together. The last few years I was lucky to get one measurement a year, and Sal had been upset with me when I refused to let him paint over the marks when we re-did the study. Then Dom looked at me, and I guess I had a perturbed look on my face. "Sorry," he said hastily. "I guess guests shouldn't be looking in closets."

"It's all right," I said. "A few of your cousins are marked there, too. The little ones get a kick out of seeing if they're as tall as Tony or Paul when they were the same age."

He nodded, smiled and nodded again. Dom started to close the closet door, then hesitated. "Would you mark me?" he asked.

I laughed. "How old are you?"

"Twenty-five," he answered sheepishly.

I laughed again, but I admit I found it kind of charming. "Let me find a pencil," I said, going over to Sal's desk. By the time I had the pencil in hand, Dom was standing with his shoulder blades against the wall, nose to nose with the sleeve of Sal's old hunting jacket. "Take off your shoes," I said.

"Oh, I forgot," he said, and slipped off his shoes.

I handed him the file while I measured, and then motioned him aside so I could write in the date and his age. I started to write his name. "Now are you a Ranalli or a Peroni?" I asked, but the room was empty. I picked up his shoes and went back to the living room. Dom was sitting with Mario and Gemma, showing them the family tree form.

"Your shoes," I said, handing them to him.

Dom looked up and smiled. "Thanks."

"Jen, I didn't know you were doing this," Mario said, gesturing to the family tree.

And Gemma said, "How come my kids aren't on here?" pointing to the empty lines under her and Don's names.

"I couldn't remember their birthdays," I admitted. "I meant to ask you, but I always forget."

"Give me a pen," Gemma demanded. "We have half the family here tonight. We can fill it in."

I got Gemma a pen, and now Marc and Kathy were hanging over her shoulder watching her write in date after date. She stopped.

"I don't know Annette and Benny's youngest boy's birthday," she said.

"October 12, Columbus Day," Kathy supplied. "He must be seven or eight, so '83 or '84."

"Ten," Gemma said. "He's the same age as my Lori."

"Is this all right that we're doing your homework, Dom?" Mario asked, chuckling because it was evident they were having a good time. Gemma was writing as fast as she could. "What kind of class makes you do a family tree over Christmas break?"

"American Peerage," he said.

"What kind of class is that?"

"Well, we don't exactly have classes," Dom said.

Mario shook his head. "We pay ten thousand dollars a year for these kids to go to school, and they don't even go to class."

"Lina is taking Outdoor Survival next semester. They build igloos or something like that," Kathy said. "She wants to be an accountant, so what I ask you is, why does an accountant need to know how to build an igloo?"

Dom was standing back from the group now, hands in his pockets, grinning. He'd put his shoes back on. I wanted to ask him where he fit in the family tree, if his last name was Ranalli or Peroni, but just then Bridgette came bursting into the living room, holding her hand out in front of her as if it was burned. Her eyes were full of tears. Bridgette's mother leaped to her feet at the sight of her daughter's obviously emotional state and reached out for her.

Alarmed, I looked around for Tony and saw him standing by the door, looking bewildered and concerned. "What's wrong?" I said.

Tony shrugged. "I asked Bridgette to marry me."

You could have knocked me over with a feather. What about school? was my first thought, but I didn't say it out loud.

"Well, what did she say?" Mario demanded to know. At that moment, he not only looked like a general but he sounded like one.

"She didn't answer me," Tony said, a bit of a tremor in his voice.

Bridgette whirled around. "Yes, yes!" she shouted from across the room. She was still standing half in her mother's arms, beet red, eyes still brimming with tears, showing the ring on her finger to everyone within ten feet, which was a lot of people.

Tony rocked back on his heels and grinned.

"Here, here! A toast is in order," Mario shouted as he raised his half-full glass of punch. "May you be as happy as your parents, and have children who behave no better than you!"

Glasses clinked and laughter rippled, and someone laughed like tinkling bells.

"Aunt Jen, look at Paul," Dom whispered.

Paul had a glass raised to his lips, but his eyes were fixed, not on Tony or Bridgette, but a pretty dark-haired girl who was laughing with Bridgette, laughing like tinkling bells.

"The laugh," Dom said. "It's her."

"Who is she?" I asked.

Dom was fidgeting with what looked like a portable CD player. The girl laughed again, I think because Bridgette was so embarrassed by all the attention.

"Angie Harris," he said. "She came with Brian. Excuse me. I want to make sure I got her laugh on the CD."

"That's a recorder?" I asked.

"New technology," he said over his shoulder.

A CD recorder. Oh, dear. Paul would want one and they were sure to be expensive. I could hope they cloned the technology before next Christmas. Fat chance.

Paul had gone over to Angie Harris, and I heard him say something about the toast Mario had made. To judge by Angie's quick laughter, it must have been a witty remark. I guess that encouraged him to keep going; Angie was still laughing prettily long after Bridgette had moved on to show others her engagement ring.

Christmas Eve parties at our house end by ten o'clock. It's not a time limit Sal or I have ever imposed; it occurs naturally. Santa Claus arrives early in the morning at households with children, even when the children are seventeen and twenty. The Eastmans were the first to leave. We didn't have to find little Nicole's coat; she was still wearing it, but now her eyes were just sleepy, no longer amazed.

"Happy anniversary, Aunt Jen," Dom said from the crush of young people heading for the door.

"Hey, Dom. Where's my mom's CD?" Paul asked, as he shook Dom's hand in farewell.

"I put it back in the case," he replied, "so I'll know right where to find it."

Paul patted Dom's shoulder, a "good man" gesture, then turned to say goodbye to Angie and Brian. Tony was helping Bridgette put on her coat, the two of them looking extremely pleased with themselves.

By ten-thirty, everyone was gone, and Sal was picking up paper plates. I went over to the table where the family tree was lying face up among the crumbs on the red tablecloth. It was pretty well filled in, Gemma's neat handwriting and Kathy's and even Mario's scrawl. He didn't write like a general.

"Did you get Dominick on there?" Sal asked me as he popped more paper plates into the trashbag.

"That's what I was looking for, and the answer is no. But not all the Ranallis and Peronis are filled in. Got all the DeRoses though." I looked at Sal. "Was he a Ranalli or a Peroni?" I never have time to get the important stuff on Christmas Eve. I shook my head.

"Ask Annette and Benny tomorrow, if they get here tomorrow."

"He's neither," Paul said.

"How do you know that?"

"I asked him, and he said, 'neither,' " Paul answered. "Did you see that CD recorder he had?"

"What did you say when he said 'neither'? " Sal asked. He held the trashbag open so that Paul could dump a paper cup in it.

Paul swigged down what was in the cup; one can only hope it was his. "Neither what?" he asked, spiking the trashbag with the cup.

"Neither a Ranalli or a Peroni."

"I said, 'Oh.' What was I supposed to say?" He frowned. "I thought they had to make CD recordings in a special environment of some kind."

"They do," Tony said. "In a clean room. The workers wear white space suits and masks over their faces. It couldn't have been a CD recorder. I'd have heard about it. Someone at school would have had one."

"He said it was a recorder."

"If he wasn't a Ranalli or a Peroni, who was he?" I asked.

No one answered.

And just how had he known that we keep our trash in the garage, I wondered. "Do you suppose he was a stranger off the streets?" Sal asked.

"You mean like a bag person?" Tony asked.

No one thought that.

"If he wasn't a Ranalli or a Peroni, he had to be a DeRose," Paul said firmly.

"He looked like a DeRose," I said.

"Grandpa's name was Dominick, wasn't it?" Paul asked.

"Yes, but . . ." Sal hesitated. "A Christmas ghost? You think my father came from the beyond to spend Christmas Eve with us?"

Paul shook his head. "Not with a CD recorder."

"What was he recording?"

"Everything. Nothing special," Tony said.

"Oh, yeah. He recorded something special," Paul said. He sat down by the Christmas tree and pulled a package out, hefting it in his hands. "He recorded me telling Brian and Angie about how when I had kids, I wasn't going to have any curfew for them, no healthy foods, and that I was going to give them big allowances." We must have given Paul blank looks. "Well, it was funny at the time. Uncle Mario made that crack about Tony and Bridgette having kids who behaved just like us. Angie kept asking me questions, like, how many kids and what were their names. That's what made me think of this. The names I gave my kids."

"Think of what?" I asked.

"I said Dominick and Rosa, first names that came to mind. I thought Dominick was Grandpa's name, not even thinking of Dom standing right there with his recorder—"

"Dominick is nice, but—Rosa DeRose?" I said. It didn't have a nice alliteration at all.

"That's about what Angie said, only she could barely get it out because she was laughing so hard."

I thought about Dom's eagerness to record that laughter. And to meet Paul's girlfriend. He'd known it wasn't Jill.

"I'd give a lot to have Dad saying he didn't believe in curfews on tape. Wouldn't you?" He was looking at Tony.

"My brother thinks he's been visited by a time traveler," Tony said solemnly. "I'm going to have to commit my own brother to an insane asylum on Christmas day. Do you think Bridgette will still marry me if there is insanity in the family?"

Paul glared at him, then he tossed the package to me. "Open this. I had to pay for it because Dom didn't have any money." He gave his brother a *take that* look. "Time travelers can't bring money with them. It doesn't have the right date."

Tony laughed.

I thought about the *scalliels*, that Dom had known the missing ingredient. And I'd said Paul liked them, and he'd said his father liked them. Paul?

"Open it," Paul insisted.

It was wrapped in tissue paper, wads of it, with a single strand of white string holding it together. I removed the string and pulled back the tissue. It was a gold star, just like the silver star Paul and Dom had gone back to the St. Nick store to get. I looked at Paul.

"Read the note," he said. "I already know what it says. I thought it was kinda hokey, but I figured you'd like it. You're into saccharine."

I found the note. "It says, 'I'll see you at your Golden Anniversary. That's a promise. Love, Dom.' "

"That doesn't mean anything," Tony said. "The guy's twenty-five years old. He'd only be fifty."

"Or that he's been to our golden wedding anniversary already," I said. And if he had, it was a message to me that Sal and I had at least another twenty-five years together.

Sal must have thought that too, for he smiled at me, a pleased and thoughtful smile. But then he shook his head. "No time travelers. One of those punk Peronis!"

I spent a lot of time with my grandma.

"My mother and my brother go nuts on Christmas," Tony said. "Come on, you don't really think . . ."

But if I couldn't remember to put the Crisco into the eggs, how could he have seen his grandmother do it? I hated conundrums, and I shook my head.

"We'll ask Annette and Benny who he is," Sal said finally. "He's going to turn out to be a second cousin twice removed."

"Maybe," I said. To Paul I said, "He's taller than you by three inches."

"You marked him on the closet wall? I'm not done growing, am I?" Paul demanded to know.

"I've been the same height since I was seventeen," Tony said.

"Great. He's recorded me saying kids shouldn't have curfews and he's going to be bigger than me, too." Suddenly he jumped up, that catlike unwind to upright that only young bodies can safely perform. "The recorder," he said. "Maybe that's why he needed the CD. Even if he couldn't take it with him, it wouldn't matter because Mom keeps *everything*."

He'd have dashed for the door, but Sal grabbed him by the collar and said, "Look, this is all very interesting, but do I have to clean this whole house by myself?"

Tony and Paul started to pick up and straighten, but I sat there with the golden star in my hands, wondering what a little boy named Dom would think of when he looked at the top mark in Sal's closet dated December 24, 1991.

I looked around to find Paul. He was gone. "Sal," I said. "What would you think of planting a piñon pine by the back door?"

He looked at me blankly for a second. "You want a piñon pine, we'll plant one. But not tonight. Who were you talking about yards with to make you think of that?"

"I never really got to talk with anyone, but I think tonight I met someone special. At least, every time I turned around, Dom seemed to be there."

Sal just grunted and went to get another trashbag.

Then I realized the stereo had come on, the Carly Simon album, which isn't Paul's taste in music at all. It was just Carly Simon, and I sighed after a while because it was still just Carly Simon. I wrapped up the golden star and put it in the china closet where it wouldn't get lost over the years. Then I picked up a paper cup half-filled with raspberry punch, humming along with the album.

I spent a lot of time with my grandmother.

It was just Carly Simon, but sometimes I thought I could hear the sound of laughter, like the tinkling of bells.

Scalliels, Theresa Felice's Italian Dunkers

1 dozen	large eggs, room temperature, (11 room temperature, 1 cold)
½ cup	Crisco
6 to 7 cups	flour, sifted (measure after sift)
1 teaspoon	salt
4 teaspoons	anise extract

Mix ingredients well to make a soft dough.

Form the dough by rolling it between your hands until it is ¼" thick, then cut into strips with knife, and shape 5-inch long strips for frying (knots, bows, etc.).

Fry until golden brown (medium-high) in Crisco.

Frost with ordinary powdered-sugar-water frosting.

Makes over 100 cookies.

THE LAST CASTLE OF CHRISTMAS

Alexander Jablokov

"The Last Castle of Christmas" was purchased by Gardner Dozois and appeared in the December 1993 issue of Asimov's, *with an interior illustration by Alan M. Clarke. In it, Jablokov takes us to the far future and across the Galaxy to an exotic alien planet where the settlers from Old Earth still keep Christmas in their hearts, sort of—although, as the evocative story that follows will demonstrate, a very strange Holiday Celebration it's become, as the centuries have passed and memories of Earth have blurred and mutated . . .*

With only a handful of elegant, cooly pyrotechnic stories and a few well-received novels, Alexander Jablokov has established himself as one of the most highly regarded and promising new writers in SF. He is a frequent contributor to Asimov's Science Fiction, Amazing, The Magazine of Fantasy & Science Fiction, *and other markets. His first novel,* Carve The Sky, *was released in 1991 to wide critical acclaim, and was followed by other successful novels such as* A Deeper Sea *and* Nimbus. *His most recent books are a collection of his short-fiction,* The Breath of Suspension, *all from the pages of* Asimov's, *and a new novel,* Red Dust. *He lives in Cambridge, Massachusetts.*

"Tessa!" Lewis's voice drifted across the wagon. "Tessa Wolholme." He windmilled his arms and fell flat on his back on the ice. Ice skates gleamed as he kicked his legs in the air.

"He wants you to celebrate with him." Dalka was contemptuous.

A gentle rein tug and the mule, splayed legs ungainly, bounced the wagon's runners out of the ice-filled ruts onto the sloping embankments. Huffing, somehow realizing that it had been granted an unexpected rest, Legume wiggled its bulging belly into the frost, stuck its head under a front leg, and was promptly asleep.

"Then I will," Tessa said. "Want to come along?"

She jumped out of the wagon. The older woman lowered her bulk after, grunting and complaining. Dalka and Tessa had spent the night in a high cleft, extracting physiologically active fractions from rare fungi. The fractionating procedure could have been carried out more easily in someone's kitchen, but Dalka held to a romantic tradition, and made it a part of Tessa's training.

Lewis lay sprawled on an irregularly shaped pond. It opened up for swimming in the summer, but densely packed leaves now closed in its surface, preserving carefully calibrated concentrations of salts and sugars. The pond was actually the bell of a subterranean flower, water storage for the dry period at the end of winter.

But pure water had seeped through the insulating leaves, and the pond was surfaced with ice. It always did, no matter how carefully the farmers grew the leaves and arranged their interlocking edges, leading Tessa to conclude that the leakage was deliberate on the part of the original plant breeders. Maybe it provided an extra seal. And maybe it was just for fun.

By the time Tessa got to Lewis, he was laughing.

"Ah, Miss Theresa Wolholme! You are too late to save me from falling. Years too late!" Lewis grinned at her, his eyes wide and blue. His white hair flopped around his head. With Tessa's help, he climbed to his feet, slipping on his skates. "That ice is cold good on the skin, ah? Keeps it tight aware against the bone." Lewis wore little under his black cloak, and Tessa could feel his sagging, stringy flesh. "Once you've seen a planet burned to death, cold makes more sense. Die with a chip of ice under your tongue, die relaxed and comfortable."

"You should get inside, Lewis," Dalka said, pleased by the unusual opportunity to play the part of conventional reason. "You look cold. The sky's clearing. The temperature will drop."

Lewis goggled at her. His hair was as white as hers, but in contrast to her carefully managed spray, his flew around like snow blown off the peak of Kardom.

"You should get *out*," he said. "Koola does not stay inside. Inside is somewhere else. Earth, maybe." His cloak flopped loosely, but he indeed didn't seem cold. Legend had it that he curled up inside of snow drifts and ice caves for days-long naps. Even knowing him as she did, Tessa could not say that the rumors weren't true.

"I've *been* out," Dalka said irritably. "We were just coming back—" She stopped herself. Boasting to Lewis about anything to do with the defiles and cliffs surrounding Calrick's Bend was as pointless as showing a bird how high you can jump. She turned her attention to the winter-hooded herbs at the pond's edge, searching for something rare and unusual to make her visit worthwhile.

"Are you all right, Lewis?" Tessa looked into his eyes, but they were the same guileless blue as always.

"I'm all right," he said. "I'm always all right. But the others—how is your father now?"

Tessa felt a moment of sadness at the question. Had it really been so long since Lewis and her father Perin had spoken? After all the years and the bonds between them?

"He's been well . . . but not the same. Not since my mother died."

"Ah, Sora. She was once his anchor. Now, you."

"You should come see him." In her younger days, Tessa would have been wary of offering such advice. Lewis was her father's wild friend, not subject to ordinary laws. When she was ten, Lewis told her and her brothers to climb the rocks naked, to feel the strength of their planet, Koola, right through their skin. She and Dom, her older brother, had stripped down and done it, to be hauled off by their furious mother and sent to their rooms. Lewis's only response was to suggest trying it a bit farther from the house.

"Perin doesn't need me," Lewis said. "He has his own way."

"You should see him." Tessa had waited for Lewis to appear at the house in the days after her mother's death. He never did, as if his old comrade's marriage and family were something insignificant, a mere bad habit. Lewis was not interested in anything that gave life comfort. But Tessa now lived with the look in her father's eyes, and if Old Man Lewis could be tamed enough to do something, she would try it.

He didn't answer her. He looked at something behind her, hard enough that she finally turned to look herself. A tiny girl had appeared in the frost-bitten field. Her head was bundled in a thick scarf, but the ends were flopping loose, not tucked into the collar of her coat.

"Hello, Malena," Dalka said, straightening up from her herbs. "What are you doing out?"

"I'm running an errand," the girl said in a high, firm voice. "Mama wants some reeds for the fire. For the cake, the castle. We're cooking it tonight."

"A small one, this year?"

"Very small." Malena Merewin was serene about the possibility. "But big enough for the Kings to stay for Christmas night. They're not proud, my father says. They'll stop if they need to."

"That's good, Malena."

Malena moved around the pond pulling up bundled reeds. She may have been going a little beyond the strict definition of permitted gleaning, but no one was about to protest. It was before Christmas, the trespasser a little girl, and the Merewins were poor. Tessa knew that she would be visiting their house tomorrow, on Christmas morning, towed there by Alta Dalhousie and the other charitable women of Cooperset Canyon.

Lewis continued to watch the little girl. She didn't acknowledge his presence openly, but stood close by him, and touched his cloak. Lewis knew Malena's father, Gorr Merewin, the same way as he knew Tessa's father Perin: they had all fought in the wars together, were all veterans of that desperate fight in the Simurad tunnels on a planet far from Koola. And each bore his own individual scars from that fight.

But why was the girl's scarf so loose? Her mother was starting to lose her grip. When children weren't taken care of, things were almost over.

"Come here," Tessa said. The little girl obediently marched up to her and stared up into her face. Her eyes had a stern wisdom that no five-year-old should have had, but her favorite doll still stuck its limp-necked head out of a pocket of her jacket. Her thick dark hair had come unbraided. It was cold, and Tessa did not have time to redo the braids, though she was tempted to take Malena home and do a decent job of it. She compromised by taking a couple of clips out of her own hair to provide some control. She tucked the head scarf into Malena's coat and buttoned it back up.

The little girl had continued staring solemnly at Tessa all through the operation. Her eyes suddenly filled with tears. "Don't blame my momma," she said. "Don't blame my momma."

Tessa, who did blame Malena's momma, put her arms around her. "It's all right, Malena. Wish your mother a good Christmas from Tessa Wolholme, and tell her I'll see her tomorrow."

The little girl caught her breath. "We're all right!" she shouted. "Don't come, we don't need you! Please." She backed away, still staring at Tessa. "Momma and poppa and I . . . we all live together. We always will. Don't try it!" And then she was running, with the frantic inefficient energy of a child, up the hill.

"She's halfway there," Lewis announced. "She's halfway to Koola."

"Please, Lewis," Tessa said, feeling a flash of fear, which she masked with anger. "She's a little girl."

"None of us is old enough to make the decisions we need to." Lewis squatted and removed his skates. He stepped out onto the ice with bare feet and stared challengingly at Tessa.

"Look at this," Dalka said. "Houndsfoot." She stood up with a tiny curled plant. "It contains a useful anthelmintic. You know how mules pick up worms from winter forage. You need a lot more than this to get a useful dose, but it might be interesting for you to examine. . . ."

Tessa allowed herself to be led away by the voluble Dalka, while Lewis slid thoughtfully on the ice in his bare feet, looking up at the snow-outlined canyon cliffs above.

Tessa slid the wagon into its slot and undid the mule. Legume, despite its unexpected nap earlier, crawled gratefully into its subterranean burrow, flicked its forked tongue out to taste the air, and promptly fell asleep again. Tessa could hear a low hum as it twisted around, seeking a comfortable position amid the sweet-smelling hummocks of lungfungus. The mule shared its quarters with the farm's bees during the winter, each providing the other with heat and, Tessa supposed, company. Tessa made sure there was enough dried herbage for it to eat when it woke again. The lungfungus, supplemented by beeswax, was supposed to be its sole diet, but for some reason Legume demanded fermented sweet herbs from the kitchen garden as a condiment. Her older brother Dom told Tessa that it was because she had spoiled the thing when she was a girl. At any rate, if the finicky Legume didn't get its borage and sweetsage with its fungus, it would climb out of its burrow and bellow its displeasure to the chef.

The Wolholme house itself climbed the canyon wall. Like many houses in Calrick Bend, it grew larger the higher up it went, supported by a tangle of trusses and brackets. It was made of wood and sheet plaster and was brightly painted red and blue and green. A dark pile of moss against the canyon wall nearby puffed smoke into the cold air. Tessa could see her father, Perin, bustling around, making sure the oven was supplied with the right air mixture to cook the cake walls without drying them out.

A large open area had been cleared near the tool sheds for the castle. Tessa's youngest brother Kevin knelt on the ground, playing with a toy wagon. His coat was unbuttoned, but he didn't seem to mind the cold. With avid concentration, he picked up any stray twigs or pieces of dry grass he found on the cleared area, loaded them into the tiny wagon, and hauled them over to a dump he was managing at the edge. The toy mule was apparently based on Legume, because it often refused to behave, necessitating whispered lectures to the tiny resin figurine. He hunched over his task, his back narrow, small boy butt stuck into the air.

Tessa couldn't stand it. She swooped down and picked him up, holding him easily over her head. He was heavier than he had been when she came back from Perala after the death of her mother, but she was stronger, too. She would see how long she could maintain the advantage.

"Hey!" He squirmed. "Put me down. I'm working!"

She laughed. "What are you doing?"

"It's important. We're going to build a castle! So I have to *work*."

Tessa hugged him, kissed him, and set him back down to his task. Once free, he grabbed her legs. "It's going to be the biggest castle in Calrick Bend! I'm going to help Poppa build it." Kevin was slyly confiding. "He needs my help."

"He needs all our help," Tessa replied. She looked over at the massive, hunch-shouldered figure of her father as he used a shovel to open up the moss-covered oven. His movements had grown more deliberate since his wife Sora's death, as if he was moving against a great resistance. "Where are Dom and Benjamin?"

"Hunting!" Kevin sat down and ran the mule and wagon back and forth on the ground until he had dug a groove. He looked up at Tessa. "I couldn't go."

"You have work to do."

"I do!"

He once again bent over his wagon, the rest of the world forgotten. Tessa started toward her father, though she knew he regarded the baking of the castle as entirely his own task, without any need of outside assistance. She just wanted to see him up close, to make sure he was all right.

There was the crunch of heavy footsteps behind her, as her brothers Dom and Benjamin strode into the yard. Their pants were frosted below the knee. Dom carried a dead telena across his shoulders. Blood from its mouth had dripped down his chest. Benjamin, not yet full grown, had had to be content with carrying both of their sling darts and the rest of their equipment. They both had the weary and joyful glaze-eyed look of men who had hunted successfully. Dom knelt, slung the telena off his back with a relieved grunt, and lowered the creature to the ground.

"So, Tessa," he said. "Been out chopping herbs with Dalka again?"

His tone was idly teasing, but recently his teasing had taken on an arrogant edge. A month before he had gone on a trading expedition to Perala with some of the other men, to negotiate purchase contracts for the next year's crops. As far as she knew, Dom had played no great role, but you couldn't tell that from his attitude.

"I finished all my work before I left." Tessa had meant to

sound merely matter-of-fact, but the tone of resentment was distinct.

"I didn't say you hadn't." Dom fussed with the dead animal, as if its limbs needed to be arranged in some aesthetic way before being carried in to be cut up and hung to age in the shed.

"He didn't see it!" Benjamin was overjoyed. "It stood right above him, and he didn't see it."

"I was too busy making sure you didn't fall into the ravine, like you did last summer."

Dom was annoyed with himself. Tessa could see that. Ben was growing up, getting faster, smarter. Dom had had a long time to have things to himself.

"Here, Tessa." Dom slapped the telena's flank. "Can you help me with this thing?" He smiled up at her.

It was a typical Dom gesture. She could carry something heavy and get blood on her clothes to prove to Dom that they were still friends. The dead animal had curved yellow tusks at its muzzle and slender, triple-toed legs. It was a native of Koola, unlike many of the other creatures of the cliffs. Its eyes were open and staring, its blue tongue was hanging out, and it didn't look peacefully dead, not at all.

The fermenthouse was above Legume's burrow. They tied the telena's legs together and wrestled it up onto a hook. It would hang there until internal enzymes had dissolved most of the carcass's connective tissue, at which time the animal would be cut up and properly stored.

"Dom," Tessa said. She had adroitly avoided all the blood while still doing her full share of the work and felt more pleased with herself than that simple achievement justified. "Can you think of any reason why Lewis would come down out of the high canyons?"

"This time of year?" Dom sniffed. The air in the shed was thick with calculated decay, ferment, and aging. Wheels of cheese were stacked in the corner, just below tightly wrapped haunches from earlier in the year. "No."

One of Dom's more frustrating virtues was his ability to state an opinion without needing to qualify it.

"I saw him, skating on a pond. Up the station road."

"Skating? Where did he get skates?"

That was a mystery that Tessa hadn't even thought of. Lewis was not a man with many possessions.

"Maybe he's down to see Poppa," Dom said hopefully. He had been as hurt by Lewis's neglect since their mother's death as anyone. "It's Christmas, after all. Maybe he just wants to see the castle."

"I don't think so, Dom. I think it's something else."

Dom shrugged. "Then we'll have to wait until he makes it clear. If he ever does."

"Let's go," Tessa said with a sigh. "I have some cooking to do."

"All right. Pull it over, pull it over. That's it . . . no, to the right a little. Good!" Perin, normally tentative, was in his true element: building. He had secretly planned the castle for months, arranging and rearranging its features. Easygoing the rest of the time, during construction he became tyrannical in traditional paternal style. "No, no! You want to snap those ramparts in half? Be gentle."

"Sorry," Benjamin puffed, as he slid a decorated, buttressed wall into its proper place. Sugar paste cemented it. He stood and contemplated his work, licking his fingers.

"Come on. We're not half-done yet."

The castle-cake smelled vividly of spice. Still warm from the ovens, it steamed slightly in the fading light of afternoon. Its upper towers were higher than Tessa was tall. When she paused in her work, she could hear the faint popping of carwa seeds within the walls. They were always baked into the cake. The heat of the oven and the acid of the stabilizers in the dough cracked the tough shells of the off-world seeds so that, next spring, they would sprout all over the fields, where the animals had carried them.

"That's enough, Kevin," Tessa said. "You'll dissolve it completely."

Kevin guiltily snatched the sugar-crystal window from his mouth and stuck it in the appropriate opening. Tessa picked one up herself and tentatively touched her tongue to it, feeling a guilty pleasure: cloying sweetness, just cut by the tartness of the binder. Despite herself, she found herself licking it. It was an unacknowledged privilege of the labor, the bits and pieces of the construction snuck into eager mouths. She remembered working with Dom and Benjamin, when Ben had been just a child Kevin's size, and the way they would frost every single castle window with their tongues. Their mother, Sora, had been there to supervise them then, indulging and disciplining with fine distinctions. She was there no longer. Tessa sometimes found herself doing some small thing wrong, so that she could turn and hear her mother's calm reprimand. No words, scolding or caring, ever came.

Tessa sighed. Kevin was munching on a piece of the crenelations that would top the castle wall. She decided to leave him alone. Things were hard enough.

"Poppa," Tessa said, coming up behind her father as he finished the elaborate sugar-and-spice decorations on one side of the castle. "What should I know about you and Old Man Lewis?"

Her father grunted. "He's not so old, Tessa. Not much older than me."

"I saw him this morning. He was ice skating on a pond. Malena Merewin was gathering rushes."

Perin paused for a long moment, considering. Tessa held her breath. There were times when he talked, and times when he didn't, and he became shy if pressed too hard. So she let him fuss with his decorations, making sure they were ready and arranged before he tackled the next wall.

"Lewis loves the cold. Not so much for what it is, but for what it isn't. Cold is not fire. Lewis has had too much fire in his life." He started spraying substrate over the hard-cake wall that surrounded the castle's triumphal entry gate. "When I met Lewis he was lying on the ground. A rock had fallen on him. A subterranean explosion, shock waves . . . there was rubble all over. We were in a tunnel, under Simurad, on the planet Trasach. Dark, underground. I was bleeding myself, a rock had hit the side of my head." He rubbed his hair. "I can still feel the lump. Here."

Tessa put her hand up to it. His hair was rough and thick. Tessa, to her dismay, had inherited it, rather than her mother's finer tresses. The lump swelled out along the left side of his head. She'd felt it every time she climbed on his shoulders when she was a little girl, and had heard the story.

"I pulled the rock up. Fire was all around. Someone helped me rescue Lewis: Gorr Merewin. And so we met, three farmers from the Eastern Shield, somewhere we should never have been.''

Perin wore the cylinder of the sprayer strapped to his right wrist. He moved his lower arm delicately, manipulating the nozzle controls with his fingers. Precise ornaments appeared, garlands, swags, the skulls of unknown horned animals.

"We were a mixed company, from all over Koola. That in itself was educational. I never understood the arrangement, really. It was all done far over our heads. All any of us were really concerned with was getting back to our homes.''

"All three of you made it.''

"Parts of us did.'' He stepped to the right and created a line of grotesque faces, their cheeks bulging out comically as they tried to blow the viewer off the face of the planet.

"Poppa. Lewis and Gorr—''

"We all helped each other, here in Cooperset Canyon as well as there at war. Lewis . . . well, you know Lewis.'' Perin smiled to himself. Lewis had tried to help raise the children, to Sora's dismay, advising them on how to slide down into ice caves and put frogs into their mouths so they knew how it felt to be a swamp. The children had taken or rejected his mad advice, but had somehow never had trouble seeing the concern that lay behind it.

"And you know Gorr as well. At least you did.'' Gorr Merewin was different. The flames of Simurad had scorched some part of his soul, leaving him bleakly silent, always angry. "He and I have not spoken for five years.''

Perin had always gone out to Gorr, not the other way around, and Tessa, who had been frightened of that dark man, had not troubled to find out what they did or talked about together, or why they had finally stopped.

"Why not?''

"His anger grew too great. It sprouted there, in Simurad, but somehow never stopped growing. And poor Malena. She is the creation of that anger. So Lewis has come down out of his mountains to watch over her. Dear Lewis.'' With his left hand, he trailed glowing stars and spheres into the setting sugar. The cake castle, already elaborate, took on another layer of fantasy. "Poor, dear Lewis. He's doing his duty, as always. I shall have to do my part too.''

Tessa, as always, had no doubt that it was the finest castle in all of upper Cooperset Canyon. Perin hunched over it, as he always did over a task, and hummed to himself, his daughter forgotten.

"Poppa—"

When he looked at her, his eyes were distant. "Something's happened. I don't know what. Only Lewis does. Whatever it is, we'll take care of Malena." It was a simple statement of fact, his duty to Gorr.

"Yes, Poppa." She paused. "Will you be in soon?"

"Just a moment. There's just a few more things I have to do. Then it will be ready."

"I don't trust him," Dalka said, sitting down by the stove. "He doesn't fit."

Tessa wasn't interested in discussing Dalka's suspicions of Old Man Lewis. Dalka had made them clear enough in the past.

"Gorr Merewin served with Poppa and Lewis in the war. About five years ago he got married to Fila. . . ." About the time Gorr and Perin had ceased communication.

"Ah, Gorr and Fila! They went and misbehaved, and that girl Malena is the unfortunate result." Dalka clucked her tongue.

After slicing the roast in a crisscross pattern with a sharp knife, Tessa misted the skin so that it would crisp up, and closed the oven. Dalka made Perin uncomfortable, but he still felt obliged to invite her to Christmas dinner, in homage to his dead wife, whose friend she had been.

"Yes, a sad story—you know, Tessa, if you had put dried quince under the skin, it would have made the meat more tender, and given it a tang."

"Yes, Dalka." Tessa pulled the top off the soup pot and checked the spices. The stew was mellowing down nicely, each sturdy winter vegetable giving its insistent piquancy to the whole.

"You might add some more winter basil," Dalka said, sniffing the air. "The turnips tend to absorb its flavor, so there's not enough in the stock when you're done. You've probably been tasting it too much to tell that."

Tessa controlled a surge of irritation and tore some leaves off the plants that grew over the sink. "Gorr and Fila . . ."

"They married for love," Dalka said. "He kidnapped her—so her family called it—from her father's house. And who knows? She might not have been entirely willing, at that. She was already pregnant with Malena at the time. She'd refused to take my advice—and paid the price for that." Dalka managed the fertility of the women of Calrick Bend, and took the responsibility seriously. Tessa had already had several lectures from her. Fila's refusal to take sensible advice obviously put her beyond the pale. "Some time later Gorr and Fila's brother Swern Toroma fought. Swern lost the use of his hand. I worked on it, but something blocked nerve regrowth, I got a lot of axonal degeneration. He went to a surgeon, got it stiffened up so he can use it to support things."

Swern Toroma wore a glove on the stiffly splayed fingers of his hand, covered with tool hooks and attachments. He acted as if he was proud of the thing, but then, what else could he do?

"And Gorr got that scar across his face," Tessa said. Rumor was, Fila had put it there defending her brother. Gorr concealed it with high collars and hoods, but even Tessa had caught a glimpse of it across his jaw, swelling purple. "It's not a normal scar. . . ."

Dalka's face went cold. "Oh, isn't it?"

"Dalka!" Tessa felt a chill at her anger. Her mother, she felt with sudden loss, was gone. Without Dalka, who would she have to talk to? Even if she was at times unpredictable. "It's important to me. Something's wrong, with the Merewins, with Malena . . . I have to know."

"Oh, do you?" Dalka was not mollified. She undid the top of a ceramic container and dipped herself a mug of spicy kitchen beer, a prerogative of cooks and their helpers, moving slowly, building tension. "Why?"

"The Merewins work the land under Pakor Spur," Tessa said. She hadn't been ready to speak her thoughts, and she fumbled at the words. "It was Carlyn land, before. It comes through Fila's family, the Toromas. Her father settled it on Fila before she ran off with Gorr. Or was kidnapped, whatever."

In the past six months, she had intensely studied the patterns of land use throughout upper Cooperset and adjoining drainages. The interrelationships were complex, and not entirely comprehensible, but she felt that she was starting to get some sort of grip on it. No one could work entirely independently, unconcerned with the behavior of his neighbors.

At the root of the Cooperset farming ecology was the network of pipe plants through which flowed, from field to field, what had once been the Cooperset River. All worked together for the common good, not because of some high-minded realization of emotional interdependence but because the system would fall apart if they didn't. Everyone, from the highest Dalhousie to the lowest Trepak in the huts down by Brant Spur, knew this and donated their labor. Refusal to participate was the one unforgivable sin.

"If something has happened to Gorr and Fila . . ."

"Why do you think something has?" Dalka was sharp. "They keep to themselves. And their daughter always wanders around the canyon. We've all seen her, we all know to watch out for her." Dalka shook her head. "Too much love between a man and a woman can squeeze their child out. It's a crime, an indecency."

"Lewis . . . don't make that face, Dalka, I grew up with him, he took care of me, of all of us, in his own way. And that's why he's down here, standing out in the open where you can see him from the road: he's down to watch after Malena, as he would be to look after us if something happened to Poppa. And if something has happened to the Merewins, well, then Malena becomes our responsibility, that of the Wolholmes."

"Along with her land?" Dalka seemed almost amused. "What about Swern Toroma?"

"He can't manage that land. That's clear to everyone. And so he can't take care of Malena." Tessa didn't need to temporize or conceal with Dalka. "Managing that land would help the Wolholmes survive. You know how hard my mother worked."

"I do, dear. And I think she would be proud to see you now."

"Oh, Dalka." Tessa blinked and felt the tears wet her eyelashes. "It's so hard, and I'm so afraid. What will happen to us? What will we do?"

"Hush, dear. Here, help with this, we should be getting it ready." Tessa leaned near Dalka's comforting bulk, and together they filled a platter with cooked vegetables, arranging their different colors in an intricate pattern. "What do you know about Gorr's scar?"

Tessa held her breath until she thought she could speak without her voice quavering. "Not much. But I overheard one of the Merewins' neighbors, Lessa Tergoran, describe Gorr's scar. She laughed at herself, said she was getting old, but she really thought it moved around, that it was never in the same place she had seen it before."

"Lessa Tergoran's an old gossip," Dalka said. "Don't encourage her, whatever you do. Your life will never be your own again. No one receives gossip without paying a price for it."

"Dalka. Fila cut Gorr, didn't she? To defend her brother, whatever. And she tipped the blade with—"

"Shh!" Dalka's eyes darted to the door. The men would soon be in to eat. "Be careful, Tessa."

"Tell me!"

"She should never have done it. It's an old piece of knowledge, almost forgotten, intended for marking animals, for making a brand without wrestling with the beast." A few still herded, Tessa knew, up on the step plateaus leading to the Boss, but no longer in the canyons. It was a precarious, severe existence. "It's a self-sustaining fungus infection of the basal layer of the dermis."

"She coated the knife with it!" She was half horrified, half delighted.

"Be quiet, please!"

"But why, Dalka? What did she say she wanted it for when she asked for it?"

Dalka looked disgusted. "Small doses of it tone up the skin, get rid of unwanted hair. Fila said she needed it, for her husband's sake. To be more beautiful for him."

"For her husband's sake. Did she plan it, do you suppose? Or did she just have it around and decide to use it on the spur of the moment?"

"I have no idea, Theresa," Dalka said. "I just know that she did, finally, use it. It's there, under his skin. It should stay in the epidermis, above the blood and lymphatic vessels, but her blade infected the vascularized dermis. The infection shifts sometimes, colonizing new areas. I'm surprised it hasn't spread and killed him. It will do that in human beings. It wasn't designed for them.

I guess he's been lucky. He'll always have it. Something to remember her by.''

The Merewin house was isolated, hanging in a shattered side
crack of Cooperset Canyon. Tessa imagined them living there, the
two of them, with their tiny daughter. She realized that, much as
she thought she knew, she didn't really understand what went on
with people. That savage coupling, a woman mutilating her husband's face but staying with him, and he agreeing to it. She wondered if she ever would understand it.

Tessa pulled the roast out of the oven. The golden skin had
crisped and pulled away from the rose-colored flesh, her slashes
forming the vivid network pattern of a proper Christmas feast.
She undid the twine holding the legs to the body and pulled them
out to their full length. It looked ready to jump.

"Come with me, tomorrow, for the Christmas visits. I'm going
out with Alta Dalhousie."

Dalka made a face. "Alta? She makes me tired. I don't even
know how she persuaded me to help make her the center of attention Christmas morning. You know the way she comes to the
door with a question and ends up in the kitchen eating your bread?
Eventually you find yourself baking it at her house, filling Dalhousia with the smells that belong in your own kitchen. You be
careful with her.''

"I need you, Dalka. We're going to be visiting the Merewins."

"Oho, it's like that, is it?" Dalka chortled. "Check them out
while being philanthropic. But why take Alta along? She has her
own interests, you know."

"I know. So I might as well have her with me from the beginning. Without her help, and the help of the Dalhousies, I don't
know if I could win a fight with Swern Toroma."

"What did you tell her?"

Tessa shrugged. "That I wanted to go up Pakor Spur, to make
it easier for me to collect the baskets after, since we're so near."

"Such a polite girl, that Tessa Wolhome is." Dalka was delighted. "Willing to help Alta Dalhousie look her best. Ah, dear,
I will go. You underestimate her, but you're doing well. I'll go."

Tessa arranged the massive top frog on the platter, surrounding
it with greenery. She thought back to the previous spring, when
this frog and all its brethren were still tiny peeping creatures,

starting their season-long climb up the tulap trees to the vines on top. This one had probably hopped across her foot with beady-eyed intentness shortly after her mother's death.

"Let's go out and light the candles," Tessa said. "Then we can come back inside and eat."

The castle glowed in the night, a candle in each of its many windows. Everyone else had gone to bed, but Tessa couldn't sleep. Or rather, she hadn't even tried, but sat up instead going over a part of her mother's fossil collection.

Families had strolled through Calrick Bend to look at the castles in the night, as was traditional. The castles were ostensibly built as a stopping place, a caravanserai, for the Traveling Kings, as they searched the endless stars for their Messiah, born but not yet found. Each family had one, some small and simple, some ridiculously elaborate, so that the Kings could freely choose. Perin's was a fine demonstration of his architectural skill, and was one of the most popular every year. A steady procession had come through the yard to examine the high ramparts, the soaring towers, the elaborately decorated screening walls. Children ran up and peered through the sugar windows at the interior passages, then ran back to their parents, who offered Perin their congratulations.

Tessa had paid more than ordinary attention to the parents and children gathering in the yard, but had seen no sign of Malena and the Merewins. She might have missed them, she thought to herself. The yard was crowded and she'd been busy. She might well have missed them.

Now Tessa stared into the darkness, her breath steaming, indecisively balanced at the door. She'd have to close it soon, they were losing too much heat, but she somehow didn't feel ready to find her coat and put it on.

Her mother Sora had always kept vigil out there by the castle. It was an old habit of hers, a tribute to her husband. Heavy shawl across her shoulders, she would walk slowly around the castle, no matter how cold it was, and admire it, for even as it was finished, it began to vanish. Animals came from beneath the fields to devour the highly edible thing: the long, elaborately spike-scaled legged snakes that dug through the soil and lived in the tulap tree roots, the field mice, the lumbering, hard-shelled land crabs, all of them in some way necessary to the functioning of the farm ecology. The castles provided them with food during the coldest and harshest months of winter, food without which they could not have survived in adequate numbers to do their work during the growing season. The castle would slowly slump down into the ground until, by the warm days of spring, when it was completely gone, the shoots of the carwa plants came up through the earth in all the fields, marking the start of planting.

Tessa gasped. A dark figure was walking slowly around the castle. But that was ridiculous. It was obviously not her mother. Taller and about twice as wide, to start with. It was her brother, Dom. And he wasn't looking at the castle, but out into the surrounding darkness, as if waiting for someone's approach.

He would be annoyed to find that she had been watching without letting him know he was being observed.

"Dom!" she said.

He gestured: come out. She grabbed her coat, feeling the cold lick at her chest and neck as she ran out into the yard still tugging it on.

"When I was little," Dom said, "Kevin's age, I would sit up and watch for the Traveling Kings. Not just because they would leave me presents, though I liked that, but because I was convinced they would come by Poppa's castle, pause . . . and go in to take a rest, since they were so tired from their years of searching. They'd be gone by morning of course, wouldn't stay for breakfast, but I wanted to see them." He looked at her. "And I was always annoyed with Momma for walking around out here. They'd see her, I knew, and go somewhere else for the night."

Tessa looked up past him. High up on the left was Kevin's window, lit by the dim glow of his night light. Was that his little head, peering down at them, worried that their unnecessary presence would frighten the Kings off, cause them to go elsewhere? There wasn't enough light to tell.

"If you'd told her, she would have stayed inside," Tessa said. "She wouldn't have wanted to scare them away."

Dom hunched gloomily in his coat. "That's true. I was always so mad at her for not realizing."

"I always wondered what you were looking at. You wouldn't tell me, and even got mad that I was asking."

"Well," Dom said. "It wasn't any of your business, little sister."

They took a turn around the castle together, just as Sora would have. Its battlements gleamed in the darkness. Dark shapes ran at the edges of their vision. To Dom and Tessa, the sight was comforting, for the appearance of these usually subterranean creatures was the first sign of the approach of the distant spring.

"I didn't want to talk about it at the table," Dom said, "but there's something I want to tell you."

Tessa knew better than to prod. Dom was giving her information to help her make a decision, and he didn't like it, feeling it should be the other way around.

"In Perala . . . you remember it, from when you were at school."

"Yes, I do." Tessa had studied at Hammerswick Academy in Perala for a year before Sora's death had brought her back to Calrick Bend, perhaps forever. She usually thought about it only late at night.

"Well, we Cooperset men were all there, and the men from the lowlands. We got good prices . . . some of the valleys west of here have had bad storms and crop damage . . . Gorr Merewin was there. So was Swern Toroma."

"How is Swern's hand?"

Dom grimaced. "Not any better after the trip. Swern and Gorr came to a fight. They always do, other people told me. It's like a regular part of the trip, that one picks a quarrel. But this one . . . Swern mentioned Lewis. That's what started it."

"They fought because of Lewis? What did Swern say?"

Dom shrugged uncomfortably. "I wasn't really paying much attention. Too much else going on . . ." He paused for a long moment. "To tell you the truth, I was drunk."

Tessa laughed, delighted by his embarrassment. "It's part of your job, Dom. Negotiations always give you a hangover. Remember when Poppa would come back, his face all green, and Momma would put him to bed for a day?"

"Yes." The memory didn't seem to comfort him.

"But it's important, what Swern said."

"I told you, I wasn't paying much attention. But it was something about Lewis and Fila. And some infection. Gorr's sick, Fila treats him, Lewis helps . . . hell, I didn't understand it, but Gorr sure did. Took a swipe at him, right at dinner. Food flying all over. Took the rest of us to hold them both down, and the lowlanders were right there, watching the canyon people beat each other up. Part of the fun for them."

"Ah," Tessa said. "That's interesting, though I don't know what it means."

Dom looked at her, his gaze sharp. "You have some plan, right? I can see it. You're smart, Tessa. We all know that. But smart isn't everything. In Calrick Bend, I'm not even sure it's much important. You went off to school, so maybe you've forgotten that."

He was trying to be helpful, but his tone grated on her nerves. The family needed protecting, and he resented her trying to do it. She could see that.

"Dom—"

He raised a hand. "You're going to be mad at me. I can tell from your eyebrows. I'm sorry. I just wanted you to know. . . ." He took her arm as they walked. "I just wanted you to know that you can count on us. All of us. If you need to. Me, Benjamin . . . Kevin too. Him most of all. He'd do anything for you. I was just trying to say that. But I don't talk good. I never have, have I?"

"Oh, I don't know. You're talking pretty good now."

Dom was embarrassed. "Okay. Just promise me one thing. Whenever you make a decision, try to imagine that you're only half as smart as you really are."

She smiled. "I'll give it a try."

Tessa slept little that night, and was up with the sun in the morning. Kevin was already circling the wrapped presents. His takings would be small enough this year, but he would make the most of it.

"Where are you going?" he said.

She gathered up her things and put on her coat. "I'll be back soon."

"But where are you *going*?"

"To Alta Dalhousie's. We're going to visit the poor families with food."

He sat on the floor and pouted. "You won't be here to open your presents. Wait until you see what I got you." He dug through the pile.

"I'll be back soon, Kevin. It's my job, now that Momma's gone. I have to go."

He pulled out something that looked like a forked tree limb wrapped in layers and layers of silver foil. Taking it from him, Tessa realized that that was exactly what it was.

"Open it!"

"Kevin, let's wait until—"

"Open it!"

She knew an irresistible command when she heard one. She pulled at the frenziedly taped foil, tight and thick as if the package were to be buried as a message to future generations, and finally managed to get it open.

The crotched limb had delicate, peeling-back bark, somewhat compressed by Kevin's packaging, and was bright with red, blue, and orange patches of lichen. Tessa wondered if any of them were of medicinal or enzymatic value. She'd have to ask Dalka.

"It's beautiful, Kevin," she said. Indeed it was. Of all the fallen branches in Cooperset Canyon, this was no doubt the best. He had probably taken a great deal of time over it. She thought it would look perfectly fine on a shelf in the room containing Sora's fossils.

"It's full of borer beetles!" he said gleefully. "I'm sure they'll come out when it gets warm. I like the way they wiggle their heads."

She looked more closely at it. The bark was pierced by countless tiny holes. If she set it on a shelf in the warm house, they would awaken early and come swarming out, to devour the furniture.

"Oh, Kevin. . . ."

Fortunately, at that moment Benjamin appeared, blinking in his pajamas, hair a mess, looking desperately young.

" 'Morning, Tessa," he said. "Where is everybody?"

"I'm in here making breakfast," Dom called from the kitchen.

"Poppa's up, Kevin's making trouble, and Tessa's going to be late for her appointment if she doesn't hurry."

"I'm not making trouble!"

Benjamin sat in a chair and Kevin climbed into his lap. Benjamin patted his brother's head. "Trouble's what you're best at."

Tessa winked and ran out the door. The landscape was frosted and silent. The mountains loomed overhead, the white dusting on their shoulders giving them extra dignity. Castles stood by their houses, proud battlements, towers, flags, and arches gaily proclaiming the holiday. Tessa followed a path she had known since childhood, a twisting way around storage barns, over fences, under hedges. Burrs stuck to her coat, and a few dried leaves got into her hair. She dirtied her stockings jumping over a narrow ravine. In their younger days Dom had always beaten her at it despite her most strenuous efforts. Now it was easy. She enjoyed it so much she jumped back and did it again.

The Dalhousie house was high and proud. Most of it had been designed by her father, Perin, in his most exuberant style, a style he could not possibly afford for his own dwelling.

Tessa passed through the front hall, which stretched up three stories to the balcony of the upper bedrooms, and into the back dining room, crowded with women readying themselves for their charitable exercises. They made room for her at a table, poured her tea, asked about her family, praised Perin's castle.

"Margen's hiding upstairs," Zabeth Trasker told her, "peeking over the balcony. I think he's waiting for *you*."

Several of the other women tittered. Tessa was of marriageable age, and had, as yet, not made any indication of her preferences. Margen Dalhousie was a possible mate for her, as she had known since they were both children.

"More likely he's waiting for Mark," Tessa said. This caused more amusement. Zabeth's son, one of the few other eligible males in Calrick Bend, was notorious for his dreamy lateness.

Tessa kept a good face on it, but it took effort. The Wolholmes were in a difficult situation, and, in a sense, it was her *duty* to marry, and soon, so as to assist their survival. These friendly, cheerful women sitting around her, ready to do their Christmas duty to the poor of the canyon, would slowly move themselves around her until it was all inevitable. The earlier she moved on her own, the more choice she would retain.

"Tessa has other things to worry about than my son, or even Zabeth's." Alta Dalhousie appeared, a signal for chairs to be pulled back and coats put on.

Alta smiled and took Tessa's arm. Despite her formidable reputation, Alta Dalhousie herself did not look particularly imposing. She was shorter than Tessa, and slight, with a mass of curling gray hair and bright blue eyes.

"Dalka's coming with us?" Alta was serene, willing to put up with irregular requests as long as they didn't interfere with any of her plans.

"Yes." Striving to imitate Dom, Tessa bit down on any following phrase like "I hope that's all right," or "she really wanted to." It left her feeling anxious, as if there was a hole in the conversation. How did Dom do it so easily? Dalka joined them at the front door.

For a moment, the women stood and laughed in the cold air of the courtyard, adjusting their hoods, tugging on their embroidered gloves, exuberantly swooping their long sleeves. This was a dignified assemblage, gathered for the purposes of charity to the weak and poor, but it was a glorious day nonetheless, the sun bright, the world sensible. Their children were gathered in their front rooms eyeing the presents left by the Traveling Kings in gratitude for assistance on their journey, their husbands were sleepily contemplating a day free of labor, and they themselves were happy to be doing good in such high style.

Tessa, Alta, and Dalka crossed a teetery plank over an ice-filled ravine, carrying heavy packs. Their mission was to the isolated houses that hid themselves in the cliff-base jambles and the high cracks at Pakor and Brant Spurs, far above the easy cart roads. Alta went first, to scatter sand, which she kept in a blue-enamel bucket on the livethorn fence. She used a small silver shovel with a delicate tracing of leaves up its handle and fork tines at its edge, so that the sand spread evenly. Then they climbed up the trail, over the root bulges of the hairy-barked oaks that grew in a line along the ridge, now almost thick enough to be cut down and turned into furniture, an old Dalhousie skill. It was steep and icy enough that Tessa considered stopping and pulling her crampons out of her pack. Instead, she reached out and took Dalka's gloved hand in hers. Together, the three women formed a snake long enough that at least two of them were always standing on firm ground. They writhed their way up the icy slope.

"We don't go up there," Swern Toroma said, snipping off a length of binding cord with an attachment on his hand. He had not stopped working the entire time he spoke, as if to show by the frenzy of his activity how little he really needed their help.

"But have you seen them?" Tessa asked.

He shook his head. He was slender and pale, and looked much like his sister Fila. "I don't see them. No reason to."

Tessa, Alta, and Dalka stood close together, fastidious in the midst of the messy kitchen. Swern's wife, a woman from up canyon, was not around, but it was clear that, whatever her duties were, they didn't extend to cleaning.

"You talk to your sister." Tessa was insistent. Somehow, she thought, Fila had told her brother about the nature of Gorr's wound, perhaps in a moment of unwise confidence. Swern had used that information against Gorr at the last trading expedition.

Swern glanced at her suspiciously, then returned to his task. "And why shouldn't I? With a husband like that . . . but I haven't talked to her in the last few days. And you know what? I hope that bastard ran off, killed himself, whatever. Then maybe she could bring the land back to the family." He gestured with his rigidly splayed fingers at their basket. "They don't deserve your help up there."

"That is not for you to decide," Alta said. "Will you be all right?"

"I'll be all right when I get my land back."

A baby started crying in a back room. Attempts to shush it just made the crying louder.

"Good day, then," Alta said crisply. "Thank you for your hospitality." The three women left, and resumed their climb up the slope.

"It's a sad situation," Alta said, as they climbed through the piled rocks of the jambles. "The Toromas were once a proud family."

"Richer than now, maybe," Dalka said. "But never rich. It's hard, high near the wall like this."

"Harder when the better part of your land leaves." Alta was making some sort of point, Tessa wasn't yet sure what. "It went with Fila, on her marriage to Gorr. Fine, it was settled on her, she was the most responsible. Still—"

"Do you think it should have been handled some other way?" Tessa asked.

"The inheritance?" Alta thought about it. "It is natural that the land should pass through the daughter, of course, but still . . . Swern and his family barely survive. Meanwhile, Gorr and Fila make little of their land, so that they're poor also. When it finally passes to Malena, its value will be much lower than it would have been. Swern, with help, could work it, but there's too much anger. So he spends his energies in manipulating the negotiations—keep this quiet, I'm not supposed to know—so that others don't get full value for their produce."

Tessa was pleased by the confidence, though she doubted she was the only one Alta had told, and suspected there was a reason she was being told.

The three women walked up to the silent, shuttered Merewin house, and knocked on the door. The sound echoed hollowly in the narrow cleft where the house hung, but there was no answer. They knocked again.

Frost had grown over the cracks of the door and the sides of the shutters. There was no mark of footsteps in the frost on the front stair. And no one had built a castle.

Alta was grim. "I was afraid of this." She looked up at the sheer walls of the cleft.

"They went for a walk!" a small voice called.

"Is that you, Malena?" Tessa said. "Where are you?"

"They went for a walk. You can leave that."

The women descended the slope from the house to the beginning of the terraced gardens. Two large trees flanked the entrance to the cleft, twining around the rock outcroppings. Tessa peered up into them and finally spotted the tiny Malena, who sat placidly on a high branch.

"Hi, Malena," Tessa said.

"Hi." Malena was as solemn as ever. Her legs dangled down.

"How long ago did your parents leave?" Alta asked.

"Not long. But they said don't wait. Just leave it, they said."

The wind blew through the top of the cleft with a high, lonely whistle. It was cold, but Malena seemed quite comfortable on her perch. Tessa wasn't even sure how she had climbed up there.

"Malena," Alta said. "Could you please come down?"

"No!" Startled by the request, Malena scrambled up another branch, small enough that it sagged even under her tiny weight. "I have to wait for Momma and Poppa."

Dalka knelt and put the tray on the front stair. "Do you promise to eat this if I leave it?"

"We'll eat it!" Malena's voice was ragged, a little frenzied. "They'll be back soon. Then we'll eat it."

The reeds she had gathered from the pond the previous morning were stacked neatly against the side of the house. The land around them was silent.

"All right, Malena," Alta said. "Say hello to your parents when they return."

"Okay."

The woman climbed back down the path until Malena was invisible behind them.

"Something's happened," Alta said. "I don't know what. Fila's run off, Gorr's done something. They may not be coming back."

"Gorr's done for Fila," Dalka said with grim relish. "Finally."

"Maybe." Alta thought. "Tessa, do you think Perin knows anything?"

"They haven't spoken in years."

"Yes, I know. I had hoped that, perhaps, recently . . . well, that leaves Old Man Lewis. He must know something." Alta stared up at the cliffs. "Finding him is something else again, of course. Do you know where he is, Tessa?" Her voice grew sharper.

"I saw him, yesterday." Tessa felt as if she was betraying a confidence, though Lewis had been out on the pond for all the world to see.

"But not since."

"No," Tessa said. "I can try to find him. Meanwhile, Malena's terrified. What shall we do?"

"I'd knock her out of that tree with a broom," Dalka said. "She's not coming down otherwise."

"Dalka!" Tessa said, startled. "You don't mean that."

"No, I don't." Dalka was reluctant. "She'll get hungry and come down on her own. Then we can get her."

"Excellent," Alta said vigorously. "Then we'll bundle her up—the poor thing must be freezing—and take her over to Dalhousia. We have a spare room, Tramt is over in Perala this term and I'm sure he won't mind." She eyed Tessa. Alta was testing her, Tessa realized, waiting for her reaction to this seizure of Malena.

Dalka stuck out her heavy lower lip. "No need for you to take care of her."

"Who else will? The Toromas?"

There was little answer to that, though they were probably her closest relatives.

Dalka glanced at Tessa and shrugged. "Well, if you want to take the trouble. . . ."

Dalka was putting up the effort for her sake, Tessa realized. For the Wolholmes. If Malena ended up at Dalhousia, eventually the management of her land would also, at least until she reached her majority. Dalka was not interested in land herself, but she knew what Tessa needed. At the moment, Tessa didn't care. She remembered the tiny girl clinging to the upper branches of a tree in winter, her parents most likely lying dead somewhere unknown, with no one to help her, and no comfort but a cooling tray of food brought by distantly dutiful neighbor ladies.

"She can climb down and go into the house if she wishes," Alta said. "I checked, and the key was hanging under the stairs. If we just leave her alone—"

"I'm not leaving her up there alone. She's a little girl!"

"Good idea," Dalka said. "We're through, aren't we, Alta? Tessa can stay up there with her."

"As you say." Alta was brisk. "We'll be back soon, Tessa. Keep the poor thing company, keep her out of trouble."

When they were out of sight, Tessa headed back up to the Merewin house. Despite herself, she sympathized with Dalka's urge to swat Malena out of her tree with a broom. There was something exasperating about the little girl's stubborn refusal to

be helped. As she crested the hill, she searched the branches for
Malena's tiny dark shape. The branches swung free in the breeze.
The food had brought her down, then.

Tessa crouched and moved more quietly, as if stalking some
wild animal. The air moved gently over her. The high cliffs rose
above, their cracks outlined by snow and frost, a few desperate
plants clinging to them. As she went, she examined the farm with
a practiced eye. There was some evidence of decay—cracked pipe
plants ready for infection, inadequately insulated roots—but nothing too dangerous yet. A little extra work in the spring could take
care of it.

She squinted into the shadows of the cleft. The tray was gone
from the front stairs. Tessa walked slowly to the house, looking
carefully around her. The girl was tiny, and clever. If she wanted
to hide, here on her own ground, it would be difficult for Tessa
to find her. But Tessa herself had been a champion at hide-and-
seek as a girl.

Tessa reached under the stairs, found the key, and opened the
door. "Malena?" she called. The girl was gone.

Tessa searched slowly through the house, looking carefully.
There was a family picture on the wall of the living room: slender
Fila looking attentively at Gorr, his hand on her shoulder as he
stared at the camera, and tiny Malena, ignored, sitting at their feet
and looking off at something out of view. The girl's space in the
house was tiny, just a bed that folded into a corner so as to be
out of the way during the day.

A shelf above held a few toys, neatly laid out in a row. Tessa
picked up a bulge-eyed duck with wheels. Its head bobbled back
and forth as she held it. Spots of paint had flaked off. She set it
back. There were no empty gaps on the shelf. Even Malena's
favorite loose-headed doll sat floppily in its place.

The house was in frantic disarray. Drawers were pulled out in
the bedroom, clothing strewn on the floor. Personal objects had
been yanked out of cabinets. It didn't look like a simple matter
of slovenly housekeeping. Everything was clean. The floor under
the piles of sweaters and pants was buffed to a dull shine, not a
spot on it. Sora herself could not have found fault. Someone had
been searching for something in a frantic hurry. Had it been

found? Tessa continued, hoping to find the place where the search had ended.

Cutlery and spices were tossed about the kitchen. A dented tea kettle lay in the corner. And in the sink, some sort of dark liquid. Scattered along the sink's edge were the sort of seedpod ampoules that Dalka used for dispensing medications. All were crushed, and the liquid oozed out of them. Tessa ran a finger down the thick whitewood sink and sniffed: a bitter smell that she could not identify. Half the kitchen was a mess. In the other half the cook pots and wood bowls stood in perfect arrangement, ready to be of service.

Tessa gathered several of the empty seedpods, and as much of the liquid as she could in one of Fila's food containers, and put it in her pack. Perhaps Dalka would be able to recognize what it was.

The back door of the kitchen opened into the pantry and the back storage area. Tessa poked around back there, though she felt that she had already found what was significant, even if she did not understand it. All the food was in order in the pantry, all the equipment in the storage area, ready for spring.

Sunlight glinted in through the window. It was late in the morning, the only time direct light made it into the cleft. She was about to turn away, to head home, when a gleam of metal caught her eye. She stepped forward. Hanging from a nail by the door, returned by the one who had borrowed them, was a pair of ice skates.

Alta Dalhousie stood in her courtyard and poured steaming tea from a towering urn. Search parties found their leaders, warmed themselves up, and headed out through the gates. Most of Calrick Bend was here, and despite the seriousness of the cause, they carried with them some of the conviviality of Christmas, strengthened by their common energy.

"Ah, Tessa." Alta poured for her as well. "You must be cold."

"Any sign?" Tessa drank slowly, trying not to burn her tongue. Warmth pulsed outward from her throat.

"None. But how far could a little girl go in such a short time? After all, you only had your eyes off her for a few minutes."

Tessa felt herself flush, and was glad that Alta had turned away as she said this, to add more hot water to the urn. Tessa—childishly—wanted to point out that Alta and Dalka had been chattering away too, while Malena escaped. That might annoy Alta, but it wouldn't alter anything. And Tessa needed Alta in as friendly a mood as possible.

"She did seem to vanish most thoroughly. Here, could you help me with this?" At her direction, Tessa carried wrapped bread, still warm from the oven, out to tables in the courtyard. "Most unusual. She's only five, and even the most energetic five-year-old has no stamina for distance. I remember when Margen tried to run away, we were in a panic, then found him on a vine trellis in the next field, eating his sandwiches as if he hadn't had food in days . . . but that was nothing compared to this."

Tessa was not going to tell Alta that Lewis had taken the girl. Lewis was tolerated in the canyon, but not truly trusted. Those search parties could easily turn to a grimmer purpose.

"Will you be going home now?" Alta was uneasy. "You must be tired."

"No, I . . ." Tessa thought about what to say. "Gorr and my father were friends. They were in the war together."

"They stopped speaking around the time Malena was born, didn't they?" Alta headed off Tessa's argument before she had even gotten to it. "Perin hated Gorr's anger. And good for Perin."

"But Malena—"

"Perin also disapproved of the way Gorr cut the Toromas off from their land," Alta continued serenely. "Gorr had the right, having married Fila, but still . . . it wasn't a good idea, do you think? Hatred is a poor basis for cooperation."

"So you think Swern and his wife could farm that land on their own?" Tessa thought she was starting to get an inkling of where Alta's argument was heading.

Alta laughed. "Oh, no, dear. Not at all. Any more than they could raise Malena. But still, they should be able to work more of the land than they do. . . ."

"I'm sure that whoever adopts Malena will allow that." Tessa was making a political agreement on behalf of her family. She'd have to explain it to them later. "It only makes sense. As long as the result does not alienate the land from the proper owner.''

Alta eyed her. "Have some sweet bread. You look hungry.''

"No thank you. I should—''

"Really, Tessa. I made it myself. I think it came out rather well.''

Alta Dalhousie, Tessa estimated, had been making sweet bread for at least twice as long as Tessa had been alive. She *better* have figured out how to make it come out well. She took a slice, smearing sugar frosting on her hands. If the tension hadn't been making her feel sick to her stomach, Tessa conceded to herself, it *would* have been good. Her mother, Sora, had had a tendency to fear underbaking it, and as a result it had always been dry. At least she hadn't slathered it with so much sugar.

"Tell me,'' Alta said. "Do *you* know where Malena is?''

"No,'' Tessa said. "But I think I can find her.'' The last words came in a rush.

"When all these search parties can't?'' Voices sounded on the path outside: searchers coming in for a break, some tea, some of Alta Dalhousie's famous sweet bread. They stacked packs at the gate. Someone made a joke, and a couple of them chuckled.

"Yes.''

Alta smiled. "Well, if you find her, you may as well keep her, right? Since Perin and Gorr agreed. And the Toromas can no doubt be persuaded.''

Tessa stared at her in wonder. "I—''

Alta waved a hand dismissively. "We can discuss it later. We both have things to do.'' She turned to the search party, and began to pour them tea.

It was late, and the mountains cast their long shadows across the farms of Cooperset Canyon. The air grew colder, and Tessa longed to move. Her blood felt as if it had pooled and crystallized. She shifted on her rock outcrop, and once again examined the Pong's Defile trail, just visible through the jambles below.

It was time to get home before the trail disappeared beneath her feet. Lit house windows already glowed in Calrick Bend, far below her. A moving line of lights descended the opposite canyon wall on a switch-blacked trail. Searchers, returning empty handed from their pursuit of a vanished little girl. Tessa had to find her and Lewis before the townspeople turned to searching for *him*.

Perhaps he wasn't going to come tonight . . . but still she sat, watching her breath puff into the steadily darkening air. Pong's Defile, up to Born Canyon, was Lewis's favorite trail. The Wolholme children had always known it. Lewis had taken Tessa some way up it when she was a child, a well-remembered first trip away from the settled logic of the canyon floor. And a trail at the edge of Cooperset Canyon, clinging high above any habitation, led straight to the cleft where the Merewin house stood.

Nothing of Malena's had been taken from the house, not her clothing, not her favorite doll, not any of the food she liked to eat. She was no doubt suffering in silence, wherever Lewis had taken her, but he would know what she needed. No one was at the Merewin house but the neighbor Lessa Tergoran, and she would most likely be asleep by now.

Tessa pulled on the chain of logic, and it held. She only hoped it was actually attached to something.

Had Alta Dalhousie actually offered to. allow Malena to be adopted by the Wolholmes if the Toromas were given access to the land? It felt that way to Tessa, though the sliding implications of Alta's offer had left Tessa dizzy. But it all made a kind of sense. If the Dalhousies themselves tried to adopt Malena, the Toromas would fight, but the rights of Perin Wolholme in the matter were well known. The solution did not actually benefit the Dalhousies, but it didn't harm them either, and settled several problems in the bargain. And it left Tessa in Alta's debt. Alta Dalhousie had always taken the long view.

That is, if Tessa managed to find Malena, and Malena herself agreed to the solution. Were things really so complicated in Calrick Bend? Tessa had never realized.

She heard a purposeful chuffing of breath on the trail below her. She swung out precariously on her rock, supported by her fingertips, and looked down the trail. The dark figure, head down, shoulders hunched, could only have been Lewis. She looked into the darkness below her feet. She'd scoped it out before, decided that a jump would be easy, but now the earth seemed to have been swallowed up, leaving her with nothing to land on.

She drew a breath. Lewis paused and raised his head. Tessa jumped. For an instant it seemed that she had indeed been right, that the ground had vanished, then it slapped her feet. She almost lost her balance, then regained it, and darted forward.

Lewis stood calmly and waited for her.

"Good evening, Theresa Wolholme," he said.

"Hello, Lewis."

"You want to ask me a question."

"What have you done with Malena Merewin?"

He turned, gestured, and she found herself walking with him, slightly behind, down the trail. She thought about putting on her head lamp, but he seemed to have no trouble finding his footing. She followed his lead.

"I haven't done anything with her. Koola has done with her. I just live here."

"Lewis!" She grabbed his shoulder and tried to swing him around. Despite the light boniness of his frame, he was immovable, as if his feet interpenetrated with the rock beneath them. "She's a little girl. She's lost her parents."

"They're not lost," Lewis said craftily. "No. We've got some absolute coordinates."

"Are they dead then?"

"Their journey is over."

Tessa felt despair at his Koolan obstinacy. "Lewis. You can't keep her."

"I'm not keeping her!" He didn't shout, but his voice grew less precise. He waved his arms. "The suns burn with their own fires. Their messages take forever to reach us, but reach us they do."

Darkness had come completely, and the clear sky was bright with stars. Tessa stared up, wondering if he could see the star around which circled the flaming Simurad Tunnels. The wind blowing down the canyon grew even colder.

"All good places are hard." Lewis had calmed down. "They slide into the flesh. Unite us."

"Lewis!"

He sidled away. "The human world has rejected her. Koola accepts her. Accepts her with gracious hardness."

"We aren't rejecting her," Tessa said in despair. She thought of the tug-of-war that Malena would return to, the tensions that pulled the net of social relations in Calrick Bend tight. And she thought of the solemn little girl in the tree, waiting for her parents to come home and knowing they never would. "We need her."

"Koola needs her more! She'll learn the ways, as I have. She'll climb to the heights."

For an instant, he almost convinced her. Malena could go with her war-uncle, learn to sleep on bare rock, to eat the edible lichens of the cliffs, to walk unafraid through the blizzards. Lewis would bring her to it, with love. It was a life as sensible as any other, more sensible than some.

"Lewis," Tessa said. "Malena did not live through Simurad. Does she need to live through this?"

For the first time, she felt she had reached him. He peered at her.

"Perin has his own service to perform for Gorr's daughter," Tessa said. "So do I. I need to talk to her. Please."

"Climb, then. Show who you are."

"Will you talk to us?"

"Us?" Lewis seemed puzzled. "Who us?"

"The Wolholmes. All of us. You know who we are."

"I'm cold," Lewis said. "It blesses my flesh. Bring Perin, if he will come. We will talk."

And with that, he was gone. He jumped up, slid over a rock, and disappeared into a silent void. Fingers shaking, Tessa pulled out her head lamp and clipped it onto her forehead. The beam showed dark-shadowed rocks and sternly undecorative plants, but Lewis was nowhere to be seen. She held her breath, but heard nothing but the wind.

Tessa began to slowly pick her way down the rough path toward home.

Dom bent over and adjusted his sister's snowshoe. Tessa had thought it was set fine on her foot, but he had another opinion. She looked ahead, at the trail that led up into the high end of Born Canyon.

"We'll be side-stepping up that slope," Dom said. "It'll be easier if it doesn't slide so much at the heel."

"You'd know that if you did much winter hunting," Benjamin said in a superior tone. "We can loosen it again at the top of the slope."

Perin said nothing. He was clearly already tired, unused to the exertions of climbing the higher canyons in midwinter, but had voiced no complaint. He wiped his red, sweaty forehead with a handkerchief, then looked up into the heights. Tessa heard the ragged pull of his breath with sorrow. Her father was growing old. Hadn't she noticed that before?

Dalka, though of an age with him, seemed unaffected by the climb. She had insisted on coming with them. She and Tessa had not had a chance to talk in private, and Tessa didn't know when they would.

"Let's *go*," Benjamin said. "We've got to move." He moved upslope with little steps, jerking his head like an animal straining against a leash. "You know where we're going, Tessa?"

"Just up Born," she said. "They're up there, somewhere." But how high? They would see.

When the going got difficult, as it did here, they roped themselves together and moved slowly. The sun was deceptively bright, glaring on the snowfields. The snowfields weren't deep: there was never much water in this part of Koola, even in winter, but they were deep enough to impede travel.

"We don't usually hunt this high at this time of year," Dom said, with the air of confiding a male secret. "The game comes lower, which actually makes it easier for us than in the summer."

"Ben didn't make it sound that way."

Dom snorted. "Well, he comes up here to prove something, not to hunt. That's dangerous, but he's been doing it since that wapiti got away from him in the summer. Hunting's not for proving, it's for food, and for fun. Or maybe I'm just saying that because I'm getting old." He turned and pointed. "But hunting helps in everything. There, those dark spots? A couple of Lewis's footprints, I think. Even he can't cross a snowfield without leaving a mark, though some people think he flies. We're still going right."

As they climbed, the countless slopes and cliffs opened out around them, their edges sharp and blue in the moody winter light. Tessa wondered what it would be like to live and farm up here, far from the density of the lower canyons. She'd heard old stories that it was possible, that at some time not long after the initial settlement of Koola, people had lived at these heights, not yet having descended to the flood-prone depths of the canyons and subdued them.

They reached the top of the steep slope and unroped. Tessa readjusted her snowshoes before Dom could come over and do it for her. He nodded his approval when he saw, thus retaining some control over the situation. The land curved gently up from this point, up to the base of a vast vertical cliff about a mile away. The top of the cliff, thousands of feet up, was cleft into three, with the middle bastion the highest, hence its name: Telena's Foot. Tessa had caught glimpses of it in the warmer months, but she had tended to climb well down-canyon. This was good territory for hunting: men's country. Women tended to stay away from it so that they would not be interrupted and annoyed during their strolls by the wails of dying animals.

"Dalka." Dalka had fallen back, and now she and Tessa were far enough away from the others to talk. "What was in those seeds?"

"Lessa Tergoran, left on watch at the Merewins', says she was attacked by ghosts last night. The house was filled with them. Actually, she fell asleep. I know her. Lewis could have lifted the entire house and taken her with it. She would never have stopped snoring."

"Dalka—"

Dalka was silent for a moment, her face stony. "Damn it, Tessa, you do give me the most difficult things, did you know that?"

"I'm sorry."

Dalka shook her head. "The High Plainsmen. They must be behind it. I see no other way."

Tessa was surprised. She looked up the canyon, toward the heights behind which the High Plainsmen lived. "Why do you say that?"

"That liquid must have been the way Fila controlled Gorr's fungal infection. It's a fairly simple enzyme blocker, keeps the fungus from spreading but doesn't kill it. Topical application, fairly straightforward. I don't think it will be too hard for me to duplicate."

"Then what—"

"I didn't make it for her! And I don't know who did, or who she got it from."

"But you think it was Lewis."

Dalka nodded. "But Lewis didn't make it. That's not his way. He got it from someone else. Someone high up-canyon. And he gave it to Fila, to control Gorr, as if he were some herd animal himself."

Tessa remembered the argument Dom had recounted for her, during the trading trip. "Swern Toroma told Gorr about it, just before all this happened, about the infection, about Lewis."

"Ah." Dalka thought about it. "It was the balance between them, that infected wound of his. Her stake."

"If he strayed from her, he would die."

"Exactly. And that, in the end, was how he punished her."

It took a moment for Tessa to realize that she'd lost track of the logic. "I don't understand."

Dalka smiled. "You don't think Fila dumped the treatment in the sink, do you? She knew exactly where it was, she didn't need to search the house for it. No, it was Gorr. Gorr, when he found out how he had been controlled, came home and destroyed his treatment. Without it, he would die, slowly and by degrees. I might have been able to help him, I don't know. He didn't give me a chance."

"He never thought about Malena," Tessa said.

"Indeed he didn't. And he never would have, his whole life. The only person who was important to him was Fila. She was the beginning and the end. As long as *he* was in control, not she. To find that, for all those years, she had held his life in her hands . . . he punished her. Punished her by taking away her control."

"And dying." Tessa looked up the slope. A jambles lay at the cliff's base, with high square blocks sticking up out of the snow. "That was how he punished her."

"She always did love him, whatever else there may have been."

"He came up here to confront Lewis," Tessa said. "He must have decided where the treatment came from."

"And Fila followed. What else could she do?"

"And what happened then?"

"That," Dalka said, "is something only Lewis can tell us."

• • •

The jambles under the cliff turned out to be the foundations of an ancient manor house, most of its structure long vanished. Tessa looked at the chisel marks on the hard rock and wondered who had built here, so long ago, and why. She climbed up on the highest part. The view down the canyon was tremendous. She could see Fulda's and Angel's Buttes in the distance, on the other side of Cooperset. The successive ranges of mountains that made up the Boss were crisp in the cloudless sky to her right.

Benjamin bounced around the rocks like an enthusiastic dog, but Tessa noticed the care with which he kept his feet on rock, off snow or soil that might hold some track or other evidence of their quarry.

Ignoring his son's outraged protest, Perin walked right into the middle of what had once been the cellar.

"Lewis!" he called. Silence. "Lewis! It's me, Perin Wolholme. I want to talk." He turned to the rest of them, who stared silently at him. "Could the rest of you please go a ways back down the slope so that we can talk, Lewis and I?"

"He hasn't even answered you," Dom said, irritated. "He's probably not even here. Why should we—"

"Please, Dom. He won't answer to a crowd, which is what we are. You know that. It won't take long, one way or another." He pointed off to a rock outcropping about a quarter mile away. "There. You can all have your lunch. It's a nice sunny spot." Perin was as decisive as Tessa had ever heard him. His tone did not accept argument or contradiction.

Dom shrugged. "All right. But look here: there's been digging at the base of these rocks." Indeed, the snow had been disturbed and there were traces of dirt in it.

"I'll discuss that with Lewis when he appears," Perin said. "Tessa—could you stay? I may need you."

"All right, Poppa." Everyone else headed out into the snow, not saying anything, Dalka most reluctantly. Tessa watched them go.

Perin stood in the middle of the foundation, black against white, not moving, staring up at the looming Telena's Foot. After a long few minutes, he bent and slung the pack from his back.

"Here, Tessa," he said. "I'm going to ask you to do some work."

He pulled out a shovel, handed it to her, and pointed to the disturbed snow and earth that Dom had noticed. Tessa accepted it. At least it would give her something to do. She started digging carefully.

Tessa warmed up as she worked, but suddenly she felt lonely. Usually she liked being alone, but not now, not with her father standing nearby, staring off at the cliffs, ignoring her. She cocked her head. Her brothers and Dalka were enjoying a companionable lunch on the outcropping, chatting over something. Probably something completely irrelevant, she thought jealously. Something that had nothing to do with life and death and adoption and land. Perhaps Dalka was retelling the story of Lessa Tergoran, mimicking her vigorous snores. Ben picked up a double handful of snow and let it glitter away in the breeze.

Something had appeared under the snow. A hand, frozen half-clenched. Tessa stared down at it, then began to dig carefully around, revealing the arm, the shoulder, and finally the head of Gorr Merewin. The details of his body were mercifully obscured by the snow. Fila lay next to him, with a wide cut in her chest.

"Perin. You shouldn't have come."

Tessa looked up from her grim labors. Old Man Lewis stood facing her father.

"I had to come, Lewis. You know I did."

"Why?" Lewis's voice was a wail of pain.

"She's not yours to take. I'm not dead. If I were, then my children too would have the choice of going with you. But I'm still here."

"This is her place. There is no other for her. Gorr—"

"Lewis!" Tessa was surprised at the strength in her father's voice as he faced his old comrade in arms. "This is intolerable. Where is she?"

"Safe." Tessa had never seen Lewis this sullen. Usually the words of people were as the wind for him, but Perin's words clearly had an impact. Lewis would have liked to disregard them, but he couldn't.

"Let me be the judge of that. Bring her out."

"But—"

"Bring her out, I said. You have breathed the air, drunk the water, eaten the earth, and slept on the rock of Koola, but you are not free of us all. Lewis!" Perin reached out his hands.

Lewis did not move away, but he did not respond either. Slowly his white-haired head rose. "You want to haul her back, hide her in a house, tear her away from her place. Is that better than the life I lead here?" Lewis spoke gently, almost humorously. "Don't speak, I know your answer. We have a duty to Gorr's blood. Both of us."

"You're right." The reluctance in Perin's voice was clear.

"Both of us. We swore, there in that flaming place. Didn't we?"

"We did." Perin spoke to Tessa over his shoulder. "Keep digging, Tessa. We still need them." He turned back to Lewis. "But if you keep her the people of the canyons will hunt you. They won't catch you, not you, Lewis, but they will hunt you because they will hate you."

Tessa resumed her excavation of the two frozen bodies. Gorr's face was peaceful. Had he died of the fungal infection? Aside from the wound on her chest, Fila's body was unmarked.

She brushed snow away from Gorr's face. The disfiguring mark of the fungus was gone. He had died, and it had no further use for him. It hid, somewhere in the bloody snow, and awaited another host. Her hands were gloved. She should be safe from infection, since it needed to penetrate the dermis to have its effect. Still, she moved away.

A shadow fell across her digging. Tessa looked up. Malena stood above her, staring down dispassionately at the bodies of her parents. Tessa almost jumped up, to grab her and screen her gaze, but stopped herself.

Malena looked at her. "They're dead, aren't they?"

Something caught in Tessa's throat, and she could only nod.

"Lewis told me . . . but I didn't see them. He dug them under himself. They loved each other very much."

"They loved you too, Malena."

"Not as much."

Malena jumped down and suffered Tessa to put her arms around her and hold her. She was wearing a hodgepodge of clothing, none of it adjusted properly, but, like Lewis, still seemed warm.

"Lewis wants me to live with him," Malena said.

"And what do you want to do?"

Malena looked up at her. Her dark eyes were wide. "I want to be with my parents."

Tessa did not glance down at the frozen bodies. "No, Malena."

Malena sighed. "They didn't want me anyway. They wanted to be by theirselves." Malena reached down and cast a handful of snow across her father's dead face. "They didn't even build a castle for the Kings. They were too busy and so the Kings passed us by."

"The Kings looked in on you, Malena. They always do, to make sure all the children are asleep. They don't need a castle to stop by."

Malena was not to be consoled. "We didn't even have a little one."

Lewis and Perin appeared above them.

"Malena." Lewis could not hide the despair in his voice. "You must choose. I was wrong."

The little girl sat down and crossed her arms, ignoring all of them. She was the same age as Kevin, now safely at a neighbor's house, being spoiled. She held her body tightly, as if the intolerable pressures on her were indeed physical, and she was being compressed into a space too small to live in. Tessa squatted down in front of her and looked her in the eyes. "I'm sorry, Malena. You shouldn't have to make decisions like this. No one should."

"I'm all right." Malena's tone was resentful. Arms still crossed, she looked away from all of them, off across the valley to the mountains beyond. "Tessa?"

"Yes, Malena?"

Malena switched her gaze to the ground. "Tell me what to do."

"I—" Tessa didn't know what to say. She looked up at the two men who loomed over her and the little girl. Perin was carefully expressionless, Lewis sad and weary. Tessa was half tempted to let Malena stay with him, so that she could learn the ways of the Shield's heights and stay completely pure, like snow and rock.

"We will adopt you. The Wolholmes. Poppa and I, and Dom and Benjamin and Kevin. Will you allow that?"

"Yes." The girl's voice was the barest whisper.

"Good." Tessa kept her voice brisk and efficient. She was getting some understanding of why Alta Dalhousie enjoyed being who she was. There was a joy in making such significant decisions, much like the feeling of jumping from a high rock down to the distant ground.

"And Lewis." She looked up at him, wondering what consequences her next decision would have. "You'll have her too, as you deserve. The canyons will not claim her entire. Malena will come to you, up here. Is that something you want to do, Malena?"

Malena looked up at Lewis, the only person who had evidenced any interest in her own personal fate, and nodded silently.

"I'm afraid you'll have to be satisfied with that, Lewis," Tessa said.

His head moving in time to Malena's, Lewis nodded also.

"But can we do that?" Crisis over, Perin was once again tentative. He looked down at Malena as if he had never seen her before. "What about—"

"Alta Dalhousie will agree," Tessa said briskly. "As long as we grant the Toromas some use of their old lands."

"Oh." Perin was still puzzled, but willing to accept his daughter's decision. "Well, that's all right then. The others will want to know." He put his fingers in his mouth and whistled shrilly.

Benjamin didn't realize that there was any mystery at all. He hugged Malena, who tolerated it, then jumped up on the rocks. They'd wanted to find her, and they'd found her, and it was a noble success.

Dom was more suspicious. Decisions had been made in his absence, significant family decisions. He accepted them, but now Tessa regretted having acted in such haste. She should have talked to him . . . but there hadn't been time, everything had moved so fast. She'd have to make it up to him later, if she could.

Dalka knelt down by Gorr and Fila. "How did they die?"

"He came up to see me, to find out why I had been giving her the medicines," Lewis said. "And to forbid me to do it any more. She came after him, much faster. They fought. He was weak, dying, but they fought, and she let him cut her, as she had cut him. The fungus went right into her, deep, even deeper than the skin. She died quickly, even more quickly than he. And after, when I found them, he had decided that his journey was over. I asked about Malena.'' Lewis sighed. ''He barely knew who I meant. Perin and I were to decide. I decided for Perin.'' He looked at his old friend. ''I was wrong.''

''Now we bury them,'' Perin said. ''We can't take them to the burial ground at Topfield until spring. So shall we build them their winter house?''

His family looked around at the high, inhospitable cliffs. They had all been looking forward to getting somewhere lower in altitude before night fell.

''They are family,'' Perin said. ''It is our duty.''

And it stakes our claim to Malena, Tessa thought, but did not say. It felt entirely too cold-blooded.

Perin knelt, gathered a small clump of snow, and began to roll it. ''Time to get to work.''

Despite the gravity of the situation, Tessa laughed and clapped her mittened hands. ''Let's go, Dom! Bet you I can roll a big one faster than you can.''

Dom shook his head. ''God. What a family I was born into.'' Then he bent over and began to roll his own snowball.

''Tessa!'' Perin whispered piercingly. ''Tessa. Get up, it's almost dawn.''

''I'm awake, Poppa.'' Tessa rolled out of her sleeping bag. Malena, who had been sharing it, got out without a sound. Tessa had listened to her steady breathing during the night, wondering if she slept.

It had been a cold night, and Perin had slept none of it. After he had sent his children to bed he had stayed up. In brief waking moments, Tessa had heard him wandering around the snow structure, adding things to it, spraying it with catalyst-warmed water to freeze in the cold night air. He'd obviously planned for this. Dom had already left his own bag without waking her. She crawled out of the tent.

A dark shape bulked in the predawn darkness: the snow structure that Perin had built for the bodies of Fila and Gorr. They were below it now, encased in ice.

''Dom!'' Tessa called. ''Help me get this tent down.'' The air was sandpaper-cold. She felt it abrading her exposed skin.

Dom bounded up, thrust a cup of steaming tea into her hand, and took down the tent before she could say anything more.

Morning light filtered around the peaks. They all stood as still as they could in the cold.

"Oh, Poppa," Tessa said. "It's beautiful!"

"That's not the point, is it?" Perin said, pleased in spite of himself. "Not the point at all. But they might as well have what I can give them, right? What I can give them."

Two days after building his magnificent structure of cake for the animals to eat, Perin had built one of ice and snow to be melted by the spring sun. It thrust up from its base in the old foundation stones. Delicate, ice-encased spires gleamed above heavy, crenelated walls. The front of the castle had huge, claw-tipped paws, as if the entire building was some gigantic, frozen animal.

Tessa sipped her tea, feeling it go quickly cold.

"Well, that's it then, isn't it?" Perin said briskly. He picked up his pack. "We'd best be down quickly. Everyone has to be told."

"But, Poppa," Tessa protested. "We can't just leave—"

"We can. We can and we will, Tessa. It's just something to keep the scavengers away from them. That's all it's for." He turned away from it without another look, tightened his snow-shoes, and started down the hill.

Dom, Benjamin, Dalka, Malena, and Tessa followed, Tessa in the rear. After taking a few steps, she stopped and turned. The castle was in full light now, gleaming as if dropped from some other world. The dark shape of Lewis moved across the tumbled rocks above it, as he walked slowly into the dark and icy mountains beyond others' knowing.

Tessa turned back and hurried to catch up with her family.

CHRISTMAS WITHOUT RODNEY

Isaac Asimov

*"Christmas Without Rodney" was purchased by Gard-
ner Dozois, and appeared in the Mid-December 1988
issue of* Asimov's, *with a cover and interior illustration
by Gary Freeman. In it, he merges his long tradition of
Robot stories with the* Asimov's *magazine tradition of
Christmas stories, to produce a slyly witty and deceptively quiet story that turns out to have a most unsettling
sting in its tail...*

*A good case could be made for the proposition that
the late Isaac Asimov was the most famous SF writer of
the last half of the twentieth century. He was the author
of almost five hundred books, including some of the best-
known novels in the genre (*The Caves of Steel, I, Robot,
and the Foundation *trilogy, for example); his last several
novels kept him solidly on the nationwide bestseller lists
throughout the '80s; he won two Nebulas and two Hugos, plus the prestigious Grandmaster Nebula; he wrote
an enormous number of nonfiction books on a bewil-
deringly large range of topics, everything from the Bible
to Shakespeare, and his many books on scientific matters
made him perhaps the best-known scientific popularizer
of our time; his nonfiction articles appeared everywhere
from* Omni *to* TV Guide; *he was one of the most sought-
after speakers in the country, and appeared on most of*

*the late-night and afternoon talk shows of his day, and
even did television commercials—and he was also the
only SF writer famous enough to have had a contem-
porary SF magazine named after him,* Asimov's Science
Fiction *magazine. A mere sampling of Asimov's other
books, even restricting ourselves to fiction alone (we
should probably say, to SF alone, since he was almost
as well-known in the mystery field), would include* The
Naked Sun, The Stars Like Dust, The Currents of Space,
The Gods Themselves, Foundation's Edge, The Robots
of Dawn, Robots and Empire, Foundation's Earth, *and
two expansions of famous Asimov short stories into
novel form,* The Ugly Little Boy *and* Nightfall, *written
in collaboration with Robert Silverberg. His most recent
fiction titles include the novel* Forward the Foundation,
and the posthumous collections Gold *and* Fantasy.

It all started with Gracie (my wife of nearly forty years) wanting
to give Rodney time off for the holiday season and it ended with
me in an absolutely impossible situation. I'll tell you about it if
you don't mind because I've got to tell *somebody*. Naturally, I'm
changing names and details for our own protection.

It was just a couple of months ago, mid-December, and Gracie
said to me, "Why don't we give Rodney time off for the holiday
season? Why shouldn't he celebrate Christmas, too?"

I remember I had my optics unfocused at the time (there's a
certain amount of relief in letting things go hazy when you want
to rest or just listen to music) but I focused them quickly to see
if Gracie were smiling or had a twinkle in her eye. Not that she
has much of a sense of humor, you understand.

She wasn't smiling. No twinkle. I said, "Why on Earth should
we give him time off?"

"Why not?"

"Do you want to give the freezer a vacation, the sterilizer, the
holoviewer? Shall we just turn off the power supply?"

"Come, Howard," she said. "Rodney isn't a freezer or a sterilizer. He's a *person*."

"He's not a person. He's a robot. He wouldn't want a vacation."

"How do you know? And he's a *person*. He deserves a chance to rest and just revel in the holiday atmosphere."

I wasn't going to argue that "person" thing with her. I know you've all read those polls which show that women are three times as likely to resent and fear robots as men are. Perhaps that's because robots tend to do what was once called, in the bad old days, "women's work" and women fear being made useless, though I should think they'd be delighted. In any case, Gracie *is* delighted and she simply adores Rodney. (That's *her* word for it. Every other day she says, "I just adore Rodney.")

You've got to understand that Rodney is an old-fashioned robot whom we've had about seven years. He's been adjusted to fit in with our old-fashioned house and our old-fashioned ways and I'm rather pleased with him myself. Sometimes I wonder about getting one of those slick, modern jobs, which are automated to death, like the one our son, DeLancey, has, but Gracie would never stand for it.

But then I thought of DeLancey and I said, "How are we going to give Rodney time off, Gracie? DeLancey is coming in with that gorgeous wife of his" (I was using "gorgeous" in a sarcastic sense, but Gracie didn't notice—it's amazing how she insists on seeing a good side even when it doesn't exist) "and how are we going to have the house in good shape and meals made and all the rest of it without Rodney?"

"But that's just it," she said, earnestly. "DeLancey and Hortense could bring *their* robot and he could do it all. You *know* they don't think much of Rodney, and they'd love to show what theirs can do and Rodney can have a rest."

I grunted and said, "If it will make you happy, I suppose we can do it. It'll only be for three days. But I don't want Rodney thinking he'll get every holiday off."

It was another joke, of course, but Gracie just said, very earnestly, "No, Howard, I will talk to him and explain it's only just once in a while."

She can't quite understand that Rodney is controlled by the three laws of robotics and that nothing has to be explained to him.

So I had to wait for DeLancey and Hortense, and my heart was heavy. DeLancey is my son, of course, but he's one of your upwardly mobile, bottom-line individuals. He married Hortense because she has excellent connections in business and can help him in that upward shove. At least, I hope so, because if she has another virtue I have never discovered it.

They showed up with their robot two days before Christmas. The robot was as glitzy as Hortense and looked almost as hard. He was polished to a high gloss and there was none of Rodney's clumping. Hortense's robot (I'm sure she dictated the design) moved absolutely silently. He kept showing up behind me for no reason and giving me heart-failure every time I turned around and bumped into him.

Worse, DeLancey brought eight-year-old LeRoy. Now he's my grandson, and I would swear to Hortense's fidelity because I'm sure no one would voluntarily touch her, but I've got to admit that putting him through a concrete mixer would improve him no end.

He came in demanding to know if we had sent Rodney to the metal-reclamation unit yet. (He called it the "bust-up place.") Hortense sniffed and said, "Since we have a modern robot with us, I hope you keep Rodney out of sight."

I said nothing, but Gracie said, "Certainly, dear. In fact, we've given Rodney time off."

DeLancey made a face but didn't say anything. He knew his mother.

I said, pacifically, "Suppose we start off by having Rambo make something good to drink, eh? Coffee, tea, hot chocolate, a bit of brandy—"

Rambo was their robot's name. I don't know why except that it starts with R. There's no law about it, but you've probably noticed for yourself that almost every robot has a name beginning with R. R for robot, I suppose. The usual name is Robert. There must be a million robot Roberts in the northeast corridor alone.

And frankly, it's my opinion that's the reason human names just don't start with R any more. You get Bob and Dick but not Robert or Richard. You get Posy and Trudy, but not Rose or Ruth. Sometimes you get unusual R's. I know of three robots called Rutabaga, and two that are Rameses. But Hortense is the only one I know who named a robot Rambo, a syllable-combination I've never encountered, and I've never liked to ask why. I was sure the explanation would prove to be unpleasant.

Rambo turned out to be useless at once. He was, of course, programmed for the DeLancey/Hortense menage and that was utterly modern and utterly automated. To prepare drinks in his own home, all Rambo had to do was to press appropriate buttons. (Why anyone would need a robot to press buttons, I would like to have explained to me!)

He said so. He turned to Hortense and said in a voice like honey (it wasn't Rodney's city-boy voice with its trace of Brooklyn), "The equipment is lacking, madam."

And Hortense drew a sharp breath. "You mean you *still* don't have a robotized kitchen, grandfather?" (She called me nothing at all, until LeRoy was born, howling of course, and then she promptly called me "grandfather." Naturally, she never called me Howard. That would tend to show me to be human, or, more unlikely, show *her* to be human.)

I said, "Well, it's robotized when Rodney is in it."

"I dare say," she said. "But we're not living in the twentieth century, grandfather."

I thought: How I wish we were—but I just said, "Well, why not instruct Rambo how to operate the controls. I'm sure he can pour and mix and heat and do whatever else is necessary."

"I'm sure he can," said Hortense, "but thank Fate he doesn't have to. I'm not going to interfere with his programming. It will make him less efficient."

Gracie said, worried, but amiable, "But if we don't interfere with his programming, then I'll just have to instruct him, step by step, but I don't know how it's done. I've never done it."

I said, "Rodney can tell him."

Gracie said, "Oh, Howard, we've given Rodney a vacation."

"I know, but we're not going to ask him to *do* anything; just tell Rambo here what to do and then Rambo can do it."

Whereupon Rambo said stiffly, "Madam, there is nothing in my programming or in my instructions that would make it mandatory for me to accept orders given me by another robot, especially one that is an earlier model."

Hortense said, soothingly, "Of course, Rambo. I'm sure that grandfather and grandmother understand that." (I noticed that DeLancey never said a word. I wonder if he *ever* said a word when his dear wife was present.)

I said, "All right, I tell you what. I'll have Rodney tell *me*, and then I will tell Rambo."

Rambo said nothing to that. Even Rambo is subject to the second law of robotics which makes it mandatory for him to obey human orders.

Hortense's eyes narrowed and I knew that she would like to tell me that Rambo was far too fine a robot to be ordered about by the likes of me, but some distant and rudimentary near-human waft of feeling kept her from doing so.

Little LeRoy was hampered by no such quasi-human restraints. He said, "I don't want to have to look at Rodney's ugly puss. I bet he don't know how to do *anything* and if he does, ol' Grampa would get it all wrong anyway."

It would have been nice, I thought, if I could be alone with little LeRoy for five minutes and reason calmly with him, with a brick, but a mother's instinct told Hortense never to leave LeRoy alone with any human being whatever.

There was nothing to do, really, but get Rodney out of his niche in the closet where he had been enjoying his own thoughts (I wonder if a robot has his own thoughts when he is alone) and put him to work. It was hard. He would say a phrase, then I would say the same phrase, then Rambo would do something, then Rodney would say another phrase and so on.

It all took twice as long as if Rodney were doing it himself and it wore *me* out, I can tell you, because everything had to be like that, using the dishwasher/sterilizer, cooking the Christmas feast, cleaning up messes on the table or on the floor, everything.

Gracie kept moaning that Rodney's vacation was being ruined, but she never seemed to notice that mine was, too, though I *did* admire Hortense for her manner of saying something unpleasant at every moment that some statement seemed called for. I noticed, particularly, that she never repeated herself once. Anyone can be nasty, but to be unfailingly creative in one's nastiness filled me with a perverse desire to applaud now and then.

But, really, the worst thing of all came on Christmas Eve. The tree had been put up and I was exhausted. We didn't have the kind of situation in which an automated box of ornaments was plugged into an electronic tree, and at the touch of one button there would result an instantaneous and perfect distribution of ornaments. On our tree (of ordinary, old-fashioned plastic) the ornaments had to be placed, one by one, by hand.

Hortense looked revolted, but I said, "Actually, Hortense, this means you can be creative and make your own arrangement."

Hortense sniffed, rather like the scrape of claws on a rough plaster wall, and left the room with an obvious expression of nausea on her face. I bowed in the direction of her retreating back, glad to see her go, and then began the tedious task of listening to Rodney's instructions and passing them on to Rambo.

When it was over, I decided to rest my aching feet and mind by sitting in a chair in a far and rather dim corner of the room. I had hardly folded my aching body into the chair when little LeRoy entered. He didn't see me, I suppose, or he might simply have ignored me as being part of the less important and interesting pieces of furniture in the room.

He cast a disdainful look on the tree and said, to Rambo, "Listen, where are the Christmas presents? I'll bet old Gramps and Gram got me lousy ones, but I ain't going to wait for no tomorrow morning."

Rambo said, "I do not know where they are, Little Master."

"Huh!" said LeRoy, turning to Rodney. "How about you, Stink-face. Do you know where the presents are?"

Rodney would have been within the bounds of his programming to have refused to answer on the grounds that he did not know he was being addressed, since his name was Rodney and not Stink-face. I'm quite certain that that would have been Rambo's attitude. Rodney, however, was of different stuff. He answered politely, "Yes, I do, Little Master."

"So where is it, you old puke?"

Rodney said, "I don't think it would be wise to tell you, Little Master. That would disappoint Gracie and Howard who would like to give the presents to you tomorrow morning."

"Listen," said little LeRoy, "who you think you're talking to, you dumb robot? Now I gave you an order. You bring those presents to me." And in an attempt to show Rodney who was master, he kicked the robot in the shin.

It was a mistake. I saw it would be that a second before and that was a joyous second. Little LeRoy, after all, was ready for bed (though I doubted that he ever went to bed before he was *good* and ready). Therefore, he was wearing slippers. What's more, the slipper sailed off the foot with which he kicked, so that he ended by slamming his bare toes hard against the solid chrome-steel of the robotic shin.

He fell to the floor howling and in rushed his mother. "What is it, LeRoy? What is it?"

Whereupon little LeRoy had the immortal gall to say, "He hit me. That old monster-robot *hit* me."

Hortense screamed. She saw me and shouted, "That robot of yours must be destroyed."

I said, "Come, Hortense. A robot can't hit a boy. First law of robotics prevents it."

"It's an *old* robot, a *broken* robot. LeRoy says—"

"LeRoy lies. There is no robot, no matter how old or how broken, who could hit a boy."

"Then *he* did it. *Grampa* did it," howled LeRoy.

"I wish I did," I said, quietly, "but no robot would have allowed me to. Ask your own. Ask Rambo if he would have remained motionless while either Rodney or I had hit your boy. Rambo!"

I put it in the imperative, and Rambo said, "I would not have allowed any harm to come to the Little Master, Madam, but I did not know what he purposed. He kicked Rodney's shin with his bare foot, Madam."

Hortense gasped and her eyes bulged in fury. "Then he had a good reason to do so. I'll still have your robot destroyed."

"Go ahead, Hortense. Unless you're willing to ruin your robot's efficiency by trying to reprogram him to lie, he will bear witness to just what preceded the kick and so, of course, with pleasure, will I."

Hortense left the next morning, carrying the pale-faced LeRoy with her (it turned out he had broken a toe—nothing he didn't deserve) and an endlessly wordless DeLancey.

Gracie wrung her hands and implored them to stay, but I watched them leave without emotion. No, that's a lie. I watched them leave with lots of emotion, all pleasant.

Later, I said to Rodney, when Gracie was not present, "I'm sorry, Rodney. That was a horrible Christmas, all because we tried to have it without you. We'll never do that again, I promise."

"Thank you, Sir," said Rodney. "I must admit that there were times these two days when I earnestly wished the laws of robotics did not exist."

I grinned and nodded my head, but that night I woke up out of a sound sleep and began to worry. I've been worrying ever since.

I admit that Rodney was greatly tried, but a robot *can't* wish the laws of robotics did not exist. He *can't*, no matter what the circumstances.

If I report this, Rodney will undoubtedly be scrapped, and if we're issued a new robot as recompense, Gracie will simply never forgive me. Never! No robot, however new, however talented, can possibly replace Rodney in her affection.

In fact, I'll never forgive myself. Quite apart from my own liking for Rodney, I couldn't bear to give Hortense the satisfaction.

But if I do nothing, I live with a robot capable of wishing the laws of robotics did not exist. From wishing they did not exist to acting as if they did not exist is just a step. At what moment will he take that step and in what form will he show that he has done so?

What do I do? What do I do?

SPACE ALIENS SAVED MY MARRIAGE

Sharon N. Farber

*"Space Aliens Saved My Marriage" was purchased by
Gardner Dozois, and appeared in the December 1990
issue of* Asimov's, *with an illustration by Laura Lakey.
It was one of more than eighteen sales that Farber has
made to the magazine since her first sale here to George
Scithers in 1978, making her one of the magazine's most
frequent contributors. She has also made sales to* Omni,
Amazing, *and other markets. Recently, for reasons of
her own, she has decided to start another writing career
under a pseudonym—and the stories written under that
name have proved equally as popular with the readership, and have shown up on major award ballots. Born
in San Francisco, she now lives in Chattanooga, Ten-
nessee.*

*Here she treats us to a holiday Close Encounter of a
very different sort—after this one, if you hear the patting
and pawing of tiny hooves on your roof Christmas Eve,
you might not be so sure that it's Santa Claus . . .*

When I got home from work, Tim was still in the kitchen, drink-
ing coffee and reading the sports page. Construction's slow in
December. The kitten began rubbing up against my leg and purr-
ing the minute I came in.

"What do you think, honey?" I asked, petting the kitten.

"Shouldn't we give Mittens two names? I mean, she does have two heads, and all."

Tim said, "Whatever you want," but Stacy stopped splashing her spoon in her Count Chockula and pointed at each head. "Muffin. Tiffany."

"Good names," I told her, pouring Muffin and Tiffany a saucer of milk. As usual, the two heads began squabbling over their treat.

"Any newspapers, Bobby June?" asked Tim.

When the new tabloids come out, I get to take home the old ones, along with the day old bread and mushy bananas. I'd already read them all, of course. The Quik-Stop-Shop gets real slow after around 2 A.M. "Look here: *HOUSEWIFE SEES ELVIS IN LAUNDROMAT*. It happened in our town!"

"Forget it," said Tim. "People are always seeing Elvis. Didn't that spaceship, Voyager or whatever it was, see his face on Mars?" This was the longest conversation we'd had since we were visiting my Aunt Martha in Austin, and saw the ghost of Uncle Edgar in the closet. So I figured, maybe this is the time to bring it up.

"Tim honey, it's Christmas Eve tomorrow. Don't you have any relatives you'd like to invite for dinner, to meet me and Stacy and all?"

"No," he said, and went off to read the papers somewhere else.

I have trouble sleeping when I work third-shift, so I took Stacy shopping for shoes. It's incredible how quick she seems to outgrow them—she's only four, and already in a grownup size 6. She has her dad's feet, I guess, but luckily she has my nose.

Anyway, the mall was pretty crowded, what with it being the day before the day before Christmas. We did a little last-minute shopping for presents, and we were buying this cute little dog and cat salt and pepper set for Jesse, my friend-at-work, when a woman shrieked.

"Oh, my god!" she yelled, pointing up at a black velvet painting of Elvis. Tears seemed to be pouring from his eyes.

"Why's he crying, Mommy?" asked Stacy.

The clerk got up on a ladder and pulled down the painting, to check for leaks or something in the wall, but nothing else was wet.

The woman who'd seen it first reached over and touched the tears, then raised her finger to her mouth. "It's salty," she said. "Those are real tears!"

I looked at the painting, and it seemed that the wet eyes were staring deep into my own. And suddenly this thought was there, in my mind. *You'd better go to County Mercy General. There's been an emergency.*

When we got to the hospital, it seemed they'd been looking for me. Grannie had had this bad stomachache, and they'd been worried she'd bled into a big old fibroid tumor she'd had for a long time, only they hadn't wanted to operate before, what with her being so old and all, but now they'd had to operate after all, and her doctor wanted to talk with me, right outside the operating room.

He was still wearing green clothes and a paper hat and booties, just like on TV. He didn't mince words, just started right out. "Your grandmother's had a baby."

"But that's impossible," I said. "Gran's seventy-eight!"

He got that narrow-eyed little look that doctors get when they think you don't believe them, and said, "Of course it's possible— it happened. It seems your grandmother had been pregnant with twins over fifty years ago, but only one of them actually got born."

Then he talked about ovulation, and hibernation, and a lot of other complicated stuff I didn't get, cause I mean, I dropped out in eleventh grade to work and all. But the long and the short of it seemed to be that this baby had been in her womb for fifty-five years, and in fact was my late daddy's twin. They'd compared footprints, and it was true.

"But that's not the end of it," the doctor continued. "I've seen a lot of weird stuff—I've delivered babies wearing ancient Egyptian amulets, or tattooed with holy symbols, and once I saw a woman give birth to a Cabbage Patch Doll. But never in all my years of practicing has one of my newborns ever spoken in the delivery room before!"

"What'd he say?"

"When I slapped his little behind, he didn't even cry, he just looked me in the eye and said 'The Twin returns. Love him tender and don't be cruel.' He wouldn't say anything more, and now he's acting just like a regular baby." The doctor took off his paper hat and scratched his head. "*The Twin.* Must be himself he means, right?"

"No. No, it isn't." I didn't know yet what he meant, back then, but I knew that something big was going on, or about to happen.

What with staying with Gran all afternoon, and then making dinner for Stacy and Tim, I only had a few hours sleep before going to work. I was a couple minutes late, but Ralph always covers for me—he's a real good guy. He was this World War II veteran who they found after drifting alone in a liferaft in the Bermuda Triangle for forty years, but he didn't let that ruin his attitude.

"Congratulate me, I'm gonna get hitched," Ralph told me while he was putting on his muffler and overcoat.

"Who to?" I didn't even know he was dating. As far as I knew, his only real friend was this guy Eddy he'd known in basic training, who'd looked him up after seeing his picture in the paper.

"I'm marrying Eddy," Ralph said, sort of blushing. "No really, it's not like that. See, he was struck by lightning last year, and it turned him into a woman!"

"Wow!" I remembered reading about it, but never realized who it had been. "Well, good luck and everything." We'd have to put on a shower for them.

Jesse had been in back, and now he came in to restock the chips. "Heard about Ralph and Eddy?" he asked. He's got this real velvety deep voice, but I never could figure out his accent.

"I hope they'll be happy," I said, started thinking about me and Tim, and choked a little. Jesse came over to hug me—we're only friends, really—and I told him how me and Tim just didn't seem to communicate anymore. Then I wiped away my tears, and looked at Jesse. "Hey! You've been losing weight."

"It's that *eat all you want and lose a pound a day diet.* Works!" A customer came in to pay for some gas, so Jesse went back to restock the Oreos and Pecan Sandies.

The customer—he was paying with a credit card—said "Your stock-clerk looks a lot like Elvis, don't you think?"

"No, not really . . ." I mean, I just thought of him as my friend Jesse, and never really thought much about his face, you know?

"Yeah," continued the customer, pointing to some cigarettes, so I had to ring him up all over again. "Yeah, they've been seeing Elvis all over—the post office in Decatur, a McDonalds in Fresno, the Baseball Hall of Fame. . . . Now I've seen him here in a convenience store. Think I'll make the papers?"

We laughed a little about that. Another customer, buying milk and bread, put her stuff down on the counter. "Don't laugh," she said. "Yesterday, totally unexpected, my cat dragged in an old monophonic record album, looking brand new. It was *Blue Hawaii!*"

We were pretty impressed by how strange that was, including Jesse, who'd come over to listen. "I tell you," the lady continued, "something's brewing. It feels kind of like a storm, about to break." She noticed Jesse. "Hey, anyone ever said you look like Elvis?"

"No ma'am. Maybe Roy Orbison," he answered.

She looked him over again. "Yeah, guess you're right. Well, Merry Christmas everyone."

Things stayed quiet for a while, and around midnight Brian the night supervisor came by to check on us. I didn't like Brian much, he was always acting like he thought you were stealing money from the store, but I was real pleasant, and didn't suspect much when he sent Jesse in back to inventory all the cookies and sodas, to see what we'd need extra to last over the holidays.

"Come here!" Brian called, from over the back aisle, where the candy and toys are.

"Uh oh," I thought. Some kids must've snuck in while I wasn't paying attention, and taken some toys and left the plastic containers behind. They do that if you don't watch careful.

But everything looked okay on the novelty rack. "What's wrong?" I asked.

"Nothing's wrong," said Brian. "I just wanted to wish you a Merry Christmas," and he started to kiss me.

"Hey!" I said, trying to make like it was a joke. I mean, I needed the job, you know? "Hey, there's no mistletoe here." I pushed him away—and then he opened his mouth and showed me these fangs like the plastic Dracula teeth we sell at Halloween, only his looked real.

"Brian, what the . . ."

And suddenly he was biting me on the throat, and I couldn't call for help. . . .

I seemed to be sliding down this long dark tunnel, and there was a light at the end, and my parents, and my grandparents (except for Gran of course), and everyone I knew who ever died including my ninth grade boyfriend who fell in the drainage ditch, and all the dogs and cats I ever owned, were there to welcome me. Only when I got to the end of the tunnel, there was this view like in an old movie house with just one big screen, and it was showing Earth, and this big old rocky asteroid heading right for it. At first I thought it was something out of a Star Trek movie, but then I realized it was for real. And then the space scene was gone, and Elvis was there—Elvis himself—smiling at me. Just smiling. And he raised up one hand and said to me, "Go back and warn them."

Next thing I knew, I was on the floor back in the Quik-Stop-Shop, and Jesse was putting cold rags on my forehead.

"I thought you'd died," he said.

"I did!" I tried to sit up, making it the second time, and noticed the floor was all wet with milk, and this slimy yellow and red gunk I didn't recognize, but smelled awful. "What happened—is that stuff Brian?"

Jesse nodded. "I threw milk on him—it dissolves vampires. Too wholesome or something, I dunno, but it works every time. Mind, you have to use whole milk. Skim or 2 percent just won't work."

"Jesse, you got to listen to this dream I just had." I told him about the tunnel, and the asteroid, and Elvis. Jesse just rocked back and forth on his heels. Finally he said, "It ain't no dream, Bobby June. It's for real, and we must act quickly if we're to save the planet."

I was still kind of dazed, what with dying and coming back and all, so I didn't hardly protest when he closed up the store, and we started driving. I didn't even really care where we were going. I just sat wrapped in a blanket—his pickup didn't have heat—and looked out the window at the big old full moon.

"You see, this is the culmination of my stay upon the Earth," Jesse said.

"Huh?"

"I'm the Twin who returned," he said. "The one your little baby uncle was talking about."

"Huh?" The night was weird enough without old Jesse getting bizarre on me. I looked at him like for the first time. He did look like Elvis. "Who are you?"

"Like I said, I'm the Twin. Elvis's twin brother Jesse, who supposedly died at birth, but who was really taken off planet and raised in a UFO."

"You mean the UFO people who steal missing children and eat them?"

"Nope—those guys're from Andromeda."

"Then, the UFO people who take your pets or lawn ornaments for company, and return them a year later?"

"Nope—Betelgeuse."

"Then how about the ones who hover outside your window and won't let you eat junk food?"

"Those busybodies? I should hope not. No, my UFO was from the Southern Cross, and they're real benevolent folk there."

I suddenly began to snuffle. "Poor Jesse. Taken away from your family and raised with weird aliens."

He took his hand off the wheel long enough to pat me on the shoulder. "It wasn't that bad. The scenery was nice, and we got Lucy reruns on the radio telescope. Besides, I'm half-space alien myself, so I had kinfolk."

His face got real sad. "Poor brother Elvis, he never even knew the truth about his heritage. That's why he ate too much, and drank, and did drugs. Earth food didn't have all the essential vitamins and minerals he needed."

"Oh!" Suddenly it made sense, Jesse's always sucking on a Tictac. "Your breath mints are from space too!"

"Right. They're to compensate for dietary deficiencies, and to protect me from the pollution."

Lots more was making sense. Like those Elvis sightings, all over the country. They'd been Jesse, just wandering about waiting for whatever it was he'd been sent to our planet to stop to happen so he could stop it. As he drove, he told me a little about how he traveled around, always one step ahead of reporters, and the KGB, and bad aliens who didn't want him to save the Earth.

Then we got to where we were going, which was the observatory up near the university. I hadn't been there since a field trip in second grade. Jesse got us inside—he could be real impressive—but the egghead types there were snooty, and wouldn't believe us.

"Asteroid coming in to destroy us? Give me a break," said the professor in charge, but then Jesse took him aside and whispered in his ear for a while, and when they came back, the man was pale. "Turn the scope around," he ordered, and began searching the sky.

"What'd you say?" I asked Jesse.

He shrugged. "I just told him things only he knew about himself—like, he really doesn't like sushi, and he always wanted to be a fireman, and he's got this secret crush on Vanna White."

It took a while, but then the professor came back, even paler, said "You were right!" and began making lots of important phone calls.

Pretty soon—well, really it was hours later, but I slept through the flight to Washington and was still half asleep when we met the President and the Joint Chiefs of Staff—pretty soon we were at the United Nations. They'd let me call Tim from the White House, and the President's wife, who was pretty nice, told them to send a plane to pick up Tim and Stacy so they could be with me.

So we were all up there at the UN. First the professor talked, and a bunch of other professors from all sorts of countries agreed with him. Then everyone got in a panic, because this asteroid was going to hit the Earth in a month or so, and smash us to bits, and we didn't have any missiles big enough to stop it.

I was kind of mad about that, thinking about Stacy not even getting old enough for kindergarten, and I said to the President, "Here I voted for you, and you spend all this money on bombs and stuff, and you can't even stop one lousy asteroid." He looked sort of upset, which got me feeling bad, so I apologized.

"It's okay," he told me. "We're all a bit on edge."

Then Jesse got up, and talked about how he had a plan and would need lots of cooperation. Our professor did some calculations and said it'd work. But lots of them still didn't believe Jesse.

"I guess I'll just have to convince you, then," he said, and asked someone to fetch him a guitar, and right there in the UN assembly hall, he started to sing. And maybe his voice wasn't much better than his brother's, who you have to admit was the greatest singer ever lived, but Jesse'd been trained by aliens, and he knew how to use that extra nine-tenths of the brain that none of the rest of us uses, so it was the best singing anyone ever thought they'd ever hear. Pretty soon everyone didn't know if they wanted to cry or applaud, and when they'd all calmed down and the medics had taken away the delegates who'd passed out or had heart attacks, everyone voted to go with Jesse's plan.

So there it was, Christmas Eve day, and Jesse had a radio hookup to everywhere on Earth. They asked if he wanted translators, but he said no—and sure enough, when he started talking, slow and kind of loud, everyone understood him, no matter what language they usually talked.

"I want everyone in the Western Hemisphere and Europe and Africa to just stand real still," he said into the radio. I was kind of awed, thinking how everyone all over the world was hearing my friend Jesse's words. And trusting and believing him too, because he sounded like his brother, and everyone on Earth knows about Elvis. "And I want everyone in the East, in China and Japan and . . ." Well, I'll just skip the list of countries, cause I don't exactly know where most of them were, or how to spell them either.

". . . I want every one of you to go get a kitchen chair exactly eighteen inches tall—that's forty-six centimeters—"

It was real impressive how smart Jesse was.

"You can put some books or plywood on the seat if it isn't exactly eighteen inches. Now I want you to get up on those chairs, every one of you. Come on now." He waited a bit, so folks who were old or young or maybe had arthritis could get onto their chairs. "Now when I say go—hold on, not yet, when I say Go, I want everyone to jump. Okay, all ready?"

He looked over at me, and I smiled and crossed my fingers.

He leaned close to his microphone. "Okay. Ready, set—jump!"

And all over China and Japan and all those other countries, people jumped off their kitchen chairs.

The ground shook a little, and Stacy began to cry. I comforted her, and Tim put his arm around my shoulder.

The professor was talking on the phone to some other scientists, who were somewhere or other doing stuff, and he put his hand over the receiver and shouted "It worked! It worked! When the Asians all jumped, they pushed the Earth slightly out of its orbit, so now that asteroid is going to miss us. We're saved!"

Everyone began to cheer and hug each other. Then we got quiet, because we'd all noticed a dayglow orange UFO hovering outside the windows.

Jesse came over and took my hands. "You've been a right good friend, Bobby June, and I'm gonna miss you."

Stacy said, "You goin' somewhere, Uncle Jesse?"

He put a hand on her head—and her hair's been blond and naturally curly ever since—and said, "My job, and my brother's, is over, Stacy. I'm going home. But first . . ."

He took Tim aside a bit. "Now Tim," he said, "I know you love your wife, but you have to talk with her."

"But if I do, if she learns the truth about me," Tim answered, "she wouldn't love me no more."

"Now, you know that isn't true. Don't be afraid," Jesse told him.

Tim said to me, "Bobby June, I wouldn't blame you if you leave me when I tell you this. The reason we never visit my relatives, and the reason I have so much trouble finding shoes that fit—sweetheart, I'm Bigfoot.

"Well, I'm not really Bigfoot," he continued. "I'm just his little brother. But you get the idea."

I said, "Honey, I wouldn't care if you were the Loch Ness Monster, you're still my man," and I hugged Tim, and Stacy jumped up and down cause she could tell things were going to be okay from now on.

Jesse went to the window, stepping onto a gangplank from the UFO. "Wouldn't you and your family like to spend the holiday with your relatives, Tim?"

"Sure would," said Tim. "But we couldn't get no flight to Oregon on Christmas Eve, and anyway, we don't have no presents either."

"Forget airplanes," grinned Jesse. "We can drop you off on our way. And I'm sure we can find something around the saucer for you to give your folks." He waved us to the gangplank.

"Oh boy!" cried Stacy. "This is going to be the best Christmas ever! And I also predict major conflict in the Mideast, a startling new career development for Linda Evans, and all the dogs in Denver will lose their hair but learn to speak . . ."

HOW TO FEED YOUR INNER TROLL

Leslie What

*"How to Feed Your Inner Troll" was purchased by
Gardner Dozois, and appeared in the December 1995
issue of* Asimov's, *along with an interior illustration by
Steve Cavallo and a delicious recipe for noodle kugle.*

*A relatively new writer whose work is often charac-
terized by madcap humor and a perspective on life
uniquely her own, Leslie What has made several sales
to* Asimov's, *as well as to* The Magazine of Fantasy &
Science Fiction, Pulphouse, Hysteria, *and* Realms of
Fantasy. *The very funny story that follows is* not *a
Christmas story, but it* is *a Holiday story nevertheless,
even if not quite the* same *Holiday (so sue us). It also
offers us, as an incidental bonus, some very good advice
on what to do if a rude and hungry troll should happen
to land on* your *doorstep late one night, especially one
that demands figgy pudding. (Just follow the* recipe,
dummy!)*

Herschel Minkowitz had barely finished writing the midterm
exam for his non-Euclidian geometry class when someone
knocked at the door. He stroked his beard, considering whether
or not to answer. Most likely, those drunken carolers from 16B
were at it again, or, worse yet, it could be that the *goyim*** from

*See "Glossary for the Goyim" on page 184.

GLOSSARY FOR THE GOYIM

Bubbe: (Pronounced bub-bee) An affectionate term for your grandmother.
Bubkes: (Pronounced sort of like that football guy.) Super-important. NOT!
Channukah: (Pronounced with the guttural "ch" a cat makes when coughing up a furball.) The Jewish festival celebrating fried foods, light, and freedom.
Dybbuk: (Pronounced dib-book) Kind of like a Santa, only scary.
Fartootst: (Pronounced just like it sounds, sorry.) Feeling kinda crazy.
Flayshig: Flesh. See Terry Bisson's "They're Made Out of Meat."
Goyim: (Other) nations. For the purpose of this story, if you need to ask, you can take it that this means you.
Kvetch: To whine or complain, frequently and with passion.

the United Way had come to collect. A sense of dread washed through him as he squinted to see the clock. "*Oy!*" he said—nearly time for *Jeopardy!*

He downed a Tums, quickly followed by another. Tonight was the first night of the Tournament of Champions, and Herschel had yet to make his final pass through the encyclopedia. The rapping persisted, annoying as an alarm.

The noise reminded Herschel of his dear *bubbe*, who used to *potch* him on the *tochis* to remind him that he'd forgotten something important. His angst had multiplied to a point where he could stand it no longer. With a longing glance at the remote control above the television, Herschel hurried across the living room to answer the door. Through the peephole he saw a furry blue triangle. "Who's there, already?" Herschel asked. There was no reply, but the blue fur wriggled. The color seemed so reassuringly familiar that Herschel opened the door part way. "Whaddaya want?" he asked, peering through the crack.

A *zaftig* little troll wearing powder-blue pajamas pushed past him and strode toward the Barcalounger that Herschel's *bubbe* had left him the year she went into the nursing home. The troll plopped into the seat cushion, making the Naugahyde squeal. It rolled up its sleeves, exposing stubby arms that were chalky as baking powder biscuits. Each hand had three short fingers, ruddy and fat as sausages. The troll reached down to pull the lever and let out the hassock. Tufts of blue fur sprouted from each of its chubby little toes.

"Comfy, isn't it?" said Herschel. As a boy he'd sat on Bubbe's lap, eating noodle kugle while the two watched *What's My Line?* How he longed to see his grandmother again!

The troll growled, "Figgy pudding!" with a trace of a Brooklyn accent. "Won't go till I get some!" It snapped its fingers and a blue ceramic mixing bowl appeared in its lap.

Herschel glanced down the hall, wondering where his uninvited guest had come from. Every door was closed, though he heard someone blaring the rap version of "Carol of the Bells" at sonic-boom volume. Before the odor of fish frying in a neighboring apartment could waft close enough to infect his whiskers, Herschel shut the door.

"Figgy pudding!" said the troll, a little louder. It pulled a blue wad of crumpled tissues from between the seat cushions and tossed them to the carpet. "Want it *now*."

Suddenly, Herschel remembered. "Oy!" he said, slapping

Latkes: (Pronounced Lot-keys) Fried potato balls (so how else would you cook potato balls?) traditionally served on Channukah.

Nu?: (Pronounced as "New?") An all-purpose greeting like "Yo."

Nudzh: (The "u" as in Bush, pronounced nuhdge) To nag or nudge with a passion.

Oy: Anagram of Yo. A two-letter word used in Scrabble. Five points.

Potch: A time-honored tradition, currently out of favor. The usual scenario involves a parent threatening to potch the child because of a disobedient act, a reprise of the disobedient act, the actual potch, and the child's questioning "Why did you potch me?"

Tochis: (Pronounced took-us) A behind.

Zaftig: The way we saw chubbiness before the times of eating disorders.

his head. Bubbe's birthday! And he'd forgotten to send so much as a card.

The troll hoisted its bowl above its head. "Figgy pudding! Figgy *pudding!*"

Herschel grew annoyed. "Are you *fartootst?* I don't know from figgy pudding," he said.

The troll snarled, baring yellow fangs. "Want it *now!*"

This was getting somewhat scary. Perhaps the troll was a *dybbuk*. Bubbe had warned him about such evil spirits, whom she'd often encountered back in the old country. Yet this dybbuk seemed more Smurf than demon, and Herschel found it difficult to take the little creature altogether seriously.

"Figgy pudding! Figgy pudding!" The troll jumped up and down on the Barcalounger. Plaster chunks fell like a plague of hail from the ceiling.

"No jumping on the furniture," Herschel said, but the troll didn't listen. In desperation, Herschel dialed his mother.

"*Nu?*" she answered. He heard the click of Mah-Jongg tiles in the background.

"Ma," Herschel said.

"You married, yet?"

"Do you have to ask every *day?*"

"So why are you calling on game night? Don't tell me you forgot your grandmother's birthday? And her all alone for the holidays."

"Cut it out, Ma," Herschel said. He felt guilty enough already. "It's just that this furry little troll stopped by and it wants me to make it some figgy pudding and I'm in a big hurry to watch my show. You got any recipes?"

"Figgy pudding, my *tochis!* What are you, fartootst? This is no accident that you're entertaining your inner troll at this time of the year," she said. He heard her cover the phone with her hand. "Five Crack," she yelled, as she discarded a tile.

"You still there, Ma? Whaddaya mean, 'inner troll'?"

"Your inner *nudzh*, your inner *kvetch*, your inner nag. Don't you remember him from childhood?" she said. "He's like an imaginary friend who's been recruited by the IRS. I wonder if your grandmother knows about this?" She sighed. "Hersh, babe. I'm telling you. There's more to life than *Jeopardy!* You're thirty-five years old. Don't you think it's time to feed the troll?'' Yet being his mother, she agreed to check for a recipe when the game ended.

She called him back quickly. ''Wall game,'' she said, meaning that nobody had won. Herschel heard her flip through the pages of her cookbook. ''Let's see here. . . . Fat, rendered, and grebenes. Fish balls. Hm. I'll try puddings. *Flayshig* Pudding? That it?''

''I don't think so,'' he said warily.

''So hire a caterer, it's not good enough,'' she said. ''Lighten up—it's almost *Channukah*. Say, I gotta go. Call me tomorrow and we'll do *latkes*.''

''Sure, Ma,'' Herschel said, sorry he had bothered calling her in the first place. ''Tomorrow.'' He said goodbye, then plodded to his tiny kitchen and opened his refrigerator. ''I could bake you maybe some schmaltz herring,'' he called.

''Figgy *pudding!* Figgy *pudding!*'' screamed the troll. The floor began to quake, and Herschel rushed out with a box of melba toast, hoping that would do. He set the box on the arm rest beside the troll.

''If you want, I've got dry curd cottage cheese,'' Herschel said. ''Low in calories. Good for the skin.''

The troll snapped his fangs at the air and hurled the melba toast across the room.

''Ouch,'' Herschel said. ''Take it easy!'' He downed another Tums, then offered one to the troll.

The troll batted its arm, knocking the roll of antacids from Herschel's grasp. ''Figgy pudding,'' it said in a growl. ''Want it now!''

Herschel began to wonder if he was in mortal danger. He backed away.

The troll reached between the Barcalounger cushions to pull out wads and wads of old tissues. Soon, the Barcalounger seemed adrift in a sea of blue. ''Want it *now!* Want it *now!*'' it screamed, then suddenly, the troll calmed down. It held up a three by five notecard. ''Figgy Pudding!'' it said. Herschel looked at the note-card, and saw Bubbe's noodle kugle recipe. So *that's* where she had hidden it!

''*Now!*'' said the troll, thrusting forward both the notecard and its mixing bowl.

Herschel hurried to warm the oven. His hands were all aquiver, but he managed to beat the eggs until silky, then start the noodles. When the noodles were soft he added raisins, lemon juice, almonds, and brown sugar, and, to that, cinnamon and just a pinch of nutmeg. A few stewed prunes were left from breakfast, and he added those as well. He set the timer, and slid the dish into the oven. Soon, the sweet smell of Bubbe's kugle filled the apartment. When the eggs were firm, Herschel scooped up a huge portion and brought it back to the troll.

The troll stuck its face down into its bowl to eat. It paused and looked up with a satisfied smile on its face. "Figgy Pudding!" it said. "We wish you," but Herschel, thinking of his grandmother, was so distracted that he paid it no attention.

"We *wish* you," it said, beginning to sound irritated.

"I sure wish my Bubbe was here," Herschel said.

The troll licked its nose with the tip of its tongue. It nodded, then jumped up to its feet and turned around thrice. It blinked hard, and, all at once—in her Barcalounger—sat Bubbe Minkowitz, dressed in a powder blue terry-cloth robe.

"Herschel!" she said, warmly. "I was hoping I'd hear from you today." She looked around the room. "You must forgive me. I'm feeling a little fartootst." She clapped her wrinkled hands together. "Who's this?" she asked, pointing to the troll. "A friend to share the holidays? And look, he's wearing your old pajamas. Well, isn't that the cutest little thing?"

The troll crept up beside her.

Bubbe closed her eyes. "What's that wonderful aroma?" she asked.

"I baked a kugle," Herschel said. He hurried into the kitchen, returning with a warm bowl filled with the sweet pudding. "Here you go. Happy birthday."

"Oh!" Bubbe said in a sigh. "You found the recipe!" She ate with gusto. "Delicious!" she said, "and so light! You don't know how much I've wanted a bowl of this stuff, lately."

"Figgy *pudding*," said the troll, approving.

"Now aren't you adorable?" Bubbe said. She reached to pat its fur and let it lick her spoon.

"*More* figgy pudding," said the troll, beginning to growl.

Herschel blanched. "All gone," he said.

"Want it *now!*" said the troll. It stomped its foot.

"Dybbuks!" Bubbe whispered to Herschel. "You have to know how to handle them." She pulled a peppermint kiss from her pocket and held it before the troll. "Make nice and you can have this," she said.

The troll obeyed and opened its mouth. "Figgy pudding," it purred as she dropped the mint upon its tongue.

"Suck, don't chew," Bubbe said.

It rubbed its head against her arm. "We *wish* you."

"All I wish is for Herschel to be happy," Bubbe said. "I don't suppose a world-traveler like you would know of any nice Jewish girls?"

The troll jumped up and turned around thrice. It blinked hard, and a young woman dressed in a rumpled beige slacks suit appeared in the center of the room. "Where am I?" she asked.

"*More* figgy pudding, *now!*" said the troll.

"Good things come to those who wait," Bubbe answered, "but I guess that our work here is done. I've got Starlight Mints and a full can of Metamucil back at the home. Why don't you come along and keep me company?"

Something about the way she winked at Herschel made him wonder if *she* had conjured up the demon in the first place.

"Bubbe?" he asked, with a wry glance her way. "Since when do dybbuks look like trolls?"

"Cultural icons gotta change with the *times*," she answered with a shrug.

"I see it as assimilation, mixed with the immigrants' desire to become more American," said the young woman, perking up.

"She's a smart one, this girl. You take good care of her," Bubbe said with a warning look to Herschel, "or, next time, I'll conjure up *Barney*."

The troll took Bubbe's arm with a gallant gesture. "Glad tidings!" it said. "And a happy New Year!" In a flash, Bubbe and the troll disappeared.

The woman picked up the box of melba toast from the floor. Assuredly, she walked over to the Barcalounger. "I always hated that figgy pudding song," she said. She nibbled on her melba toast. "Cottage cheese would taste good with this," she said, looking at Herschel. "Say, don't I know you from the University? Math department, right? I'm in sociology."

He shook her hand, pleased to see her blush.

"You gotta excuse me," she said. "I'm fartootst. One minute I'm in Jersey watching *Jeopardy*, the next minute I'm *here*. Oy! And tonight is the Tournament of Champions!"

Herschel grinned and brought her the remote. "I was just about to turn on the television," he said, crossing his fingers for luck. "I'm glad you're here." He felt more relaxed than he had in years. Surprisingly, he no longer cared *bubkes* about *Jeopardy*. Who knew? His inner troll had eaten. With the little guy temporarily out of the picture, maybe Herschel could finally get around to some serious romance!

—the author wishes to thank Martha Bayless for her contributions to this story.

BUBBE MINKOWITZ'S NOODLE KUGLE RECIPE

Ingredients:
½ pound egg noodles
2 eggs separated
½ cup brown sugar
¼ teaspoon cinnamon
⅛ teaspoon salt
3 tablespoons butter
½ cup raisins
¼ cup chopped almonds
juice of ¼ fresh lemon

1. Preheat oven to 400 degrees.

2. Cook noodles according to package directions until tender and drain.

3. Beat egg yolks with sugar, cinnamon, nutmeg, and salt. Add drained noodles, butter, raisins, and almonds and mix well.

4. Beat egg whites until stiff and gently fold into noodle mixture. Pour into casserole dish, dot with butter and bake 45 minutes.

Serves 4 adults, or one hungry inner troll.

THE NUTCRACKER COUP

Janet Kagan

"The Nutcracker Coup" was purchased by Gardner
Dozois, and appeared in the December 1992 issue of
Asimov's, with a cover and an interior illustration by
David Cherry. It was one of a number of well-received
stories by Kagan that have appeared in the magazine
over the last few years, since her first sale there in 1989,
several of which have won the Asimov's Reader's
Award poll by large margins. After its appearance in
Asimov's, the compelling story that follows, "The Nutcracker Coup," went on to win Kagan a Hugo Award
in 1993. In it, she takes us to a distant planet for the
wry and yet poignant story of a homesick diplomat from
Earth who teaches some inquisitive resident aliens about
some old Earth customs, with some very surprising re-
sults, including a few that are literally world-shaking . . .

Although she has only been selling for a few years,
Janet Kagan has rapidly built a large and enthusiastic
audience for her work, and has become a figure of note
in the '90s. Her first novel, a Star Trek book called
Uhura's Song, was a nationwide bestseller, and her second novel Hellspark (not a Star Trek novel) was also
widely acclaimed. Her most recent novel Mirabile was
also greeted with similar warmth and enthusiasm. She
is a frequent contributor to Asimov's Science Fiction,

and has also sold to Analog, Pulphouse, *and* Pirate Writings. *She lives in Lincoln Park, New Jersey, with her husband Ricky, several computers, and* lots *of cats, and is at work on a new novel.*

Marianne Tedesco had "The Nutcracker Suite" turned up full blast for inspiration, and as she whittled she now and then raised her knife to conduct Tchaikovsky. That was what she was doing when one of the locals poked his delicate snout around the corner of the door to her office. She nudged the sound down to a whisper in the background and beckoned him in.

It was Tatep, of course. After almost a year on Rejoicing (that was the literal translation of the world's name), she still had a bit of trouble recognizing the Rejoicers by snout alone, but the three white quills in Tatep's ruff had made him the first real "individual" to her. Helluva thing for a junior diplomat *not* to be able to tell one local from another—but there it was. Marianne was desperately trying to learn the snout shapes that distinguished the Rejoicers to each other.

"Good morning, Tatep. What can I do for you?"

"Share?" said Tatep.

"Of course. Shall I turn the music off?" Marianne knew that *The Nutcracker Suite* was as alien to him as the rattling and scraping of his music was to her. She was beginning to like pieces here and there of the Rejoicer style, but she didn't know if Tatep felt the same way about Tchaikovsky.

"Please, leave it on," he said. "You've played it every day this week—am I right? And now I find you waving your knife to the beat. Will you share the reason?"

She *had* played it every day this week, she realized. "I'll try to explain. It's a little silly, really, and it shouldn't be taken as characteristic of human. Just as characteristic of Marianne."

"Understood." He climbed the stepstool she'd cobbled together her first month on Rejoicing and settled himself on his haunches comfortably to listen. At rest, the wicked quills adorning his ruff and tail seemed just that: adornments. By local standards, Tatep was a handsome male.

He was also a quadruped, and human chairs weren't the least bit of use to him. The stepstool let him lounge on its broad upper platform or sit upright on the step below that—in either case, it put a Rejoicer eye to eye with Marianne. This had been so successful an innovation in the embassy that they had hired a local artisan to make several for each office. Chornian's stepstools were a more elaborate affair, but Chornian himself had refused to make one to replace "the very first." A fine sense of tradition, these Rejoicers.

That was, of course, the best way to explain the Tchaikovsky. "Have you noticed, Tatep, that the further away from home you go, the more important it becomes to keep traditions?"

"Yes," he said. He drew a small piece of sweetwood from his pouch and seemed to consider it thoughtfully. "Ah! I hadn't thought how very strongly you must need tradition! You're very far from home indeed. Some thirty light years, is it not?" He bit into the wood, shaving a delicate curl from it with one corner of his razor sharp front tooth. The curl he swallowed, then he said, "Please, go on."

The control he had always fascinated Marianne—she would have preferred to watch him carve, but she spoke instead. "My family tradition is to celebrate a holiday called Christmas."

He swallowed another shaving and repeated, "Christmas."

"For some humans Christmas is a religious holiday. For my family, it was more of . . . a turning of the seasons. Now, Esperanza and I couldn't agree on a date—her homeworld's calendar runs differently than mine—but we both agreed on a need to celebrate Christmas once a year. So, since it's a solstice festival, I asked Muhammed what was the shortest day of the year on Rejoicing. He says that's Tamemb Nap Ohd."

Tatep bristled his ruff forward, confirming Muhammed's date.

"So I have decided to celebrate Christmas Eve on Tamemb Nap Ohd and to celebrate Christmas Day on Tememb Nap Chorr."

"Christmas is a revival, then? An awakening?"

"Yes, something like that. A renewal. A promise of spring to come."

"Yes, we have an Awakening on Tememb Nap Chorr as well."

Marianne nodded. "Many peoples do. Anyhow, I mentioned that I wanted to celebrate and a number of other people at the embassy decided it was a good idea. So, we're trying to put together something that resembles a Christmas celebration—mostly from local materials.''

She gestured toward the player. ''That piece of music is generally associated with Christmas. I've been playing it because it—gives me an anticipation of the Awakening to come.''

Tatep was doing fine finishing work now, and Marianne had to stop to watch. The bit of sweetwood was turning into a pair of tommets—the Embassy staff had dubbed them ''notrabbits'' for their sexual proclivities—engaged in their mating dance. Tatep rattled his spines, amused, and passed the carving into her hands. He waited quietly while she turned it this way and that, admiring the exquisite workmanship.

''You don't get the joke,'' he said, at last.

''No, Tatep. I'm afraid I don't. Can you share it?''

''Look closely at their teeth.''

Marianne did, and got the joke. The creatures were tommets, yes, but the teeth they had were not tommet teeth. They were the same sort of teeth that Tatep had used to carve them. Apparently, ''fucking like tommets'' was a Rejoicer joke.

''It's a gift for Hapet and Achinto. They had *six* children! We're all pleased and amazed for them.''

Four to a brood was the usual, but birthings were few and far between. A couple that had more than two birthings in a lifetime was considered unusually lucky.

''Congratulate them for me, if you think it appropriate,'' Marianne said. ''Would it be proper for the embassy to send a gift?''

''Proper and most welcome. Hapet and Achinto will need help feeding that many.''

''Would you help me choose? Something to make children grow healthy and strong, and something as well to delight their senses.''

''I'd be glad to. Shall we go to the market or the wood?''

''Let's go chop our own, Tatep. I've been sitting behind this desk too damn long. I could use the exercise.''

As Marianne rose, Tatep put his finished carving into his pouch and climbed down. ''You will share more about Christmas with me while we work? You can talk and chop at the same time.''

Marianne grinned. ''I'll do better than that. You can help me choose something that we can use for a Christmas tree, as well.

If it's something that is also edible when it has seasoned for a few weeks' time, that would be all the more to the spirit of the festival.''

The two of them took a leisurely stroll down the narrow cobbled streets. Marianne shared more of her Christmas customs with Tatep and found her anticipation growing apace as she did.

At Tatep's suggestion they paused at Killim the glassblower's, where Tatep helped Marianne describe and order a dozen ornamental balls for the tree. Unaccustomed to the idea of purely ornamental glass objects, Killim was fascinated. "She says," reported Tatep when Marianne missed a few crucial words of her reply, "she'll make a number of samples and you'll return on Debem Op Chorr to choose the most proper."

Marianne nodded. Before she could thank Killim, however, she heard the door behind her open, heard a muffled squeak of surprise, and turned. Halemtat had ordered yet another of his subjects clipped—Marianne saw that much before the local beat a hasty retreat from the door and vanished.

"Oh, god," she said aloud. "Another one." That, she admitted to herself for the first time, was why she was making such an effort to recognize the individual Rejoicers by facial shape alone. She'd seen no less than fifty clipped in the year she'd been on Rejoicing. There was no doubt in her mind that this was a new one—the blunted tips of its quills had been bright and crisp. "Who is it this time, Tatep?"

Tatep ducked his head in shame. "Chornian," he said.

For once, Marianne couldn't restrain herself. "Why?" she asked, and she heard the unprofessional belligerence in her own voice.

"For saying something I dare not repeat, not even in your language," Tatep said, "unless I wish to have *my* quills clipped."

Marianne took a deep breath. "I apologize for asking, Tatep. It was stupid of me." Best thing to do would be to get the hell out and let Chornian complete his errand without being shamed in front of the two of them. "Though," she said aloud, not caring if it was professional or not, "it's Halemtat who should be shamed, not Chornian."

Tatep's eyes widened, and Marianne knew she'd gone too far.

She thanked the glassblower politely in Rejoicer and promised to return on Debem Op Chorr to examine the samples.

As they left Killim's, Marianne heard the scurry behind them—Chornian entering the shop as quickly and as unobtrusively as possible. She set her mouth—her silence raging—and followed Tatep without a backward glance.

At last they reached the communal wood. Trying for some semblance of normalcy, Marianne asked Tatep for the particulars of an unfamiliar tree.

"*Huep*," he said. "Very good for carving, but not very good for eating." He paused a moment, thoughtfully. "I think I've put that wrong. The flavor is *very* good, but it's very low in food value. It grows prodigiously, though, so a lot of people eat too much of it when they shouldn't."

"Junk food," said Marianne, nodding. She explained the term to Tatep and he concurred. "Youngsters are particularly fond of it—but it wouldn't be a good gift for Hapet and Achinto."

"Then let's concentrate on good *healthy* food for Hapet and Achinto," said Marianne.

Deeper in the wood, they found a stand of the trees the embassy staff had dubbed gnomewood for its gnarly, stunted appearance. Tatep proclaimed this perfect, and Marianne set about to chop the proper branches. Gathering food was more a matter of pruning than chopping down, she'd learned, and she followed Tatep's careful instructions so she did not damage the tree's productive capabilities in the process.

"Now this one—just here," he said. "See, Marianne? Above the bole, for new growth will spring from the bole soon after your Awakening. If you damage the bole, however, there will be no new growth on this branch again."

Marianne chopped with care. The chopping took some of the edge off her anger. Then she inspected the gnomewood and found a second possibility. "Here," she said. "Would this be the proper place?"

"Yes," said Tatep, obviously pleased that she'd caught on so quickly. "That's right." He waited until she had lopped off the second branch and properly chosen a third and then he said, "Chornian said Halemtat had the twining tricks of a *talemtat*. One of his children liked the rhyme and repeated it."

"*Talemtat* is the vine that strangles the tree it climbs, am I right?" She kept her voice very low.

Instead of answering aloud, Tatep nodded.

"Did Halemtat—did Halemtat order the child clipped as well?"

Tatep's eyelids shaded his pupils darkly. "The entire family. He ordered the entire family clipped."

So that was why Chornian was running the errands. He *would* risk his own shame to protect his family from the awful embarrassment—for a Rejoicer—of appearing in public with their quills clipped.

She took out her anger on yet another branch of the gnomewood. When the branch fell—on her foot, as luck would have it—she sat down of a heap, thinking to examine the bruise, then looked Tatep straight in the eye. "How long? How long does it take for the quills to grow out again?" After much of a year, she hadn't yet seen evidence that an adult's quills regenerated at all. "They do regrow?"

"After several Awakenings," he said. "The regrowth can be quickened by eating *welspeth*, but . . ."

But *welspeth* was a hot-house plant in this country. Too expensive for somebody like Chornian.

"I see," she said. "Thank you, Tatep."

"Be careful where you repeat what I've told you. Best you not repeat it at all." He cocked his head at her and added, with a rattle of quills, "I'm not sure where Halemtat would clip a human, or even if you'd feel shamed by a clipping, but I wouldn't like to be responsible for finding out."

Marianne couldn't help but grin. She ran a hand through her pale white hair. "I've had my head shaved—that was long ago and far away—and it was intended to shame me."

"Intended to?"

"I painted my naked scalp bright red and went about my business as usual. I set something of a new fashion and, in the end, it was the shaver who was—quite properly—shamed."

Tatep's eyelids once again shaded his eyes. "I must think about that," he said, at last. "We have enough branches for a proper gift now, Marianne. Shall we consider the question of your Christmas tree?"

"Yes," she said. She rose to her feet and gathered up the branches. "And another thing as well. . . . I'll need some more wood for carving. I'd like to carve some gifts for my friends, as well. That's another tradition of Christmas."

"Carving gifts? Marianne, you make Christmas sound as if it were a Rejoicing holiday!"

Marianne laughed. "It is, Tatep. I'll gladly share my Christmas with you."

Clarence Doggett was Super Plenipotentiary Representing Terra to Rejoicing and today he was dressed to live up to his extravagant title in striped silver tights and a purple silk weskit. No less than four hoops of office jangled from his belt. Marianne had, since meeting him, conceived the theory that the more stylishly outré his dress the more likely he was to say yes to the request of a subordinate. Scratch that theory . . .

Clarence Doggett straightened his weskit with a tug and said, "We have no reason to write a letter of protest about Emperor Halemtat's treatment of Chornian. He's deprived us of a valuable worker, true, but . . ."

"Whatever happened to human rights?"

"They're not human, Marianne. They're aliens."

At least he hadn't called them "Pincushions" as he usually did, Marianne thought. Clarence Doggett was the unfortunate result of what the media had dubbed "the Grand Opening." One day humans had been alone in the galaxy, and the next they'd found themselves only a tiny fraction of the intelligent species. Setting up five hundred embassies in the space of a few years had strained the diplomatic service to the bursting point. Rejoicing, considered a backwater world, got the scrapings from the bottom of the barrel. Marianne was trying very hard not to be one of those scrapings, despite the example set by Clarence. She clamped her jaw shut very hard.

Clarence brushed at his fashionably large mustache and added, "It's not as if they'll *really* die of shame, after all."

"Sir," Marianne began.

He raised his hands. "The subject is closed. How are the plans coming for the Christmas bash?"

"Fine, sir," she said without enthusiasm. "Killim—she's the

local glassblower—would like to arrange a trade for some dyes, by the way. Not just for the Christmas tree ornaments, I gather, but for some project of her own. I'm sending letters with Nick Minski to a number of glassblowers back home to find out what sort of dye is wanted.''

"Good work. Any trade item that helps tie the Rejoicers into the galactic economy is a find. You're to be commended."

Marianne wasn't feeling very commended, but she said, "Thank you, sir."

"And keep up the good work—this Christmas idea of yours is turning out to be a big morale booster."

That was the dismissal. Marianne excused herself and, feet dragging, she headed back to her office. " 'They're not human,' " she muttered to herself. " 'They're aliens. It's not as if they'll *really* die of shame. . . .' " She slammed her door closed behind her and snarled aloud, "But Chornian can't keep up work and the kids can't play with their friends and his mate Chaylam can't go to the market. What if they starve?"

"They won't starve," said a firm voice.

Marianne jumped.

"It's just me," said Nick Minski. "I'm early." He leaned back in the chair and put his long legs up on her desk. "I've been watching how the neighbors behave. Friends—your friend Tatep included—take their leftovers to Chornian's family. They won't starve. At least, Chornian's family won't. I'm not sure what would happen to someone who is generally unpopular."

Nick was head of the ethnology team studying the Rejoicers. At least he had genuine observations to base his decisions on.

He tipped the chair to a precarious angle. "I can't begin to guess whether or not helping Chornian will land Tatep in the same hot water, so I can't reassure you there. I take it from your muttering that Clarence won't make a formal protest."

Marianne nodded.

He straightened the chair with a bang that made Marianne start. "Shit," he said. "Doggett's such a pissant."

Marianne grinned ruefully. "God, I'm going to miss you, Nick. Diplomats aren't permitted to speak in such matter-of-fact terms."

"I'll be back in a year. I'll bring you fireworks for your next Christmas." He grinned.

"We've been through that, Nick. Fireworks may be part of your family's Christmas tradition, but they're not part of mine. All that banging and flashing of light just wouldn't *feel* right to me, not on Christmas."

"Meanwhile," he went on, undeterred, "you think about my offer. You've learned more about Tatep and his people than half the folks on my staff; academic credentials or no, I can swing putting you on the ethnology team. We're short-handed as it is. I'd rather have skipped the rotation home this year, but . . ."

"You can't get everything you want, either."

He laughed. "I think they're afraid we'll all go native if we don't go home one year in five." He preened and grinned suddenly. "How d'you think I'd look in quills?"

"Sharp," she said and drew a second burst of laughter from him.

There was a knock at the door. Marianne stretched out a toe and tapped the latch. Tatep stood on the threshold, his quills still bristling from the cold. "Hi, Tatep—you're just in time. Come share."

His laughter subsiding to a chuckle, Nick took his feet from the desk and greeted Tatep in high-formal Rejoicer. Tatep returned the favor, then added by way of explanation, "Marianne is sharing her Christmas with me."

Nick cocked his head at Marianne. "But it's not for some time yet. . . ."

"I know," said Marianne. She went to her desk and pulled out a wrapped package. "Tatep, Nick is my very good friend. Ordinarily, we exchange gifts on Christmas Day, but since Nick won't be here for Christmas, I'm going to give him his present now."

She held out the package. "Merry Christmas, Nick. A little too early, but—"

"You've hidden the gift in paper," said Tatep. "Is that also traditional?"

"Traditional but not necessary. Some of the pleasure is the surprise involved," Nick told the Rejoicer. With a sidelong glance and a smile at Marianne, he held the package to his ear and shook it. "And some of the pleasure is in trying to guess what's in the package." He shook it and listened again. "Nope, I haven't the faintest idea."

He laid the package in his lap.

Tatep flicked his tail in surprise. "Why don't you open it?"

"In my family, it's traditional to wait until Christmas Day to open your presents, even if they're wrapped and sitting under the Christmas tree in plain sight for three weeks or more."

Tatep clambered onto the stool to give him a stare of open astonishment from a more effective angle.

"Oh, no!" said Marianne. "Do you really mean it, Nick? You're *not* going to open it until Christmas Day?"

Nick laughed again. "I'm teasing." To Tatep, he said, "It's traditional in my family to wait—but it's also traditional to find some rationalization to open a gift the minute you lay hands on it. Marianne wants to see my expression; I think that takes precedence in this case."

His long fingers found a cranny in the paper wrapping and began to worry it ever so slightly. "Besides, our respective home-worlds can't agree on a date for Christmas. . . . On some world *today* must be Christmas, right?"

"Good rationalizing," said Marianne, with a sigh and a smile of relief. "Right!"

"Right," said Tatep, catching on. He leaned precariously from his perch to watch as Nick ripped open the wrapping paper.

"Tchaikovsky made me think of it," Marianne said. "Although, to be honest, Tchaikovsky's nutcracker wasn't particularly traditional. This one *is*: take a close look."

He did. He held up the brightly painted figure, took in its green weskit, its striped silver tights, its flamboyant mustache. Four metal loops jangled at its carved belt and Nick laughed aloud.

With a barely suppressed smile, Marianne handed him a "walnut" of the local variety.

Nick stopped laughing long enough to say, "You mean, this is a genuine, honest-to-god, *working* nutcracker?"

"Well, of course it is! My family's been making them for years." She made a motion with her hands to demonstrate. "Go ahead—crack that nut!"

Nick put the nut between the cracker's prominent jaws and, after a moment's hesitation, closed his eyes and went ahead. The nut gave with an audible and very satisfying craaack! and Nick began to laugh all over again.

"Share the joke," said Tatep.

"Gladly," said Marianne. "The Christmas nutcracker, of which that is a prime example, is traditionally carved to resemble an authority figure—particularly one nobody much likes. It's a way of getting back at the fraudulent, the pompous. Through the years they've poked fun at everybody from princes to policemen to"—Marianne waved a gracious hand at her own carved figure—"well, surely you recognize *him*."

"Oh, my," said Tatep, his eyes widening. "Clarence Doggett, is it not?" When Marianne nodded, Tatep said, "Are you about to get your head shaved again?"

Marianne laughed enormously. "If I do, Tatep, this time I'll paint my scalp red and green—traditional Christmas colors—and hang one of Killim's glass ornaments from my ear. Not likely, though," she added, to be fair. "Clarence doesn't go in for head shaving." To Nick, who had clearly taken in Tatep's "again," she said, "I'll tell you about it sometime."

Nick nodded and stuck another nut between Clarence's jaws. This time he watched as the nut gave way with an explosive bang. Still laughing, he handed the nutmeat to Tatep, who ate it and rattled his quills in laughter of his own. Marianne was doubly glad she'd invited Tatep to share the occasion—now she knew exactly what to make *him* for Christmas.

Christmas Eve found Marianne at a loss—something was missing from her holiday and she hadn't been able to put her finger on precisely what that something was.

It wasn't the color of the tree Tatep had helped her choose. The tree was the perfect Christmas tree shape, and if its foliage was a red so deep it approached black, that didn't matter a bit. "Next year we'll have Killim make some green ornaments," Marianne said to Tatep, "for the proper contrast."

Tinsel—silver thread she'd bought from one of the Rejoicer weavers and cut to length—flew in all directions. All seven of the kids who'd come to Rejoicing with their ethnologist parents were showing the Rejoicers the "proper" way to hang tinsel, which meant more tinsel was making it onto the kids and the Rejoicers than onto the tree.

Just as well. She'd have to clean the tinsel off the tree before she passed it on to Hapet and Achinto—well-seasoned and just the thing for growing children.

Nick would really have enjoyed seeing this, Marianne thought. Esperanza was filming the whole party, but that just wasn't the same as being here.

Killim brought the glass ornaments herself. She'd made more than the commissioned dozen. The dozen glass balls she gave to Marianne. Each was a swirl of colors, each unique. Everyone oohed and aaahed—but the best was yet to come. From her side-pack, Killim produced a second container. "Presents," she said. "A present for your Awakening Tree."

Inside the box was a menagerie of tiny, bright glass animals: notrabits, fingerfish, wispwings. . . . Each one had a loop of glass at the top to allow them to be hung from the tree. Scarcely trusting herself with such delicate objects of art, Marianne passed them on to George to string and hang.

Later, she took Killim aside and, with Tatep's help, thanked her profusely for the gifts. "Though I'm not sure she should have. Tell her I'll be glad to pay for them, Tatep. If she'd had them in her shop, I'd have snapped them up on the spot. I didn't know how badly our Christmas needed them until I saw her unwrap them."

Tatep spoke for a long time to Killim, who rattled all the while. Finally, Tatep rattled too. "Marianne, three humans have commissioned Killim to make animals for them to send home." Killim said something Marianne didn't catch. "Three humans in the last five minutes. She says, Think of this set as a—as an advertisement."

"No, you may not pay me for them," Killim said, still rattling. "I have gained something to trade for my dyes."

"She says," Tatep began.

"It's okay, Tatep. That I understood."

Marianne hung the wooden ornaments she'd carved and painted in bright colors, then she unsnagged a handful of tinsel from Tatep's ruff, divided it in half, and they both flung it onto the tree. Tatep's handful just barely missed Matsimoto, who was hanging strings of beads he'd bought in the bazaar, but Marianne's got Juliet, who was hanging chains of paper cranes it must have taken her the better part of the month to fold. Juliet laughed and pulled the tinsel from her hair to drape it—length by length and *neatly*—over the deep red branches.

Then Kelleb brought out the star. Made of silver wire delicately filigreed, it shone just the way a Christmas tree star should. He hoisted Juliet to his shoulders and she affixed it to the top of the tree and the entire company burst into cheers and applause.

Marianne sighed and wondered why that made her feel so down. "If Nick had been here," Tatep observed, "I believe he could have reached the top without an assistant."

"I think you're right," said Marianne. "I wish he *were* here. He'd enjoy this." Just for a moment, Marianne let herself realize that what was missing from this Christmas was Nick Minski.

"Next year," said Tatep.

"Next year," said Marianne. The prospect brightened her.

The tree glittered with its finery. For a moment they all stood back and admired it—then there was a scurry and a flurry as folks went to various bags and hiding places and brought out the brightly wrapped presents. Marianne excused herself from Tatep and Killim and brought out hers to heap at the bottom of the tree with the rest.

Again there was a moment's pause of appreciation. Then Clarence Doggett—of all people—raised his glass and said, "A toast! A Christmas toast! Here's to Marianne, for bringing Christmas thirty light years from old Earth!"

Marianne blushed as they raised their glasses to her. When they'd finished, she raised hers and found the right traditional response: "A Merry Christmas—and God bless us, every one!"

"Okay, Marianne. It's your call," said Esperanza. "Do we open the presents now or"—her voice turned to a mock whine—"do we *hafta* wait till tomorrow?"

Marianne glanced at Tatep. "What day is it now?" she asked. She knew enough about local time reckoning to know what answer he'd give.

"Why, today is Tememb Nap Chorr."

She grinned at the faces around her. "By Rejoicer reckoning, the day changes when the sun sets—it's been Christmas Day for an hour at least now. But stand back and let the kids find their presents first.''

There was a great clamor and rustle of wrapping paper and whoops of delight as the kids dived into the pile of presents.

As Marianne watched with rising joy, Tatep touched her arm. "More guests," he said, and Marianne turned.

It was Chornian, his mate Chaylam, and their four children. Marianne's jaw dropped at the sight of them. She had invited the six with no hope of response and here they were. "And all dressed up for Christmas!" she said aloud, though she knew Christmas was *not* the occasion. "You're as glittery as the Christmas tree itself," she told Chornian, her eyes gleaming with the reflection of it.

Ruff and tail, each and every one of Chornian's short-clipped quills was tipped by a brilliant red bead. "Glass?" she asked.

"Yes," said Chornian. "Killim made them for us."

"You look magnificent! Oh—how wonderful!" Chaylam's clipped quills had been dipped in gold; when she shifted shyly, her ruff and tail rippled with light. "You sparkle like sun on the water," Marianne told her. The children's ruffs and tails had been tipped in gold and candy pink and vivid yellow and—the last but certainly not the least—in beads every color of the rainbow.

"A kid after my own heart," said Marianne. "I think that would have been my choice too." She gave a closer look. "No two alike, am I right? Come—join the party. I was afraid I'd have to drop your presents by your house tomorrow. Now I get to watch you open them, to see if I chose correctly."

She escorted the four children to the tree and, thanking her lucky stars she'd had Tatep write their names on their packages, she left them to hunt for their presents. Those for their parents she brought back with her.

"It was difficult," Chornian said to Marianne. "It was difficult to walk through the streets with pride but—we did. And the children walked the proudest. They give us courage."

Chaylam said, "If only on their behalf."

"Yes," agreed Chornian. "Tomorrow I shall walk in the sunlight. I shall go to the bazaar. My clipped quills will glitter, and *I* will not be ashamed that I have spoken the truth about Halemtat."

That was all the Christmas gift Marianne needed, she thought to herself, and handed the wrapped package to Chornian. Tatep gave him a running commentary on the habits and rituals of the human Awakening as he opened the package. Chornian's eyes shaded and Tatep's running commentary ceased abruptly as they peered together into the box.

"Did I get it right?" said Marianne, suddenly afraid she'd committed some awful faux pas. She'd scoured the bazaar for *welspeth* shoots and, finding none, she'd pulled enough strings with the ethnology team to get some imported.

Tatep was the one who spoke. "You got it right," he said. "Chornian thanks you." Chornian spoke rapid-fire Rejoicer for a long time; Marianne couldn't follow the half of it. When he'd finished, Tatep said simply, "He regrets that he has no present to give you."

"It's not necessary. Seeing those kids all in spangles brightened up the party—that's present enough for me!"

"Nevertheless," said Tatep, speaking slowly so she wouldn't miss a word. "Chornian and I make you this present."

Marianne knew the present Tatep drew from his pouch was from Tatep alone, but she was happy enough to play along with the fiction if it made him happy. She hadn't expected a present from Tatep and she could scarcely wait to see what it was he felt appropriate to the occasion.

Still, she gave it the proper treatment—shaking it, very gently, beside her ear. If there was anything to hear, it was drowned out by the robust singing of carols from the other side of the room. "I can't begin to guess, Tatep," she told him happily.

"Then open it."

She did. Inside the paper, she found a carving, the rich wine-red of burgundy-wood, bitter to the taste and therefore rarely carved but treasured because none of the kids would gnaw on it as they tested their teeth. The style of carving was so utterly Rejoicer that it took her a long moment to recognize the subject, but once she did, she knew she'd treasure the gift for a lifetime.

It was unmistakably Nick—but Nick as seen from Tatep's point of view, hence the unfamiliar perspective. It was Looking Up At Nick.

"Oh, Tatep!" And then she remembered just in time and

added, "Oh, Chornian! Thank you both so very much. I can't *wait* to show it to Nick when he gets back. Whatever made you think of doing Nick?"

Tatep said, "He's your best *human* friend. I know you miss him. You have no pictures; I thought you would feel better with a likeness."

She hugged the sculpture to her. "Oh, I do. Thank you, both of you." Then she motioned, eyes shining. "Wait. Wait right here, Tatep. Don't go away."

She darted to the tree and, pushing aside wads of rustling paper, she found the gift she'd made for Tatep. Back she darted to where the Rejoicers were waiting.

"I waited," Tatep said solemnly.

She handed him the package. "I hope this is worth the wait."

Tatep shook the package. "I can't begin to guess," he said.

"Then open it. *I* can't stand the wait!"

He ripped away the paper as flamboyantly as Nick had—to expose the brightly colored nutcracker and a woven bag of nuts.

Marianne held her breath. The problem had been, of course, to adapt the nutcracker to a recognizable Rejoicer version. She'd made the Emperor Halemtat sit back on his haunches, which meant far less adaptation of the cracking mechanism. Overly plump, she'd made him, and spiky. In his right hand, he carried an oversized pair of scissors—of the sort his underlings used for clipping quills. In his left, he carried a sprig of *talemtat*, that unfortunate rhyme for his name.

Chornian's eyes widened. Again, he rattled off a spate of Rejoicer too fast for Marianne to follow . . . except that Chornian seemed anxious.

Only then did Marianne realize what she'd done. "Oh, my God, Tatep! He wouldn't clip your quills for *having* that, would he?"

Tatep's quills rattled and rattled. He put one of the nuts between Halemtat's jaws and cracked with a vengeance. The nut-meat he offered to Marianne, his quills still rattling. "If he does, Marianne, you'll come to Killim's to help me choose a good color for *my* glass beading!"

He cracked another nut and handed the meat to Chornian. The next thing Marianne knew, the two of them were rattling at each other—Chornian's glass beads adding a splendid tinkling to the merriment.

Much relieved, Marianne laughed with them. A few minutes later, Esperanza dashed out to buy more nuts—so Chornian's children could each take a turn at the cracking.

Marianne looked down at the image of Nick cradled in her arm. "I'm sorry you missed this," she told it, "but I promise I'll write everything down for you before I go to bed tonight. I'll try to remember every last bit of it for you."

"Dear Nick," Marianne wrote in another letter some months later. "You're not going to approve of this. I find I haven't been ethnologically correct—much less diplomatic. I'd only meant to share my Christmas with Tatep and Chornian and, for that matter, whoever wanted to join in the festivities. To hear Clarence tell it, I've sent Rejoicing to hell in a handbasket.

"You see, it does Halemtat no good to clip quills these days. There are some seventy-five Rejoicers walking around town clipped and beaded—as gaudy and as shameless as you please. I even saw one newly male (teenager) with beads on the ends of his unclipped spines!

"Killim says thanks for the dyes, by the way. They're just what she had in mind. She's so busy, she's taken on two apprentices to help her. She makes 'Christmas ornaments' and half the art galleries in the known universe are after her for more and more. The apprentices make glass beads. One of them—one of Chornian's kids, by the way—hit upon the bright idea of making simple sets of beads that can be stuck on the ends of quills cold. Saves time and trouble over the hot glass method.

"What's more—

"Well, yesterday I stopped by to say 'hi' to Killim, when who should turn up but Koppen—you remember him? He's one of Halemtat's advisors? You'll never guess what he wanted: a set of quill tipping beads.

"No, he hadn't had his quills clipped. Nor was he buying them for a friend. He was planning, he told Killim, to tell Halemtat a thing or two—I missed the details because he went too fast—and he expected he'd be clipped for it, so he was planning ahead. Very expensive *blue* beads for him, if you please, Killim!

"I find myself unprofessionally pleased. There's a thing or two Halemtat *ought* to be told. . . .

"Meanwhile, Chornian has gone into the business of making nutcrackers. —All right, so sue me, I showed him how to make the actual cracker work. It was that or risk his taking Tatep's present apart to find out for himself.

"I'm sending holos—including a holo of the one I made— because you've got to see the transformation Chornian's worked on mine. The difference between a human-carved nutcracker and a Rejoicer-carved nutcracker is as unmistakable as the difference between Looking Up At Nick and . . . well, *looking up at Nick*.

"I still miss you, even if you do think fireworks are appropriate at Christmas.

"See you soon—if Clarence doesn't boil me in my own pudding and bury me with a stake of holly through my heart."

Marianne sat with her light pen poised over the screen for a long moment, then she added, "Love, Marianne," and saved it to the next outgoing Dirt-bound mail.

Rejoicing
Midsummer's Eve
(Rejoicer reckoning)

Dear Nick—

This time it's not my fault. This time it's Esperanza's doing. Esperanza decided, for *her* contribution to our round of holidays, to celebrate Martin Luther King Day. (All right—if I'd known about Martin Luther King I'd probably have suggested a celebration myself—but I didn't. Look him up; you'll like him.) And she invited a handful of the Rejoicers to attend as well.

Now, the final part of the celebration is that each person in turn "has a dream." This is not like wishes, Nick. This is more on the order of setting yourself a goal, even one that looks to all intents and purposes to be unattainable, but one you will strive to attain. Even Clarence got so into the occasion that he had a dream that he would stop thinking of the Rejoicers as "Pincushions" so he could start thinking of them as Rejoicers. Esperanza said later Clarence didn't quite get the point but for him she supposed that was a step in the right direction.

Well, after that, Tatep asked Esperanza, in his very polite fashion, if it would be proper for him to have a dream as well. There was some consultation over the proper phrasing—Esperanza says her report will tell you all about that—and then Tatep rose and said, "I have a dream . . . I have a dream that someday no one will get his quills clipped for speaking the truth."

(You'll see it on the tape. Everybody agreed that this was a good dream, indeed.)

After which, Esperanza had her dream "for human rights for all."

Following which, of course, we all took turns trying to explain the concept of "human rights" to a half-dozen Rejoicers. Esperanza ended up translating five different constitutions for them—*and* an entire book of speeches by Martin Luther King.

Oh, god. I just realized . . . maybe it *is* my fault. I'd forgotten till just now. Oh. You judge, Nick.

About a week later Tatep and I were out gathering wood for some carving he plans to do—for Christmas, he says, but he wanted to get a good start on it—and he stopped gnawing long enough to ask me, "Marianne, what's 'human'?"

"How do you mean?"

"I think when Clarence says 'human,' he means something different than you do."

"That's entirely possible. Humans use words pretty loosely at the best of times—there, I just did it myself."

"What do you mean when you say 'human'?"

"Sometimes I mean the species *homo sapiens*. When I say, Humans use words pretty loosely, I do. Rejoicers seem to be more particular about their speech, as a general rule."

"And when you say 'human rights,' what do you mean?"

"When I say 'human rights,' I mean *Homo sapiens* and *Rejoicing sapiens*. I mean any *sapiens*, in that context. I wouldn't guarantee that Clarence uses the word the same way in the same context."

"You think I'm human?"

"I *know* you're human. We're friends, aren't we? I couldn't be friends with—oh, a notrabbit—now, could I?"

He made that wonderful rattly sound he does when he's amused. "No, I can't imagine it. Then, if I'm human, I ought to have human rights."

"Yes," I said, "You bloody well ought to."

Maybe it is all my fault. Esperanza will tell you the rest—she's had Rejoicers all over her house for the past two weeks—they're. watching every scrap of film she's got on Martin Luther King.

I don't know how this will all end up, but I wish to hell you were here to watch.

Love, Marianne

Marianne watched the Rejoicer child crack nuts with his Halemtat cracker and a cold, cold shiver went up her spine. That was the eleventh she'd seen this week. Chornian wasn't the only one making them, apparently; somebody else had gone into the nutcracker business as well. This was, however, the first time she'd seen a child cracking nuts with Halemtat's jaw.

"Hello," she said, stooping to meet the child's eyes. "What a pretty toy! Will you show me how it works?"

Rattling all the while, the child showed her, step by step. Then he (or she—it wasn't polite to ask before puberty) said, "Isn't it funny? It makes Mama laugh and laugh and laugh."

"And what's your mama's name?"

"Pilli," said the child. Then it added, "With the green and white beads on her quills."

Pilli—who'd been clipped for saying that Halemtat had been overcutting the imperial reserve so badly that the trees would never grow back properly.

And then she realized that, less than a year ago, no child would have admitted that its mama had been clipped. The very thought of it would have shamed both mother *and* child.

Come to think of it . . . she glanced around the bazaar and saw no less than four clipped Rejoicers shopping for dinner. Two of them she recognized as Chornian and one of his children, the other two were new to her. She tried to identify them by their snouts and failed utterly—she'd have to ask Chornian. She also noted, with utterly unprofessional satisfaction, that she *could* ask Chornian such a thing now. That too would have been unthinkable and shaming less than a year ago.

Less than a year ago. She was thinking in Dirt terms because of Nick. There wasn't any point dropping him a line; mail would cross in deep space at this late a date. He'd be here just in time for "Christmas." She wished like hell he was already here. He'd know what to make of all this, she was certain.

As Marianne thanked the child and got to her feet, three Rejoicers—all with the painted ruff of quills at their necks that identified them as Halemtat's guards—came waddling officiously up. "Here's one," said the largest. "Yes," said another. "Caught in the very act."

The largest squatted back on his haunches and said, "You will come with us, child. Halemtat decrees it."

Horror shot through Marianne's body.

The child cracked one last nut, rattled happily, and said, "I get my quills clipped?"

"Yes," said the largest Rejoicer. "You will have your quills clipped." Roughly, he separated child from nutcracker and began to tow the child away, each of them in that odd three-legged gait necessitated by the grip.

All Marianne could think to do was call after the child, "I'll tell Pilli what happened and where to find you!"

The child glanced over its shoulder, rattled again, and said, "Ask her could I have silver beads like Hortap!"

Marianne picked up the discarded nutcracker—lest some other child find it and meet the same fate—and ran full speed for Pilli's house.

At the corner, two children looked up from their own play and galloped along beside her until she skidded to a halt by Pilli's bakery. They followed her in, rattling happily to themselves over the race they'd run. Marianne's first thought was to shoo them off before she told Pilli what had happened, but Pilli greeted the two as if they were her own, and Marianne found herself blurting out the news.

Pilli gave a slow inclination of the head. "Yes," she said, pronouncing the words carefully so Marianne wouldn't miss them, "I expected that. Had it not been the nutcracker, it would have been words." She rattled. "That child is the most outspoken of my brood."

"But—" Marianne wanted to say, Aren't you afraid? but the question never surfaced.

Pilli gave a few coins to the other children and said, "Run to Killim's, my dears, and ask her to make a set of silver beads, if she doesn't already have one on hand. Then run tell your father what has happened.''

The children were off in the scurry of excitement.

Pilli drew down the awning in front of her shop, then paused. "I think you are afraid for my child."

"Yes," said Marianne. Lying had never been her strong suit; maybe Nick was right—maybe diplomacy wasn't her field.

"You are kind," said Pilli. "But don't be afraid. Even Halemtat wouldn't dare to order a child *hashay*."

"I don't understand the term."

"*Hashay?*" Pilli flipped her tail around in front of her and held out a single quill. "Chippet will be clipped here," she said, drawing a finger across the quill about halfway up its length. "*Hashay* is to clip here." The finger slid inward, to a spot about a quarter of an inch from her skin. "Don't worry, Marianne. Even Halemtat wouldn't dare to *hashay* a child."

I'm supposed to be reassured, thought Marianne. "Good," she said aloud, "I'm relieved to hear that." In truth, she hadn't the slightest idea what Pilli was talking about—and she was considerably less than reassured by the ominous implications of the distinction. She'd never come across the term in any of the ethnologists' reports.

She was still holding the Halemtat nutcracker in her hands. Now she considered it carefully. Only in its broadest outlines did it resemble the one she'd made for Tatep. This nutcracker was purely Rejoicer in style and—she almost dropped it at the sudden realization—peculiarly *Tatep's* style of carving. Tatep was making them too?

If *she* could recognize Tatep's distinctive style, surely Halemtat could—what then?

Carefully, she tucked the nutcracker under the awning—let Pilli decide what to do with the object; Marianne couldn't make the decision for her—and set off at a quick pace for Tatep's house.

On the way, she passed yet another child with a Halemtat nutcracker. She paused, found the child's father and passed the news to him that Halemtat's guards were clipping Pilli's child for the "offense." The father thanked her for the information and, with much politeness, took the nutcracker from the child.

This one, Marianne saw, was *not* carved in Tatep's style or in

Chornian's. This one was the work of an unfamiliar set of teeth.

Having shooed his child indoors, the Rejoicer squatted back on his haunches. In plain view of the street, he took up the bowl of nuts his child had left uncracked and began to crack them, one by one, with such deliberation that Marianne's jaw dropped.

She'd never seen an insolent Rejoicer but she would have bet money she was seeing one now. He even managed to make the crack of each nut resound like a gunshot. With the sound still ringing in her ears, Marianne quickened her steps toward Tatep's.

She found him at home, carving yet another nutcracker. He swallowed, then held out the nutcracker to her and said, "What do you think, Marianne? Do you approve of my portrayal?"

This one wasn't Halemtat, but his—for want of a better word—grand vizier, Corten. The grand vizier always looked to her as if he smirked. She knew the expression was due to a slightly malformed tooth but, to a human eye, the result was a smirk. Tatep's portrayal had the same smirk, only more so. Marianne couldn't help it . . . she giggled.

"Aha!" said Tatep, rattling up a rainstorm's worth of sound. "For once, you've shared the joke without the need of explanation!" He gave a long grave look at the nutcracker. "The grand vizier has earned his keep this once!"

Marianne laughed, and Tatep rattled. This time the sound of the quills sobered Marianne. "I think your work will get you clipped, Tatep," she said, and she told him about Pilli's child.

He made no response. Instead, he dropped to his feet and went to the chest in the corner, where he kept any number of carvings and other precious objects. From the chest, he drew out a box. Three-legged, he walked back to her. "Shake this! I'll bet you can guess what's inside."

Curious, she shook the box: it rattled. "A set of beads," she said.

"You see? I'm prepared. They rattle like a laugh, don't they?— a laugh at Halemtat. I asked Killim to make the beads red because that was the color you painted your scalp when you were clipped."

"I'm honored. . . ."

"But?"

"But I'm afraid for you. For *all* of you."

"Pilli's child wasn't afraid."

"No. No, Pilli's child wasn't afraid. Pilli said even Halemtat wouldn't dare hashay a child." Marianne took a deep breath and said, "But you're not a child." And I don't know what hashaying does to a Rejoicer, she wanted to add.

"I've swallowed a talpseed," Tatep said, as if that said it all.

"I don't understand."

"Ah! I'll share, then. A talpseed can't grow unless it has been through the"—he patted himself—"stomach? digestive system? of a Rejoicer. Sometimes they don't grow even then. To swallow a talpseed means to take a step toward the growth of something important. I swallowed a talpseed called 'human rights.' "

There was nothing Marianne could say to that but: "I understand."

Slowly, thoughtfully, Marianne made her way back to the embassy. Yes, she understood Tatep—hadn't she been screaming at Clarence for just the same reason? But she was terrified for Tatep—for them all.

Without consciously meaning to, she bypassed the embassy for the little clutch of domes that housed the ethnologists. Esperanza—it was Esperanza she had to see.

She was in luck. Esperanza was at home writing up one of her reports. She looked up and said, "Oh, good. It's time for a break!"

"Not a break, I'm afraid. A question that, I think, is right up your alley. Do you know much about the physiology of the Rejoicers?"

"I'm the expert," Esperanza said, leaning back in her chair. "As far as there is one in the group."

"What happens if you cut a Rejoicer's spine"—she held up her fingers—"*this* close to the skin?"

"Like a cat's claw, sort of. If you cut the tip, nothing happens. If you cut too far down, you hit the blood supply—and maybe the nerve. The quill would bleed most certainly. Might never grow back properly. And it'd hurt like hell, I'm sure—like gouging the base of your thumbnail."

She sat forward suddenly. "Marianne, you're shaking. What is it?"

Marianne took a deep breath but couldn't stop shaking. "What would happen if somebody did that to all of Ta''—she found she couldn't get the name out—''all of a Rejoicer's quills?''

''He'd bleed to death, Marianne.'' Esperanza took her hand and gave it a firm squeeze. ''Now, I'm going to get you a good stiff drink and you are going to tell me all about it.''

Fighting nausea, Marianne nodded. ''Yes,'' she said with enormous effort. ''Yes.''

''Who the *hell* told the Pincushions about 'human rights'?'' Clarence roared. Furious, he glowered down at Marianne and waited for her response.

Esperanza drew herself up to her full height and stepped between the two of them. ''Martin Luther King told the *Rejoicers* about human rights. You were there when he did it. Though you seem to have forgotten *your* dream, obviously the Rejoicers haven't forgotten theirs.''

''There's a goddamned revolution going on out there!'' Clarence waved a hand vaguely in the direction of the center of town.

''That is certainly what it looks like,'' Juliet said mildly. ''So why are we here instead of out there observing?''

''You're here because I'm responsible for your safety.''

''Bull,'' said Matsimoto. ''Halemtat isn't interested in clipping *us*.''

''Besides,'' said Esperanza. ''The supply ship will be landing in about five minutes. Somebody's got to go pick up the supplies—and Nick. Otherwise, he's going to step right into the thick of it. The last mail went out two months ago. Nick's had no warning that the situation has''—she frowned slightly, then brightened as she found the proper phrase—''changed *radically*.''

Clarence glared again at Marianne. ''As a member of the embassy staff, you are assigned the job. You will pick up the supplies and Nick.''

Marianne, who'd been about to volunteer to do just that, suppressed the urge to say, ''Thank you!'' and said instead, ''Yes, sir.''

Once out of Clarence's sight, Marianne let herself breathe a sigh of relief. The supply transport was built like a tank. While Marianne wasn't any more afraid of Halemtat's wrath than the ethnologists, she was well aware that innocent *Dirt* bystanders might easily find themselves stuck—all too literally—in a mob of Rejoicers. When the Rejoicers fought, as she understood it, they used teeth and quills. She had no desire to get too close to a lashing tail-full. An unclipped quill was needle-sharp.

Belatedly, she caught the significance of the clipping Halemtat had instituted as punishment. Slapping a snout with a tail full of glass beads was not nearly as effective as slapping a snout with a morning-star made of spines.

She radioed the supply ship to tell them they'd all have to wait for transport before they came out. Captain's gonna love that, I'm sure, she thought, until she got a response from Captain Tertain. By reputation he'd never set foot on a world other than Dirt and certainly didn't intend to do so now. So she simply told Nick to stay put until she came for him.

Nick's cheery voice over the radio said only, "It's going to be a very special Christmas this year."

"Nick," she said, "you don't know the half of it."

She took a slight detour along the way, passing the narrow street that led to Tatep's house. She didn't dare to stop, but she could see from the awning that he wasn't home. In fact, nobody seemed to be home . . . even the bazaar was deserted.

The supply truck rolled on, and Marianne took a second slight detour. What Esperanza had dubbed "the Grande Allez" led directly to Halemtat's imperial residence. The courtyard was filled with Rejoicers. Well-spaced Rejoicers, she saw, for they were—each and every one—bristled to their fullest extent. She wished she dared to go for a closer look, but Clarence would be livid if she took much more time than normal reaching the supply ship. And he'd be checking—she knew his habits well enough to know that.

She floored the accelerator and made her way to the improvised landing field in record time. Nick waved to her from the port and stepped out. Just like Nick, she thought. She'd told him to wait in the ship until she arrived; he'd obeyed to the letter. It was all she could do to keep from hugging him as she hit the ground beside him. With a grateful sigh of relief, she said, "We've got to move fast on the transfer, Nick. I'll fill you in as we load."

By the time the two of them had transferred all the supplies from the ship, she'd done just that.

He climbed into the seat beside her, gave her a long thoughtful look, and said, "So Clarence has restricted all of the *other* ethnologists to the embassy grounds, has he?" He shook his head in mock sadness and clicked his tongue. "I see I haven't trained my team in the proper response to embassy edicts." He grinned at Marianne. "So the embassy advises that I stay off the streets, does it?"

"Yes," said Marianne. She hated being the one to tell him but he'd asked her. "The Super Plenipotentiary Etc. has issued a full and formal Advisory to all non-governmental personnel. . . ."

"Okay," said Nick. "You've done your job: I've been Advised. Now I want to go have a look at this revolution-in-progress." He folded his arms across his chest and waited.

He was right. All Clarence could do was issue an Advisory; he had no power whatsoever to keep the ethnologists off the streets. And Marianne wanted to see the revolution as badly as Nick did.

"All right," she said. "I *am* responsible for your safety, though, so best we go in the transport. I don't want you stuck." She set the supply-transport into motion and headed back toward the Grande Allez.

Nick pressed his nose to the window and watched the streets as they went. He was humming cheerfully under his breath.

"Uh, Nick—if Clarence calls us . . ."

"We'll worry about that when it happens," he said.

Worry is right, thought Marianne, but she smiled. He'd been humming Christmas carols, like some excited child. Inappropriate as all hell, but she liked him all the more for it.

She pulled the supply-transport to a stop at the entrance to the palace courtyard and turned to ask Nick if he had a good enough view. He was already out the door and making his way carefully into the crowd of Rejoicers. "Hey!" she shouted—and she hit the ground running to catch up with him. "Nick!"

He paused long enough for her to catch his arm, then said, "I need to see this, Marianne. It's my *job*."

"It's *my* job to see you don't get hurt—"

He smiled. "Then you lead. I want to be over there where I can see and hear everything Halemtat and his advisors are up to."

Marianne harbored a brief fantasy about dragging him bodily

back to the safety of the supply-transport, but he was twice her weight and, from his expression, not about to cooperate. Best she lead, then. Her only consolation was that, when Clarence tried to radio them, there'd be nobody to pick up and receive his orders.

"Hey, Marianne!" said Chornian from the crowd. "Over here! Good view from here!"

And safer too. Grateful for the invitation, Marianne gingerly headed in that direction. Several quilled Rejoicers eased aside to let the two of them safely through. Better to be surrounded by beaded Rejoicers.

"Welcome back, Nick," said Chornian. He and Chaylam stepped apart to create a space of safety for the two humans. "You're just in time."

"So I see. What's going on?"

"Halemtat just had Pilli's Chippet clipped for playing with a Halemtat cracker. Halemtat doesn't *like* the Halemtat crackers."

Beside him, a fully quilled Rejoicer said, "Halemtat doesn't like much of anything. I think a proper prince ought to rattle his spines once or twice a year at least."

Marianne frowned up at Nick, who grinned and said, "Roughly translated: Hapter thinks a proper prince ought to have a sense of humor, however minimal."

"Rattle your spines, Halemtat!" shouted a voice from the crowd. "Let's see if you can do it."

"Yes," came another voice—and Marianne realized it was Chornian's—"Rattle your spines, Great Prince of the Nutcrackers!"

All around them, like rain on a tin roof, came the sound of rattling spines. Marianne looked around—the laughter swept through the crowd, setting every Rejoicer in vibrant motion. Even the grand vizier rattled briefly, then caught himself, his ruff stiff with alarm.

Halemtat didn't rattle.

From his pouch, Chornian took a nutcracker and a nut. Placing the nut in the cracker's smirking mouth, Chornian made the bite cut through the rattling of the crowd like the sound of a shot. From somewhere to her right, a second crack resounded. Then a third. . . . Then the rattling took up a renewed life.

Marianne felt as if she were under water. All around her spines shifted and rattled. Chornian's beaded spines chattered as he cracked a second nut in the smirking face of the nutcracker.

Then one of Halemtat's guards ripped the nutcracker from Chornian's hands. The guard glared at Chornian, who rattled all the harder.

Looking over his shoulder to Halemtat, the guard called, "He's already clipped. What shall I do?"

"Bring me the nutcracker," said Halemtat. The guard glared again at Chornian, who had not stopped laughing, and loped back with the nutcracker in hand. Belatedly, Marianne recognized the smirk on the nutcracker's face.

The guard handed the nutcracker to the grand vizier—Marianne knew beyond a doubt that he recognized the smirk too.

"Whose teeth carved this?" demanded Halemtat.

An unclipped Rejoicer worked his way to the front of the crowd, sat proudly back on his haunches, and said, "Mine." To the grand vizier, he added, with a slight rasp of his quills that was a barely suppressed laugh, "What do you think of my work, Corten? Does it amuse you? You have a strong jaw."

Rattling swept the crowd again.

Halemtat sat up on his haunches. His bristles stood straight out. Marianne had never seen a Rejoicer bristle quite that way before. "Silence!" he bellowed.

Startled, either by the shout or by the electrified bristle of their ruler, the crowd spread itself thinner. The laughter had subsided only because each of the Rejoicers had gone as bristly as Halemtat. Chornian shifted slightly to keep Marianne and Nick near the protected cover of his beaded ruff.

"Marianne," said Nick softly. "That's Tatep."

"I know," she said. Without meaning to, she'd grabbed his arm for reassurance.

Tatep. . . . He sat back on his haunches, as if fully at ease—the only sleeked Rejoicer in the courtyard. He might have been sitting in Marianne's office discussing different grades of wood, for all the excitement he displayed.

Halemtat, rage quivering in every quill, turned to his guards and said, "Clip Tatep. *Hashay.*"

"*No!*" shouted Marianne, starting forward. As she realized she'd spoken Dirtside and opened her mouth to shout it again in

Rejoicer, Nick grabbed her and clapped a hand over her mouth.

"*No!*" shouted Chornian, seeming to translate for her, but speaking his own mind.

Marianne fought Nick's grip in vain. Furious, she bit the hand he'd clapped over her mouth. When he yelped and removed it—still not letting her free—she said, "It'll kill him! He'll bleed to death! Let me *go*." On the last word, she kicked him hard, but he didn't let go.

A guard produced the ritual scissors and handed them to the official in charge of clipping. She held the instrument aloft and made the ritual display, clipping the air three times. With each snap of the scissors, the crowd chanted, "No. No. No."

Taken aback, the official paused. Halemtat clicked at her and she abruptly remembered the rest of the ritual. She turned to make the three ritual clips in the air before Halemtat.

This time the voice of the crowd was stronger. "No. No. No," came the shout with each snap.

Marianne struggled harder as the official stepped toward Tatep. . . .

Then the grand vizier scuttled to intercept. "No," he told the official. Turning to Halemtat, he said, "The image is mine. *I* can laugh at the caricature. Why is it, I wonder, that you can't, Halemtat? Has some disease softened your spines so that they no longer rattle?"

Marianne was so surprised she stopped struggling against Nick's hold—and felt the hold ease. He didn't let go, but held her against him in what was almost an embrace. Marianne held her breath, waiting for Halemtat's reply.

Halemtat snatched the ritual scissors from the official and threw them at Corten's feet. "You," he said. "You will hashay Tatep."

"No," said Corten. "I won't. *My* spines are still stiff enough to rattle."

Chornian chose that moment to shout once more, "Rattle your spines, Halemtat! Let us hear you rattle your spines!"

And without so much as a by-your-leave the entire crowd suddenly took up the chant: "Rattle your spines! Rattle your spines!"

Halemtat looked wildly around. He couldn't have rattled if he'd wanted to—his spines were too bristled to touch one to another.

He turned his glare on the official, as if willing her to pick up the scissors and proceed.

Instead, she said, in perfect cadence with the crowd, "Rattle your spines!"

Halemtat made an imperious gesture to his guard—and the guard said, "Rattle your spines!"

Halemtat turned and galloped full tilt into his palace. Behind him the chant continued—"Rattle your spines! Rattle your spines!"

Then, quite without warning, Tatep rattled his spines. The next thing Marianne knew, the entire crowd was laughing and laughing and laughing at their vanished ruler.

Marianne went limp against Nick. He gave her a suggestion of a hug, then let her go. Against the rattle of the crowd, he said, "I thought you were going to get yourself killed, you little idiot."

"I couldn't—I couldn't stand by and do *nothing*; they might have killed Tatep."

"I thought doing nothing was a diplomat's job."

"You're right; some diplomat I make. Well, after this little episode, I probably don't have a job anyhow."

"My offer's still open."

"Tell the truth, Nick. If I'd been a member of your team fifteen minutes ago, would you have let me go?"

He threw back his head and laughed. "Of course not," he said. "But at least I understand why you bit the hell out of my hand."

"Oh, god, Nick! I'm so sorry! Did I hurt you?"

"Yes," he said. "But I accept your apology—and next time I won't give you that option."

" 'Next time,' huh?"

Nick, still grinning, nodded.

Well, there was that to be said for Nick: he was realistic.

"Hi, Nick," said Tatep. "Welcome back."

"Hi, Tatep. Some show you folks laid on. What happens next?"

Tatep rattled the length of his body. "Your guess is as good as mine," he said. "I've never done anything like this before. Corten's still rattling. In fact, he asked me to make him a grand vizier nutcracker. I think I'll make him a present of it—for Christmas."

He turned to Marianne. "Share?" he said. "I was too busy to watch at the time. Were you and Nick mating? If you do it again, may I watch?"

Marianne turned a vivid shade of red, and Nick laughed entirely too much. "You explain it to him," Marianne told Nick firmly. "Mating habits are not within my diplomatic jurisdiction. And I'm still in the diplomatic corps—at least, until we get back to the embassy."

Tatep sat back on his haunches, eagerly awaiting Nick's explanation. Marianne shivered with relief and said hastily, "No, it wasn't mating, Tatep. I was so scared for you I was going to charge in and—well, I don't know what I was going to do after that—but I couldn't just stand by and let Halemtat hurt you." She scowled at Nick and finished, "Nick was afraid I'd get hurt myself and wouldn't let me go."

Tatep's eyes widened in surprise. "Marianne, you would have fought for me?"

"Yes. You're my friend."

"Thank you," he said solemnly. Then to Nick, he said, "You were right to hold her back. Rattling is a better way than fighting." He turned again to Marianne. "You surprise me," he said. "You showed us how to rattle at Halemtat."

He shook from snout to tail-tip, with a sound like a hundred snare drums. "Halemtat turned tail and *ran* from our rattling!"

"And now?" Nick asked him.

"Now I'm going to go home. It's almost dinner time and I'm hungry enough to eat an entire tree all by myself." Still rattling, he added, "Too bad the hardwood I make the nutcrackers from is so bitter—though tonight I could almost make an exception and dine exclusively on bitter wood."

Tatep got down off his haunches and started for home. Most of the crowd had dispersed as well. It seemed oddly anticlimactic, until Marianne heard and saw the rattles of laughter ripple through the departing Rejoicers.

Beside the supply-transport, Tatep paused. "Nick, at your convenience—I really *would* like you to share about human mating. For friendship's sake, I should know when Marianne is fighting and when she's mating. Then I'd know whether she needs help or—or what kind of help she needs. After all, some trees need help to mate. . . .''

Marianne had turned scarlet again. Nick said, ''I'll tell you all about it as soon as I get settled in again.''

''Thank you.'' Tatep headed for home, for all the world as if nothing unusual had happened. In fact, the entire crowd, laughing as it was, might have been a crowd of picnickers off for home as the sun began to set.

A squawk from the radio brought Marianne back to business. No use putting it off. Time to bite the bullet and check in with Clarence—if nothing else, the rest of the staff would be worried about both of them.

Marianne climbed into the cab. Without prompting, Nick climbed in beside her. For a long moment, they listened to the diatribe that came over the radio, but Marianne made no move to reply. Instead, she watched the Rejoicers laughing their way home from the palace courtyard.

''Nick,'' she said. ''Can you really laugh a dictator into submission?''

He cocked a thumb at the radio. ''Give it a try,'' he said. ''It's not worth cursing back at Clarence—you haven't his gift for bureaucratic invective.''

Marianne also didn't have a job by the time she got back to the embassy. Clarence had tried to clap her onto the returning supply ship, but Nick stepped in to announce that Clarence had no business sending anybody from his ethnology staff home. In the end, Clarence's bureaucratic invective had failed him and the ethnologists simply disobeyed, as Nick had. All Clarence could do, after all, was issue a directive; if they chose to ignore it, the blame no longer fell on Clarence. Since that was all that worried Clarence, that was all right.

In the end, Marianne found that being an ethnologist was considerably more interesting than being a diplomat . . . especially during a revolution.

She and Nick, with Tatep, had taken time off from their mutual studies to choose this year's Christmas tree—from Halemtat's reserve. ''Why,'' said Marianne, bemused at her own reaction, ''do I feel like I'm cutting a Christmas tree with Thomas Jefferson?''

''Because you are,'' Nick said. ''Even Thomas Jefferson did

ordinary things once in a while. Chances are, he even hung out
with his friends. . . ." He waved. "Hi, Tatep. How goes the revolution?"

For answer, Tatep rattled the length of his body.

"Good," said Nick.

"I may have good news to share with you at the Christmas
party," added the Rejoicer.

"Then we look forward to the Christmas party even more than
usual," said Marianne.

"And I brought a surprise for Marianne all the way from Dirt,"
Nick added. When Marianne lifted an eyebrow, he said, "No, no
hints."

"Share?" said Tatep.

"Christmas Eve," Nick told him. "After you've shared your
news, I think."

The tree-trimming party was in full swing. The newly formed Ad
Hoc Christmas Chorus was singing Czech carols—a gift from
Esperanza to everybody on both staffs. Clarence had gotten so
mellow on the Christmas punch that he'd even offered Marianne
her job back—if she was willing to be dropped a grade for in-
subordination. Marianne, equally mellow, said no but said it politely.

Nick had arrived at last, along with Tatep and Chornian and
Chaylam and their kids. Surprisingly, Nick stepped in between
verses to wave the Ad Hoc Christmas Chorus to silence. "Attention, please," he shouted over the hubbub. "Attention, *please*!
Tatep has an announcement to make." When he'd finally gotten
silence, Nick turned to Tatep and said, "You have the floor."

Tatep looked down, then looked up again at Nick.

"I mean," Nick said, "go ahead and speak. Marianne's not
the only one who'll want to know your news, believe me."

But it was Marianne Tatep chose to address.

"We've all been to see Halemtat," he said. "And Halemtat
has agreed: no one will be clipped again unless five people from
the same village agree that the offense warrants that severe a
punishment. *We* will choose the five, not Halemtat. Furthermore,
from this day forward, anyone may say anything without fear of
being clipped. Speaking one's mind is no longer to be punished."

The crowd broke into applause. Beside Tatep, Nick beamed.

Tatep took a piece of parchment from his pouch. "You see, Marianne? Halemtat signed it and put his bite to it."

"How did you get him to agree?"

"We laughed at him—and we cracked our nutcrackers in the palace courtyard for three days and three nights straight, until he agreed."

Chornian rattled. "He said he'd sign anything if we'd all just go away and let him sleep." He hefted the enormous package he'd brought with him and rattled again. "Look at all the shelled nuts we've brought for your Christmas party!"

Marianne almost found it in her heart to feel sorry for Halemtat. Grinning, she accepted the package and mounded the table with shelled nuts. "Those are almost too important to eat," she said, stepping back to admire their handiwork. "Are you sure they oughtn't to go into a museum?"

"The important thing," Tatep said, "is that I can say anything I want." He popped one of the nuts into his mouth and chewed it down. "Halemtat is a talemtat," he said, and rattled for the sheer joy of it.

"Corten looks like he's been eating too much briarwood," said Chornian—catching the spirit of the thing.

Not recognizing the expression, Marianne cast an eye at Nick, who said, "We'd say, 'Been eating a lemon.' "

One of Chornian's brood sat back on his/her haunches and said, "I'll show you Halemtat's guards—"

The child organized its siblings with much pomp and ceremony (except for the littlest who couldn't stop rattling) and marched them back and forth. After the second repetition, Marianne caught the rough import of their chant: "We're Halemtat's guards/We send our regards/We wish you nothing but ill/Clip! we cut off your quill!"

After three passes, one child stepped on another's tail and the whole troop dissolved into squabbling amongst themselves and insulting each other. "You look like Corten!" said one, for full effect. The adults rattled away at them. The littlest one, delighted to find that insults could be funny, turned to Marianne and said, "Marianne! You're spineless!"

Marianne laughed even harder. When she'd caught her breath,

she explained to the child what the phrase meant when it was translated literally into Standard. "If you want a good Dirt insult," she said, mischievously, "I give you 'birdbrain.' " All the sounds in that were easy for a Rejoicer mouth to utter—and when Marianne explained why it was an insult, the children all agreed that it was a very good insult indeed.

"Marianne is a birdbrain," said the littlest.

"No," said Tatep. "*Halemtat* is a birdbrain, not Marianne."

"Let the kid alone, Tatep," said Marianne. "The kid can say anything it wants!"

"True," said Tatep. "True!"

They shooed the children off to look for their presents under the tree, and Tatep turned to Nick. "Share, Nick—your surprise for Marianne."

Nick reached under the table. After a moment's searching, he brought out a large bulky parcel and hoisted it onto the table beside the heap of Halemtat nuts. Marianne caught a double-handful before they spilled onto the floor.

Nick laid a protective hand atop the parcel. "Wait," he said. "I'd better explain. Tatep, every family has a slightly different Christmas tradition—the way you folks do for Awakening. This is part of my family's Christmas tradition. It's *not* part of Marianne's Christmas tradition—but, just this once, I'm betting she'll go along with me." He took his hand from the parcel and held it out to Marianne. "Now you can open it," he said.

Dropping the Halemtat nuts back onto their pile, Marianne reached for the parcel and ripped it open with enough verve to satisfy anybody's Christmas unwrapping tradition. Inside was a box, and inside the box a jumble of gaudy cardboard tubes—glittering in stars and stripes and polka dots and even an entire school of metallic green fish. "Fireworks!" said Marianne. "Oh, Nick. . . ."

He put his finger to her lips. "Before you say another word—you chose today to celebrate Christmas because it was the right time of the Rejoicer year. You, furthermore, said that holidays on Dirt and the other human worlds don't converge—"

Marianne nodded.

Nick let that slow smile spread across his face. "But they *do*.

This year, back on Dirt, today is the Fourth of July. The dates won't coincide again in our lifetimes but, just this once, they do. So, just this once—fireworks. You do traditionally celebrate Independence Day with fireworks, don't you?''

The pure impudence in his eyes made Marianne duck her head and look away but, in turning, she found herself looking right into Tatep's bright expectant gaze. In fact, all of the Rejoicers were waiting to see what Nick had chosen for her and if he'd chosen right.

"Yes," she said, speaking to Tatep but turning to smile at Nick. "After all, today's Independence Day right here on Rejoicing, too. Come on, let's go shoot off fireworks!''

And so, for the next twenty minutes, the night sky of Rejoicing was alive with Roman candles, shooting stars and all the brightness of all the Christmases and all the Independence Days in Marianne's memory. In the streets, humans ooohed and aaahed and Rejoicers rattled. The pops and bangs even woke Halemtat, but all he could do was come out on his balcony and watch.

A day later Tatep reported the rumor that one of the palace guards even claimed to have heard Halemtat rattle. "I don't believe it for a minute," Nick added when he passed the tale on to Marianne.

"Me neither," she said, "but it's a good enough story that I'd *like* to believe it."

"A perfect Christmas tale, then. What would you like to bet that the story of The First Time Halemtat Rattled gets told every Christmas from now on?''

"Sucker bet," said Marianne. Then the wonder struck her. "Nick? Do traditions start that easily—that quickly?''

He laughed. "What kind of fireworks would you like to have *next* year?''

"One of each," she said. "And about five of those with the gold fish–like things that swirl down and then go *bam!* at you when you least expect it."

For a moment, she thought he'd changed the subject, then she realized he'd answered her question. Wherever she went, for the rest of her life, her Christmas tradition would include fireworks—not just any fireworks, but Fourth of July fireworks. She smiled.

"Next year, maybe we should play Tchaikovsky's *1812 Overture* as well as *The Nutcracker Suite*."

He shook his head. "No," he said, "*The Nutcracker Suite* has plenty enough fireworks all by itself—at least *your* version of it certainly did!"